LA FAMIGLIA: DANTE

THE DIRUGGIERO MAFIA FAMILY SAGA

LAURA SUTTON

Printed in the United States of America
408 hwy 77 South
Robstown, Texas 78380
First Edition Published March 2021

Cover design by Michelle Ruggiero
Formatting by The Nutty Formatter

CHAPTER

ONE

Cassie sighed as she pulled her beat-up little car into the nearly empty parking lot. It was only nine am and already over ninety degrees, the summer sun already high in the Dallas sky. Unfortunately for Cassie, her car's air conditioning had decided that that morning, in the middle of a heatwave in July, was the perfect time to call it quits.

She wasn't shocked. Her beloved Camry, affectionately named Betsy, was almost as old as she was... and she was turning twenty-six that year. She should probably start shopping around for a new car, but she and Betsy had been through a lot together. She had worked throughout high school, saving every penny to afford the car when she turned eighteen. Since then, Betsy had gotten her through college, to every job she'd had thus far, and even one long-but-fun road trip to Florida.

Cassie took her hair down from the messy bun and tried to run her fingers through the wind-knotted curls. She wasn't sure she was ready to say goodbye to her beloved Betsy just yet, but she was afraid she just might have to.

She pulled down her visor and checked her reflection in the mirror and saw a flushed, sweaty mess. Her pale skin, red from the heat, and the dusting of freckles only seemed to stand out further in contrast. It was *not* how she had wanted to present herself that morning. She needed it to go well– not for herself, but for her little sister. Amber was three years younger than Cassie and the only family she had in the world, anymore.

Amber was the reason Cassie was parked outside *Aphrodite's Palace*, the largest and possibly the most infamous strip club in all of Dallas. Everyone who lived in Dallas– hell, probably in all of North Texas– knew about the *Palace*. It had been open for something like fifty years, with many a bachelor party or divorce party celebrated here. It was known to employ the most beautiful women in town, and it was where her sister had gotten into big trouble.

Amber was twenty-three, beautiful, and always in the center of some kind of catastrophe. This time, the catastrophe was owing some guy at the club, Tony, ten thousand dollars. She and her loser boyfriend had gotten mixed up in something illegal again, and had made some arrangement to sell some new club drugs. But something had happened, this time. Cassie wasn't sure what, but a week earlier Amber had called her in a panic from a seedy motel in a bad part of town, needing her help.

Cassie had rushed over and taken her away from the motel, appalled to see the state her sister was in. She'd held Amber, a shadow of herself, thin and strung-out, and then she'd started making a few calls. Cassie had a good friend who ran a drug treatment facility in Colorado who, amazingly, had a spare bed. So she'd bought her sister a one-way plane ticket to Fort Collins and sent her off to get some help.

Maybe this time it would stick.

Amber had been willing to go, after spending the weekend slumped on the bathroom floor, shaking and vomiting her way through the early withdrawals. That was when she had admitted to Cassie about the money.

"How were you going to pay it back?" Cassie asked, handing her sister a bowl of chicken noodle soup.

"I was going to start dancing at the club," Amber said with a shrug and took a sip, her appetite seeming to have recovered a bit.

"Dance?" Cassie asked, aghast. She couldn't imagine taking her clothes off for strangers. She barely liked to get naked for her boyfriends, though there had only been two in her entire life.

"Yes, silly, dance." Amber rolled her eyes and grinned. "The girls there make a lot of money. I would've paid back the ten K in no time."

"Well, yeah, but you'd have to– to get *naked*," Cassie said, her tone scandalized. Amber laughed, blue eyes dancing, at Cassie's obvious discomfort.

Cassie wasn't on Amber's level of beauty, but she was pretty enough... when she tried, when she did her hair and makeup and wore something other than the baggy pants and shapeless tops that were her uniform.

But Cassie *didn't* try, and that was on purpose. She'd seen the kind of trouble Amber's looks got her into, and it wasn't as if Cassie was comfortable displaying them, anyway. She always felt exposed and vulnerable in revealing clothes, and styled hair and cosmetics always made her feel like she was wearing a big sign screaming 'pay attention to me!'. Attention was the opposite of what Cassie sought out of life.

"Maybe Tony will let me work when I get back from Colorado," Amber mused, her gaze distant.

No. Alarm flared in Cassie's gut. Amber couldn't go to a drug treatment facility just to come back and work in the same environment where she'd gotten the drugs. Even if the drugs weren't dealt out of the club, that world was the one Amber had been immersed in for the last year. It was the world that had encouraged her to start using in the first place. No, she would go to Colorado and get clean and stay as far away from *Aphrodite's Palace* as humanly possible.

"No, Amber, absolutely not."

"But, Cass, you don't understand," Amber said, her voice small and her face pinched with fear. "If I don't pay... these are dangerous people."

Cassie leaned across her small kitchen table and patted her

sister's hand.

"Don't worry, sissy." 'Sissy' had been their pet name for each other as children. Amber smiled at Cassie's use of it. "I'll take care of it. You just focus on getting well."

Amber stared at Cassie, something in her eyes old and tired, and finally nodded.

Cassie's relief had been immense, at that moment, but it waned as she watched a man get out of a sleek black car and enter the club. He wasn't especially tall or brawny, but there was a flatness to his expression that sent a chill up her spine.

Amber had told her Tony always went to the club early on Tuesdays to do ordering and... whatever else people who ran clubs had to do. Cassie gathered her hair back up in a messy bun and grabbed her purse. She had two thousand dollars in cash in her purse, all she could comfortably afford to pull from her savings.

Her job as an accountant for a mid-sized firm paid her decently, but not enough to come up with ten thousand dollars at the drop of a hat. She hoped the two thousand would be enough to keep Tony happy enough to let her pay the rest back on a monthly basis. If she lived on peanut butter and ramen, she could probably come up with $800 a month, though it would mean keeping Betsy even longer... which meant no new AC for the foreseeable future.

Cassie's light green shirt, sweat-damp, clung to her skin as she got out of the car. She pinched some of the fabric, pulling it back and forth in a vain attempt to get some air flowing under it, and stared at her surroundings as she approached the club.

If she were honest, the exterior didn't really look like a strip club. The building was tall and square, almost industrial, with no windows. An enormous neon sign with the words *Aphrodite's Palace Gentlemen's Lounge* in a florid script unfurled across the place, just waiting for nightfall to be turned on... much like the patrons.

The front door and its deep red awning were the only thing that distinguished the place from the countless warehouses in that part of town. The awning– jet black with gold trim– looked like it belonged on a Hollywood red carpet, and the lacquered door boasted a fancy gold handle.

Entering the club was like stepping into a whole different world, with chairs covered in red velvet encircling dozens of tables. Three stages ranged around the perimeter of the club; the largest was in the middle of the room and looked like a model's catwalk... except that at the end of this runway, a long metal pole rose at least 20 feet in the air.

Cassie couldn't even imagine what tricks– or the guts– it would take to dance on a pole that high in the air. It might be the first time Cassie was stepping foot in a strip club, but she wasn't completely ignorant. The pole before her was definitely taller than those depicted in movies and on television.

Across the large open room were two smaller stages, round, with what Cassie would call normal-sized stripper poles ringed by bar stools. There seemed to be three bar areas, and sitting at one of them was the man she had observed walking into the club earlier.

"Excuse me?" she called out to him.

"We're closed," the man answered absently, not even bothering to lift his head from whatever his head was bent over.

Cassie ignored the rebuff and ventured further inside. The sound of people talking and the clanging of pots and pans came louder to her. Through the dim lighting, the bluish light of a tablet told her what had the man so distracted.

"Are you Tony?" Cassie asked him, moving closer.

He huffed in irritation. "Yeah, I'm Tony. And Thursdays are try-out days," he bit out, finally turning to look at her.

"I'm– I'm not here to try out," she stammered, horrified that he'd think she was there to be a *stripper*.

He looked her up and down and smirked. Behind her, the door to the bar opened and for a second Tony's attention was taken from her. He nodded at the person who must have just entered the club.

"Are you sure?" Tony asked with a grin. It wasn't a pleasant grin.

Cassie knew that men often found her confusing. She purposefully dressed to hide her appeal, not enhance it, and that tended to baffle them– they were used to women doing everything possible to make themselves attractive, to appeal to them. Sometimes, though, a man saw past her intentional disguise and became a pest. Amber was able to handle men with an ease and confidence Cassie envied... but it seemed to come at the expense of wisdom and reliability. No, Cassie would stick with being prudent and safe, even if it meant she seemed awkward and strange.

She flushed in annoyance. "No, I'm here about my sister, Amber."

Tony's brown eyes narrowed. "What about Amber?"

Cassie's grip on the strap of her purse tightened. For the first time, she realized how dangerous this task might be, how dangerous these people might be, and an anxious sweat broke out on the back of her neck, even in the chill of the dark club.

"I– she–" Cassie stumbled over the words. She took a deep breath and started again. "I know she owes you a substantial sum."

"She does," Tony agreed, an edge of suspicion in his tone.

Cassie reached into her purse and pulled out the envelope containing the two thousand dollars, thrusting it at the man.

"Here are two thousand dollars as a down payment on what she owes. I was hoping I could work out some sort of payment plan."

Tony took the envelope from her and began counting the money in front of her, not acknowledging her words at all.

"I was thinking five hundred a month..." Cassie trailed off, waiting for the man to say something.

"Your sister already worked out a deal with me. She's going to work off her debt here in the club. A girl like her will have the fifteen K paid down in no time." Tony gave a careless shrug, tossing the envelope on the bar next to his tablet.

Cassie sucked in a shocked gasp. "*Fifteen?* Amber said it was ten." Fifteen thousand dollars was a third of her yearly salary. What was Amber thinking? Had she been thinking at all?

"Well, your sister lied to you. It's fifteen– well, thirteen, now." He picked up the envelope and wagged it at her for emphasis. "She'll have less ass-shaking to do when she gets back, thanks to you." He laughed at his own joke.

Cassie curled her fists in anger but managed to keep her face blank. "Well, she can't do any 'shaking' for you anymore. She's gone to rehab."

"That's unfortunate. Amber could've done well here." Tony reached out and ran a finger down her cheek. Cassie flinched back. "Guess you'll have to take over the ass-shaking. Some guys like that good girl shtick, but if you're Amber's sister, I bet there's a hellion buried under those boring clothes." He smirked, staring baldly at her chest. "Though your tits leave a lot to be desired."

"No, I won't be 'ass-shaking', either. I can pay you five hundred dollars a month, guaranteed, until it's paid off." She kept her chin high. He wasn't the first disgusting man she'd dealt with in her life, and she doubted he would be last.

"That's not gonna work, sweetheart, I'm not waiting that long for my money."

Cassie bit her lip and weighed her options. She thought about what she had, and what she could do without. "I can pay eight hundred a month."

He shook his head. "No, that's not going to work. You can have the same deal Amber had, or I'll track her down and... *convince...* her it's for her own good that she pays me back quickly."

Cassie's anger flared. Amber needed to stay in that rehab. She needed to get clean so she could work on her other problems. She could not come back to this cesspool. Cassie wouldn't allow it.

"If you so much as breathe in my sister's direction, I will hurt you," Cassie said, stepping into Tony's space. She couldn't physically hurt him, but she was smart. She was resourceful. She would find a way, like she always had when she and Amber were kids.

"Oh, the kitten has claws," he said, laughing. "Honey, you don't scare me. These receipts from last weekend scare me more than you do." Tony jerked a thumb toward the tablet discarded on the table.

Cassie recognized the application. It was a simple bookkeeping app, too simple for such a large club, honestly, and she bit back a smile.

"I don't doubt that," she shot back. Tony cocked his head like a confused puppy. "You've added that first column incorrectly." She couldn't bite back a smug smile.

"What? That can't be." He grabbed up the tablet, confused, and scrolled through the app. "All you do is put in the totals. It adds them up on its own."

"That app is terrible. It's marketed for dummies, but its code is flawed. No decent bookkeeper would use it."

"And how, pray tell, do you know that?" he demanded.

"Because I'm an accountant. And I was a bookkeeper during college, at night, for several locally-owned hotels. Read the reviews on that app, I bet you're coming up over and you can't figure out why."

Tony stared at her. "What– how?"

"It randomly adds in extra numbers, but the ease of entry fools people who don't really understand what they're doing wrong."

Tony started to say something else but behind her someone gave a huff of laughter.

"She's got you there, Tony," said a smooth voice.

Cassie turned. If Tony had been intimidating at first, this man was downright menacing. Seated in one of the red velvet chairs, he was dressed sharply in a dark grey suit without a tie, just a black shirt with the first few buttons unbuttoned, revealing a strong, tanned neck.

He was handsome. His hair was coffee-brown and his jaw was beautifully angular and sharp. It was his eyes that caught her, though; they were serious, dark– not only in color, but in the way of a man who had seen things, had done things. *Dark* things. It was a darkness Cassie recognized; she saw it when she looked in the mirror.

"Boss, I–" Tony started, but the man silenced him with a wave of his hand and stood from the chair, his body unfolding with an elegance not often seen in a man of his height. He was large and powerful and she knew he didn't merely expect deference. He commanded it.

"Give me the tablet and the envelope, Tony," the man said.

Tony did as he was told, without question. Cassie turned her gaze back to Tony, expecting to see fear on his face, but there was none. He respected this boss. No, not just respected. His gaze was almost... reverent. It made a shiver of unease skitter up her spine.

"Come upstairs with me, Ms...?"

"Lockheart. Cassie Lockheart." She held out her hand for him to shake, as if he were any other colleague or potential client, and she didn't miss his small smile when he took her hand. It wasn't pleasant; he was amused by her, somehow. His hand engulfed hers, making her feel every bit as tiny as she was in comparison to him.

"I'm Dante di Ruggiero, Ms. Lockheart." He smiled fully, this time, and her heart thudded in her chest. He was very handsome... and even more dangerous.

"Cassie," she whispered, still looking into his eyes.

He peered at her, as if trying to solve a puzzle. "Cassie." He headed for the stairs. "Tony, when you're done with the delivery, please have the kitchen send up lunch for myself and Ms. Lockheart."

"Sure thing, boss. The regular?" Tony asked.

Dante slanted a glance her way. "Do you eat steak, Cassie?"

If Cassie were someone else, another woman, she would've sworn he was flirting with her. But his kind didn't flirt with her kind. He was perfect, charming and confident, and she was... far from perfect.

"I do," she answered, despite her misgivings, and he shot her a grin.

"Yes, the usual, Tony," he called back, and then headed up the stairs without a backwards glance, trusting Cassie to follow.

As she climbed the steps behind him, eyes trained on the muscular backside and thighs filling out his suit *so* nicely, she couldn't tamp down the feeling that he was leading her somewhere she wasn't entirely prepared to go.

CHAPTER

TWO

Dante muttered a curse as he pulled his Range Rover into the parking lot of *Aphrodite's Palace*. It was too fucking early for him to be awake and dealing with bullshit. He'd spent the prior night going over truck routes with two of his highest-ranking lieutenants. The second shipment in six months had been confiscated at the border, just outside of Laredo, and it was becoming a problem.

If he were honest, everything was a problem, the last few years. It had started with his mother's murder, and the shit just kept rolling downhill. Then that morning, a call had woken him: the books at *Aphrodite's* were fucked up, and Tony didn't know why.

It was Tuesday, the first day of the new week, and that meant Tony would go through the receipts from the weekend. The fact that he had called Dante at eight fucking o'clock in the fucking morning told Dante that Tony was in over his head. He couldn't blame the man; it wasn't his job to balance the books, but the club had come up short during the last audit.

Aphrodite's Palace was the face of the family business, one of the many legitimate businesses necessary to keep the other not-so-legitimate businesses running. It was an intricate machine; if one part was going off the rails, it wouldn't be long before the entire thing was imploding. It was like Dante was in the middle of a train wreck and he was floundering, trying to find a way to stop it before it truly went out of control.

Inside the club, Tony was by the bar, talking to a petite redhead Dante didn't think he recognized. Dante didn't know every dancer or waitress by heart, but then, he didn't need to: Tony did. His grandfather, his *nonno*, had taught him early the importance of finding good, reliable people to rely on in their line of work.

Upon approach, Dante knew for sure that the woman didn't work at *Aphrodite's Palace*. She didn't fit the aesthetic of the club at all. Oh, they had all shapes, all sizes, all races of dancers; the best strip clubs always offered a variety of fantasies for their clientele. But every woman who did work there exuded a sense of being comfortable, of having an ease, in their own skin that the redhead lacked.

So why was she there?

Nonno had also taught him the value of watching, of listening, of waiting, of having the patience to see how a situation developed instead of barging in, guns a-blazin'. Dante had perfected the technique. He chose a table where he could easily overhear their conversation while remaining unseen... at least by her.

Once seated, he studied her. At first glance, one would think she wasn't much of anything to look at, from the back. She was tiny, both short and slight, and her hair was a vibrant red. Not a dark auburn, but not carroty orange, and Dante wondered how long it was– impossible to know, from how she'd stuffed it into an untidy knot. He always enjoyed a beautiful redhead.

The sweat-damp cling of her shirt made him wonder why she was so overheated. Was she strung out? It would explain why she was talking to Tony, but she wasn't jittery or twitchy in the way of most addicts. Instead, she seemed clear-headed, her words precise instead of slurred.

She was dressed like a frumpy college student, her body swallowed up in a loose shirt and baggy jeans. That was unusual; the women that surrounded Dante all dressed to show off their assets, not hide them. It made him wonder about this girl, her shoulders hunched forward as though she were trying to make herself even smaller. *Any smaller, and she would be invisible,* he thought, interested in spite of himself.

Then she mentioned her sister, Amber. Dante knew that name; an Amber had been fucking her way through some of his muscle. She seemed to like the danger almost as much as she liked the heroin his men had access to. In fact, Amber had convinced one of the newer men, Angel, that she could help him move some weight. Tony thought it might be a good idea, a way to test Angel's mettle, so to speak.

Well, Amber had helped him move it, all right: moved it right up her nose. Then Angel had managed to get busted with the rest. Angel had failed Tony's test in a big way, and Amber– well, Amber owed them fifteen large.

And this little mouse of a woman was the beautiful Amber's sister. *Huh.* Talk about a quirk of genetics.

It wasn't looks, though; it was her carriage. Amber wore her beauty like a badge of honor and accepted her due that was given because of that beauty. This woman purposely concealed her appeal, hid it from the world, and that was curious.

Dante grinned and thought briefly of Elias. They looked alike, he and his younger brother, but Elias was weak. He couldn't handle the life, didn't want the challenge. Wanted a picket fence and a passel of kids out in DC with his girl.

How boring. How fucking *mundane.*

A person would have to be crazy, to have a life of wealth and influence at their fingertips and pass it all up out of some squeamish sense of right and wrong.

Like Elias giving up his power for the suburbs, Dante wondered why this woman wouldn't use her looks to take advantage of those who wanted to bask in it. Why wouldn't a woman capitalize on that power? She could gain so much more from it, would make things easier for herself.

"I could make payments," the girl was telling Tony. Telling, not begging. Dante had to give her credit for that. She didn't look scared, either, which was surprising. The conservative way she was dressed, her lack of cosmetics and jewelry... she could have stepped straight out of a convent and into the club. If she made herself up a bit, used some of her beauty as a bargaining chip, she might get somewhere... but she wasn't. It could only mean one thing.

She had morals. Ethics. Scruples, and she held herself to them fastidiously, it would seem.

It wasn't very often Dante came across scrupulous person, especially a beautiful woman. They just didn't swim in the same waters he did, so to see one going toe-to-toe with his right hand man was fascinating. She wasn't scared of Tony, who looked like he chewed nails for breakfast and followed it up with rebar for lunch. She was a church mouse, but she didn't run from the big bad tom cat– no, she took him on, head to head.

Interesting.

The two went back and forth about the debt, getting nowhere fast, and Dante was becoming bored and about to intervene when the girl mentioned something about the tablet Tony had been working on.

"I put myself through college as a bookkeeper," she said, a smugness to her tone that amused him– to be proud of working as a bookkeeper?

But, he then considered, she'd obviously worked hard to achieve a goal. He could respect that. He knew a little something about having goals, himself. Earning what you had was the only way to know the worth of it. Dante had earned his keep with the family early. He had been young the first time he helped his father collect debts for the family, not even a teenager. That was when he learned how everything had a price and that sacrifices had to be made, if you were to achieve what you wanted in life.

The germ of an idea was forming in his mind. If she knew so damned much about bookkeeping, and she was looking for a solution to what her sister owed, they could have a mutually beneficial relationship. Her fear for her sister's safety would keep her in line, keep her loyal to the family, and if she could unsnarl the tangle the finances were in...

Dante listened a bit longer, enjoying how that little scrap of a woman put Tony in his place, reducing him to sheepish embarrassment.

"She's got you there, Tony," Dante said, speaking at last. He had come into the club in a bear of a mood, but watching this woman hold her own and show up a lifelong mobster had been the best thing Dante had seen all week... hell, probably all month.

"Boss, I–" Tony started, but Dante waved off whatever he was about to say and stood. He knew Tony was frustrated by his own incompetence when it came to the bookkeeping, but it wasn't his expertise. Dante needed and used Tony's talents around the club for other things. And, well, this unassuming woman might be exactly the answer to their problem.

"Give me the tablet and the envelope, Tony," Dante said as he took the few steps to the bar and purposely crowded the redhead's space. Something in Dante was satisfied when she didn't cower at his nearness; curiosity shifted deeper, into intrigue.

They both needed something: he needed a competent person looking at his books, but also one willing to keep their mouth shut, should they see something not-exactly-legal, and she wanted to pay off her sister's debt. Dante always enjoyed a little mutually-assured destruction, as long as he could stack the cards in his favor.

"Come upstairs with me, Ms...?"

"Lockheart. Cassie Lockheart."

He smiled as he shook her hand. It was tiny in his; he could crush it easily, if he chose... or perhaps not. Something told him it might not be as easy as he thought. He had the feeling that Ms. Lockheart had some hidden steel in her spine.

"I'm Dante, Ms. Lockheart." Her smile deepened as a faint blush colored her fair cheeks.

"Cassie," she whispered in response.

"Cassie." He released her hand and headed for the stairs, tossing over his shoulder, "Tony, when you're done with the delivery, please have the kitchen send up lunch for myself and Ms. Lockheart."

"Sure thing, boss. The regular?" Tony asked.

Dante flicked a look at Cassie, gauging her mood and level of agreeability. He noted that she, like he himself, had brown eyes... but hers were prettier than his own. Though his *were* very pretty.

"Do you eat steak, Cassie?" Dante pitched his voice toward the flirtatious. He wanted to tease her, to coax her, to lure her in. She wasn't the usual kind of woman he fucked, but something about her, her fire and determination, was interesting enough to warrant a second look. And perhaps a third, and even a fourth.

"I do."

He shot her a grin. "Yes, the usual, Tony," he called back, and then proceeded up the stairs without a backwards glance, confident Cassie was right at his heels.

The second floor of the club held the business offices for the club. The building that housed *Aphrodite's Palace* was huge– 20,000 square feet– and the second floor took up half of that. A counting room took up a lot of the space, because strip clubs still dealt in large amounts of cash, even in the age of plastic. And then there were the offices, the largest being Dante's.

Dante led her to his office and typed his number into the keypad at the door. His office was locked at all times, and only he had the entry code. He trusted several people to varying degrees and Tony, his father, and two younger brothers ranked at the top of the list, but he trusted no one implicitly and was taking no chances.

"Please come in," Dante said, holding open the door for Cassie.

He had not changed much of the room's opulence since the old *don*, his grandfather, Nonno Gio, had passed away almost two years earlier. He hadn't seen much need to; the dark oak bookcase, the black leather tuxedo-style couch with its brass tacks, and the gilding on everything from the legs of the furniture to the crown and base mouldings all screamed of old Italian mafia wealth and power, just the way he wanted and needed it to. It intimidated those needing to be intimidated, and impressed those needing to be impressed.

She took a step closer to the large painting that dominated his office. It was his family's coat of arms, Nonno Gio swearing it went back centuries, but Dante doubted that. He knew they had been little more than peasants back in Sicily before his great-great-grandfather had boarded a crowded steamer and set across the Atlantic in the late 1800s.

"Do you like it?" Dante asked as he stepped up behind her, close enough to smell the light floral scent of her perfume, and he almost laughed when she jumped at the sound of his voice.

She turned her head, wide brown eyes meeting his for just a second before they were back on the painting. The rampant eagle was especially menacing with the two spears crossing behind it. It grew more terrifying as one looked at it and came to understand its implications.

"It sure makes a statement, doesn't it?" she replied with diplomacy, adroitly side-stepping his question.

He wasn't satisfied with that non-answer.

"What does it say to you?" Dante persisted, leaning in even closer to whisper it into her ear.

"It says 'here be monsters'," she said flatly, and Dante couldn't stop his bark of laughter.

She eyed him as he laughed, deadpan, and it made him laugh harder. Dante hardly ever found anything genuinely funny. This little nothing of a woman had to have, by this point, some idea of who he was and what he was capable of. But she had called him and his family 'monsters' without a glimmer of fear. It was as astounding as it was amusing.

"Are you alright?" she asked as he wiped the tears of laughter from his eyes.

"I am, it was just your very apt description of my family's gaudy heraldry," he said with a faint gasp as he caught his breath. "Not many would dare to say it to my face."

She paled at his words but didn't flinch, even when Dante slipped an arm behind her back and gently guided her to the small dining table. He held the chair out for her to sit just as someone knocked on the door, signaling the arrival of their lunch.

"Come in," Dante called and took his seat across from her as two of the kitchen staff entered and set up their lunch. They placed two plates on the table, each loaded with prime rib steaks covered in a red-wine sauce, honey-buttered carrots, and mashed potatoes. A pitcher of sweet tea was set in the center of the table. Dante only drank alcohol sparingly, when he drank at all, and never so early in the day. He did not enjoy the loss of faculties that came with intoxication.

"Tea?" Dante asked, holding up the pitcher and, when Cassie nodded, poured both of them a glass.

"This looks and smells wonderful." She sounded both awed and bewildered.

"Come on, Cassie. You didn't expect the premiere gentleman's club in Dallas to serve chicken wings and fries, did you?" He knew by the wry look she shot him that she had, and he grinned as he picked up his fork and steak knife.

"Well, I've never been in a gentleman's club, full stop, so I didn't know what to expect. I will say it wasn't this, especially at ten in the morning."

Dante shrugged. He wasn't one for breakfast foods, and he wasn't usually in the club that early, anyway.

"Well, don't let it get cold," Dante said and tucked a bite of steak, dripping with sauce and juices, into his mouth. It was delicious, of course; Dante hired none but the most skilled and talented kitchen staff. Selling food made the club far less liable, should a patron overindulge and then get behind the wheel of a car. Plus, *Aphrodite's Palace* was the highest of high-end clubs. They provided only the best.

"So, how long have you been a bookkeeper?" He took a leisurely sip of his tea.

Cassie dabbed at her mouth with her napkin and replaced it in her lap. "I'm actually an accountant, now, because I got a degree in accounting, but I started bookkeeping in high school."

She took another careful bite of her lunch. He didn't think she went without, but this kind of luxury was obviously a treat for her, and Dante enjoyed watching her take pleasure in it. The more he watched her, the more obvious it became that she was attractive and she actively worked to hide it. The more he watched her, the more he enjoyed the idea of discovering the beautiful woman under all the frumpy clothing.

"Why bookkeeping in high school, instead of some fast-food joint?"

He himself had never worked a regular job, at a fast-food joint or anywhere else. He had apprenticed under his father and grandfather, groomed from birth to lead the family and all its enterprises. But he knew most teenagers worked at more menial kinds of jobs, not as a bookkeeper.

She shrugged and took a sip of tea before answering. She didn't seem compelled to rush an answer or fill the conversation with unnecessary chatter, nor did she speak without thinking– another thing to appreciate about Cassie Lockheart, it seemed.

"My foster mother did taxes and some bookkeeping at home. It allowed her to be able to both work and take care of us kids. When she realized I had an aptitude for math, she had me help her." Cassie smiled a little, clearly fond of the memory.

"Oh, did she use you to do her work for you?" Dante poked, wanting to needle her, just a little, to see how she'd react.

Cassie sat up straighter, her grip tightening on her fork, the faint smile fading instantly. It was like a kitten glaring down a lion, but such a visceral reaction spoke of love for her foster mother.

"Absolutely not. Carol and Mike were probably the first adults never to use me, for once. She just noticed I was good at math and encouraged me to take the bookkeeping classes offered by my high school and junior college. They even paid for them out of their own pocket."

Her tone hardened as her defense of her parents went on, her eyes blazing the whole while, and Dante held up his hands in mock surrender. Getting her that riled up served no purpose but to antagonize, and that was not what he wanted to do to her.

"I'm sorry, Cassie. It's just not what I've come to expect from those who grew up in the system. I meant no disrespect."

The anger retreated from her brown eyes like the tide in the morning. After a moment, her shoulders visibly relaxed and she continued.

"Yeah, Carol and Mike were extraordinary. Every child they cared for was lucky. I was very lucky." She stared down at her plate, deliberately not looking at him. He figured Carol and Mike must be dead, judging by her downcast expression.

"So, they fostered your strengths?" he asked, trying to turn the conversation back to something positive or at least neutral.

"They did, Carol especially," she confirmed. "It's because of them that I was able to finish college."

He nodded, pleased they'd overcome that conversational hurdle. Dante liked to push people, to make them uncomfortable and see how far they could go before breaking, but he also knew when to stop. There was only so far Cassie would go before she bolted, and he didn't want her to run. He wanted to learn her, figure out every nook and cranny of her mind... and he wanted her body too, that was for sure.

"Where did you go to school?" Perhaps that would help him figure her out.

"Nowhere fancy. I got my basics out of the way at the community college and then finished up at the University of Texas - Dallas. You?"

"I didn't go to college. My father and grandfather taught me how to take over the club and I went straight to work, much to the disap-

pointment of my mother." He ran much more than just the club, but
she didn't need to know that... yet. He just wanted to see her reaction
to the knowledge of what he was worth, what he controlled.

"Your mom wanted you to go to college?" she asked, to his
surprise not latching on to the implication that he was rich and
powerful. Most women did; most women were attracted to his wealth
and influence but again, Cassie was an outlier.

"She attended some fancy school like my brother... they studied
literature and history, but that wasn't me." He stopped abruptly,
sipping at his tea to give a more natural pause to his sudden halt. He
had very few weak points, and his mother was one of them.
Mentioning her had been a mistake, and far more than he ever
revealed to anyone, much less a stranger, but he was disarmed by
Cassie's lack of coyness, her failure to attempt a seduction.

"Carol and Mike didn't push me into some notion of what they
thought I should be. They let me figure out what I wanted." Then she
gave a hollow little laugh. "Or at least they tried, more than anyone
else did."

Dante nodded at that. He had been raised with no freedom whatsoever to choose his own path. It was sheer idiot luck that the family's
expectations suited him just fine. They didn't suit Elias, though, and
he had run to the other side of the country to distance himself from
them. Dante was born to be the *don*, to take control, and he enjoyed
that– thrived on it, even.

"Well, you seem to have done well, at least better than your
sister," Dante quipped, prodding at Cassie once again, searching for
another sore spot.

"Leave her out of this, she's not– she's fragile," Cassie retorted,
eyes flashing once more.

Dante was quickly learning that Cassie was fierce despite her
weakness. He admired that in others... as long as they weren't more
powerful than he. But that was a lesson he didn't need to teach
Cassie. Not yet, at least.

Dante picked up his glass and tipped it towards her, an unspoken agreement to cede the point and leave the matter of Amber alone... for now.

"I can leave her out of this, Cassie, since you've agreed to work off her debt." Cassie nodded shortly, and he continued. "As you can see, the club needs someone to keep the books... and the privacy of our business."

She opened her mouth to say something, probably that she wouldn't do anything illegal, and he held up his hand, silencing her.

"Don't worry your pretty head, Cassie. The club's books are all above-board. The *Palace* is a legal enterprise, but the bar and the restaurant receipts have been coming up short for months. Tony took them over, to try to figure out who is stealing and why, but he's a mess at the books and I don't have the time to do it myself. I run this club and three others, besides."

"Among your other enterprises," she murmured with a hint of teasing, but he smiled.

"Cassie, darlin', we all have a boss." The lie fell from his lips with ease and her shoulders relaxed. *Good.* He wanted her to feel at ease with him, and if she didn't know he was the big bad mob boss that led her sister astray, all the better.

"So you'll come in three nights a week and do the books, figure out what or who is losing my money."

"I don't have to come in, you can have someone else enter the receipts and I can do the balancing at home." she protested, but he shook his head.

"Absolutely not. You will do the entry and balance the books. Everything." He eyed her over the rim of the glass he held, noting her irritation but also how she held it back. "You can start today, since you seem free, and then we can work out the nights you'll come back and continue. The club is closed on Mondays, so our week is from Tuesday to Sunday."

She nodded. "I'll do it, but only for six months. That should be more than enough of my time and expertise to pay off my sister's debt," she countered.

Dante lips curved in a faint smile. He enjoyed a woman who knew her worth.

"It's a deal." He extended his hand over the table and she gave it a firm shake, returning his smile. She obviously felt like she had won this round. It was funny, how wrong she was. As always, Dante knew he had gotten the better end of the bargain.

When they finished their meal, Dante showed her to a room that was no better than an old storage room, holding a desk and chair and nothing else, unless you counted the boxes and dust. The sole window was begrimed with decades of dirt and outside's broiling sunlight could barely pass through it.

"You can work here," he told her, watching to see if she'd take offense, to be given such a shabby space. When she only nodded in comprehension, he escorted her back to the stairs and watched as she descended. Then he went back to his office and called Tony.

"Yes, boss," Tony answered on the first ring.

"Find out anything and everything about Cassandra Lockheart. I want the information by tomorrow." Dante ended the call before Tony could respond.

She was an enigma, one he would study and learn... and conquer. She might not realize it, but she'd caught his attention.

How long she kept it remained to be seen.

CHAPTER

THREE

"What do you mean, you have to work tonight? It's Friday night, Cassie!" Sarah complained through the cell phone as Cassie pulled Betsy into the parking lot of *Aphrodite's Palace*. Even though it was only eight o'clock on, yes, a Friday night, the parking lot was already more than half full.

"Sarah, I told you I took a side job." Cassie turned the car off and looked down at her clothes. She had hoped eight p.m. was early enough to come in and it would still be slow. She didn't want people gawking at her as she moved through the club. The people she'd met on Tuesday, after her strange lunch with Dante, had been polite, and the dancers had been friendly enough, but she still felt like an oddity among them. It was a world where she didn't belong, and she knew it showed on her face.

"Yeah, but I thought it was freelance, like a few of your other projects. I wanted to have dinner and then go dancing," Sarah whined and Cassie laughed at her sulky tone.

"Then go, Sarah. I know you have other friends besides me." It was true. Sarah was a social butterfly, vivacious and lively, and people flocked to her. It was still a wonder that Sarah ever picked Cassie as a friend, when they had met in college. From that first moment in class, it was like Sarah knew Cassie needed someone fun and light-hearted, and Sarah had been that for Cassie: someone to smile with, watch stupid movies and do facials with. Someone she didn't have to worry about.

She had even stuck around when things got so bad for Cassie sophomore year, when so many hadn't. Sarah was special.

"Yes, but I love you the most of all of them," Sarah grumbled.

"I'm sorry, sweetie. But I can make it up to you."

"Shopping?" Sarah was already perking back up.

"Yes, we can go shopping." Sarah was always trying to get Cassie into tighter, more flattering and stylish clothes but she didn't and would never understand. She knew Sarah's concern came from a good place, but it wouldn't change who Cassie was.

"Now... I gotta go." Cassie hung up as a limo unloaded at least a dozen men, all rowdy and noisy as they entered the club. Their boisterous antics reinforced her lack of enthusiasm for the night ahead, but she knew the longer she waited, the harder it would be to talk herself into doing it.

Cassie gathered up her courage and her purse and got out of the car. One deep breath and quick jog later, she was standing in front of one very large, very formidable bouncer.

"No single ladies," the bouncer said, barely looking at her before motioning her away like some gnat.

"No, I– I'm–"

"I don't care if you're here looking for your husband, either. You need an escort to get in, baby girl." The bouncer laughed down at her.

Cassie gritted her teeth. His disregard of her wasn't new; many people did. Her small size and drab presentation seemed to declare that to them that she was inconsequential. While that was usually true, it wasn't in this case, and she would be damned if she would be late on her first night. She needed to make a good impression– for Amber.

"I'm not here for fun," she told him. The 'you idiot' at the end she left unsaid, but the implication was clear. "I'm the new bookkeeper, Cassie."

Finally the man actually looked at her, instead of only giving a dismissive glance, and swore under his breath.

"Shit, Ms. Lockheart. I'm sorry, ma'am." The bouncer straightened from where he'd been slouching against the wall and looked at her with something approaching respect. It was a total 180 to his behavior just moments before, and it threw Cassie for a loop.

"I'm sorry, I'm Bruno. I work the door on the weekends. The boss said to be on the lookout for you, but you weren't..." Bruno trailed off and inexplicably looked worried again.

What the hell, Cassie wondered, but forced a smile anyway.

"It's okay, simple mistake," she replied. The big bouncer smiled back at her, clearly relieved, and opened the door for her. Cassie had little time to worry about the bouncer because stepping through the door to *Aphrodite's Palace* was like entering a different dimension.

A popular song, sultry and intense, pounded through the club, sending a subtle vibration through Cassie, and it looked very different in full swing, at night, than it had when empty and quiet in the middle of day on Tuesday. At that time, all she could see was a sea of red velvet chairs and black tables.

Now, no matter where she looked, all she saw were people. They were mainly men, but some women were present, too. Cassie tried her best not to stare, but it was hard; everyone was dressed and coiffed and made up to make their best romantic impression, with trendiness and sexiness being the priority. The extent of Cassie's 'clubbing' was going to Cliff's for karaoke on Fridays, when Sarah or her work friends could talk her into it, but that was just a small neighborhood pub. This was the polar opposite in every way.

Resolutely, Cassie kept her eyes from the main stage, because she knew she would be helpless to keep from gawking at the woman dancing there. The smaller stage by the packed main bar was distracting enough. Oh, she wasn't attracted to women, but it was an amazing feat, the way she swung around the pole and then stopped, seeming to defy gravity by holding her body parallel to the floor with just her arms, which looked entirely too twig-like to be able to support her weight in that way.

"Are you lost, hon?"

Cassie jumped at the feminine voice in her ear and turned to see a beautiful brunette. She wore a slinky black robe, a friendly smile, and very little else.

"H– hi." Cassie closed her eyes for a second and took a deep, steadying breath before reopening them. The woman was still standing there, looking amused, Cassie returned her smile weakly.

"Are you Cassie?" the woman asked. How did she know–? Cassie nodded her head, even more confused than she had been outside, with the bouncer.

"I'm Miranda. I'm kind of an unofficial manager for the girls." Miranda put out her hand and Cassie shook it, unsurprised to see her fingers tipped with long, expertly manicured nails. Everything about this woman screamed 'sexy'.

"Manager?" Cassie asked, raising her voice over the music of the club. Miranda nodded and threaded her arm through one of Cassie's, leading her toward the bar as another sizable crowd of men came in the entrance behind them.

"I've worked here almost seven years, and I have a decent head on my shoulders, so I help Tony and Mr. Dante, as most of the girls like to call him. I do the schedule and make sure the new girls are trained properly. I was supposed to meet with your sister Amber last night. That was when Tony told me you've put her in rehab."

Cassie wasn't thrilled to have her sister's business known so publicly but she nodded as they made their way through the crowd, Miranda smiling at various men and even waving at a few. Everyone seemed to know her.

"Yes, I'm sorry if that was an inconvenience for anyone expecting her," Cassie said, but Miranda waved her words off with a smile.

"Don't be. If rehab is what Amber needs, then this isn't the place for her."

A feeling of relief and validation trickled through Cassie's apprehension; she hadn't thought anyone would agree with her, had believed everyone would think her overprotective. Cassie found herself liking Miranda for agreeing with her on the issue.

"So you're going to be doing the books for the club?" Miranda continued. She tilted up her chin to one of the bartenders; he nodded and began to approach them through the busy group of workers behind the bar.

"Yes. Amber–" Cassie started to explain, but Miranda held up her hand to stop her.

"I don't need to know. I've seen Amber around, more and more, the past few months. I can imagine what happened– she got in some trouble, and you're being a good sister...?" Cassie nodded at Miranda's implied question. "Came to the rescue and saved her," Miranda finished, and all Cassie could do was stare at the woman.

Miranda gave a little shrug. "I'm good at reading people. Have to be; I'm working on my PhD in psychology right now..." Miranda leaned in and stage-whispered, "...but don't let that get around." Cassie nodded with a laugh.

"Who's your friend, Miranda?" The bartender asked, finally arriving in front of them. He was handsome, dark, with longish hair in a low ponytail and a charming smile.

"This is Cassie, the new bookkeeper," Miranda replied.

His smile dropped, just a bit, so quickly that Cassie wondered if maybe she had imagined it. But he definitely seemed more wary of her than he had been moments earlier.

"Nice to meet you, Cassie." He reached across the bar to shake her hand. "I'm Juan."

"Nice to meet you, Juan," Cassie said with a smile, returning his handshake.

"Juan's not just one of the bartenders, he's the *head* bartender," Miranda told Cassie with exaggerated, teasing awe. "He's been here even longer than I have."

"Can I get you two lovely ladies anything to drink?" he asked, using a cloth to wipe down the long bar, his attention seemingly transfixed by the search for water spots on the already-gleaming wood. Cassie tried not to take it personally, that he seemed to be avoiding eye contact with her. Maybe he knew Amber and her troubles. Maybe he thought Cassie was the same.

She mentally shrugged. It didn't matter what Juan thought about her– or didn't think about her. She had a job to do, and that was all she was there for. Not to make friends.

"I'll take my usual Long Island iced tea, Juan. And charge it to Mike's tab." Miranda turned to Cassie. "Do you want anything? A water or a soda, maybe?"

The question shook Cassie from her pondering Juan's behavior. She smiled, glad that Miranda, at least, seemed genuinely nice. "A bottle of water would be great."

Cassie reached into her purse to pull out some cash, but Juan waved her off, handing her a bottle from one of the coolers under the bar.

"Water is free around these parts, ma'am," he teased with an exaggerated Texas accent that made Cassie laugh a little. Maybe she had imagined his coolness to her, after all. She was nervous, and she felt like she stuck out like a sore thumb. It would be easy to imagine that the new girl was an unwelcome interloper.

"Thanks." Cassie opened the bottle and took a long sip, trying to be surreptitious as she glanced around. A part of her had been both fearing and hoping to run into Dante tonight.

"Are you looking for someone?" Miranda asked, and Cassie jumped and shook her head quickly.

"No!" she said, a little too loudly even in the noisy club, and cleared her throat. "No I–" Cassie dropped her voice and leaned a little closer to Miranda's ear. "I've never been in a strip club before," she admitted, and felt her face heat from the embarrassment.

"Oh, hon, it's a culture shock, for sure, but you get used to it." Miranda accepted her drink from Juan, who had already turned away to other customers, and threaded her arm through Cassie's to walk towards a familiar set of stairs.

"Come find me if you get hungry or need a break," Miranda said with a companionable squeeze of the arm. "It's busy tonight, but I'll happily take a break and spend some more time talking with you, if you like."

"Thank you, Miranda, so much," Cassie replied, meaning it. Having a friendly face leading her through the club had helped ease a lot of her fears and worries about how she'd have managed it alone.

"No problem at all! I look forward to getting to know you better." With one last squeeze of Cassie's arm she was off, fluttering through the club, a sultry butterfly in black satin, smiling and greeting everyone she passed before sitting on the lap of an older, well-dressed gentleman and whispering something in his ear.

Cassie observed her for a few moments, wondering what it was like to be a woman like Miranda, so confident in herself, in her sensuality. Cassie finally shook her head, laughing internally at herself, before starting the climb up the stairs.

She needed to keep her head on straight; she just had to do the job, figure out who might steal from the club, and get her sister out of trouble. She couldn't afford to focus on anything else. It was a job, and a short-term one, at that. Soon she would be back to her regular, boring life... just the way she liked it.

...Or so she told herself, as she entered the dinky little office that would be hers for the next few months and sighed.

CHAPTER

FOUR

Dante observed Cassie's arrival from one of his preferred booths. It was almost hidden in an alcove, swathed in shadows, and had a perfect view of the entire club. From there he could watch the patrons of *Aphrodite's Palace*, the bartenders at their craft, and the girls as they went about ensuring the customers were happy, all at once.

He had learned plenty about her from the file that Ricardo, his best investigator, had been able to put together... plenty, and at the same time, not nearly enough.

He was itching to get her alone again, to see if the goodness and the loyalty were a façade or not. It had been his experience that everyone lied, even to themselves. He wanted to know if she really were the savior of his books that she touted herself to be, or if it were about what she could gain.

Though her being in the club at all was a check in her favor; she seemed genuine in her care and concern for her sister, at least.

Cassie was early for her scheduled shift, no doubt hoping to miss some of the crowd that she had had to wade through the night before. She was dressed to blend in, with a baggy long-sleeved shirt that covered much of her pale skin and dark jeans, but whatever anonymity she gained with her clothes was negated by the riotous red curls pulled back into another messy bun on the top of her head.

Every time a beam of light glanced off her hair, she glowed like a torch... a human torch, and he was more like a moth drawn to her flame than he'd like. She was just a slip of a woman, tiny and easily broken, with her slight frame and hunched shoulders, walking with her head down. He wanted to peel off her layers and discover why she hid her beauty.

His gaze followed her as Miranda put herself in Cassie's path. He had asked the shrewd stripper to introduce herself to the meek bookkeeper.

"Of course, Dante, but why?" Miranda had asked in his office the prior afternoon, before she changed for her shift on the floor. She folded herself into a chair and crossed her denim-clad legs, an indication she wasn't going anywhere until he explained.

Over the years, she had become a staple at the *Palace*. She had first started there during her sophomore year in college, needing the money and also wanting to study the culture of the club. Dante had hired her, over Tony's protests, and he was glad he had. Miranda was an asset to the club, one he hoped wouldn't leave even once she eventually aged out of the industry.

They had an interesting relationship. He had never tried to bed her, no matter how beautiful she was, even if half the club thought they had fucked at least once. She was too astute, too valuable to the club. "Don't shit where you eat," was one of Nonno's favorite pieces of advice, and Dante followed it scrupulously. He knew better than to let his dick do his thinking. Nothing came before the business.

"No real reason," Dante replied, paging through a pile of documents and reports, before glancing up to meet her eyes. "I don't understand her. And I don't like when I don't understand something. It bears investigation, don't you think?"

Miranda studied him in silence for a moment. Dante was well aware of the challenge he presented to a psychology student; she'd never truly comprehend him– no one could, not really– but he had to give her credit for trying. And then more credit for knowing when not to push him.

"Alright," Miranda said eventually, proving just that. "So why do I need to befriend her?"

Because he wanted to fuck her. That was the simple answer, but the complicated one was that he wanted to know Cassie. He wanted to peer under her façade and see if she were as good and sweet as she seemed. It was unlikely. Women in his experience were crafty and at times deceptive creatures, and yet... and yet, there was a beguiling hint of genuine decency about her that he couldn't simply write off.

"Because you have a better chance of getting information out of her than I do." Dante was not one to inspire easy friendship and open revelations, but Miranda was a master of making people feel comfortable, of ingratiating herself and rendering others compliant. She mostly used it to get men to open their wallets in the club, but Dante was not above using it for his own purposes.

"So what kind of information am I supposed to be weaseling out of her?" Miranda asked, her tone gently teasing. "I'm not doing anything illegal for you, boss. I look horrible in prison orange."

Dante barked out a laugh as he rose and went to his office door, opening it to indicate their meeting was over.

"Don't worry, I have others who don't mind prison orange," he said with a grin. "Just get her to open up a little, share why she's here, why it matters so much to her that her sister not come back. Why she seems so horrified to see a naked person every time she walks in the door."

Miranda gave a laugh of her own as she passed him while leaving. "She's not *that* bad, is she?"

"No," Dante had replied, mostly to himself. "She's not that bad at all."

Now Miranda was escorting Cassie around, introducing her to a few of the waitresses and a couple of the other strippers who hadn't been in the previous night. Then she led Cassie to the bar where they talked to Juan once again. The bartender tucked a drink umbrella behind Cassie's ear with a flirty grin and an itchy little niggle of displeasure uncurled in Dante's belly. If Juan thought though he was going to count Cassie as one of his sexual conquests, he had another thing coming. Cassie was far too good for the likes of him.

Miranda's gaze skimmed over the club's inhabitants, seeming to be searching for someone in particular. Dante knew it was him when their eyes met and hers widened. She gave him a subtle nod and turned back to the bar, pulling Cassie away and grabbing the bottle of water from Juan herself. They disappeared up the stairs, and Dante turned his attention to the bartender, now wiping down the bar, oblivious to how he'd just irked his boss.

Dante had wanted to fire Juan for a while; he liked to fuck his way through the dancers, and more than once it had been a problem in the club, but the man was a distant cousin on his mother's side, so he had been making exceptions for family. Juan was also a decent dealer who moved a lot of weight with good connections. He made the family a lot of money, but not so much that he wasn't as expendable as any other employee who annoyed Dante more than he was worth.

"Boss?" He turned his attention from the bar and toward Tony, who had approached while Dante had been focused on Juan.

"Yes?"

"They're here." Tony gesturing to two men filling the door of the club. They represented a motorcycle club out of Arizona, having approached one of Dante's men in hopes of a meeting. They needed a new source of heroin, and the di Ruggieros were the largest and best heroin distributors in the southern United States. This was the first meeting, and an important one. It could be very lucrative for the family if this worked out, extending their reach well out into the southwest.

Dante stood as the two rough-looking bikers, clad in leather vests with their precious insignia embroidered over their chests. Dante never understood organisations like that, flaunting themselves in front of whoever was watching, like a lay person... or law enforcement. It just invited unnecessary and unwanted trouble, but biker gangs, street gangs and even fucking college fraternities thrived on announcing who and how bad they were, wherever they went.

"Gentlemen," Dante said to the men, extending his hand first to the older-looking of the two. If his information was correct, this was Lake, the president of their chapter, a powerful and, some said, cruel leader.

"*Don* di Ruggiero." The man took his hand in a firm shake, his dark eyes and bronze-toned skin giving away his Native American heritage if the long, straight black hair pulled away from his face hadn't already.

"Please call me Dante. The *don* was my grandfather." Dante kept his tone pleasant. He wanted them to feel welcome. Moreover, he wanted their money. "You must be Lake."

Lake nodded. Dante extended his hand to the other, much larger, biker. Tattoos covered almost every visible bit of skin on the man's arms, hands, neck and even crept up over his jaws. He looked like the muscle Dante's information had painted him to be.

"And you must be Kane." The large man simply nodded and said nothing. "Please have a seat." Dante gestured to the table he had just risen from. There were only three seats at the table, but Dante wasn't alone. His men dotted the club, all watching. Marco was the closest, sitting just a table over, within earshot should Dante need the help of his dangerous younger brother.

"Thank you for taking this meeting with us," Lake said.

Dante gave him a slight smile in response. "Tony said that you and he have a mutual friend?"

Lake nodded. "Yeah, Kane and I served in the Marine Corps with Tony's younger brother, Joey, so I knew through him that Tony worked here at your club." He shrugged. "I took a chance calling Tony since Joey isn't exactly of our world."

It was true; Tony's brother was a straight as an arrow, a football coach for a high school outside of Houston. Joey lived one of those boring, normal lives Dante rolled his eyes at... until he needed a little blow for his bachelor party a few years back, or a few dancers to cele-brate his thirty-fifth birthday, and then he wasn't quite the straight arrow his wife and co-workers thought him to be.

"Well, I'm glad you did. Your proposition is tempting, but I'm curious why you need so much weight. I hate to look a gift horse in the mouth, but trust is not something I extend to strangers, as a rule." Dante pretended to sip his scotch, then waved over a waitress. "Would you like a drink while we talk?"

Maribel approached the table. "Good evening, gentlemen. What can I get you?" She placed two napkins on the table in front of Lake and Kane.

"I'll get a beer, something domestic in a bottle," Kane answered her. Dante was unsurprised to find his voice as gruff as his appearance.

"And for you, sir?" Maribel asked Lake with a smile, and as the more obviously personable of the two, he returned it.

"I'll have a whiskey, neat," he answered. She nodded and departed for the bar.

"So how did you come to need my services? And such a large supply?" Dante asked once she had gone, getting straight to the point. He didn't need to seduce them to buy from him. They needed his merchandise, and that gave him the upper hand in the negotiations.

"Here you are, gentlemen." Maribel's chipper voice interrupted Lake before he could answer. "One beer, domestic, in a bottle." She set the brown bottle on the napkin in front of Kane, who may have grunted something resembling a 'thank you', but Dante couldn't be sure.

"And one whiskey neat," she said, placing the drink in front of Lake. "Need anything else?"

"Not right now, thank you, Maribel," Dante answered her with a smile that told her he was done with her. She smiled back her under-standing and vanished into the surrounding crowd.

Like all parts of this meeting, Dante had chosen her to wait on them, because she was one his best and most professional waitresses. She had worked there long enough to read when someone needed something... and when not to interrupt. She had perfect timing, dropping off the drinks before they got down to the real business.

"Sorry about that," Dante said easily. His smile and charm seemed to put at least Lake at ease, though Kane still looked pissed off at the world.

Lake took a slug of his whiskey before answering. "We had been buying from an MC out of California that had some good connections in South America, but they've had a regime change and are no longer a viable option for us," Lake answered, his tone casual but tension seemed to hold him taut.

Dante studied how the other man's hand clenched and relaxed around his whiskey glass. He didn't think Lake was lying– in fact, he was sure he wasn't– but that wasn't the real story. It wasn't the *why*. And whys were what mattered in their business. The whys earned you money... or sent you behind bars, or to an early grave.

"When you say 'regime change', is this someone you're now at war with?" Dante asked, and Lake tossed back the rest of his whiskey in one swallow.

"We aren't at war with them, but we will never work with them again. It's–" Lake cut his eyes to Kane so quickly that a less perceptive person might have missed it, but Dante missed nothing.

"It's personal. We aren't at war, but we cannot work together anymore," Lake finally finished and Dante relaxed back into the red velvet of his chair and regarded the two men. He could tell Lake wasn't lying, but he also knew he wouldn't get the entire story, and that was fine. He just wanted to make sure there wouldn't be new heat brought down on the family from this deal. They were still recovering from their own bullshit.

Dante nodded once and straightened once more. "And you have a set network of dealers? Ready to get this out onto the streets in your territory?" he asked.

Lake nodded, his brawny frame loosening in a clear sign of relief flooding his body. Damn, the fucker was a mess of tells. No wonder they did little business outside their square of sand in Arizona.

"We do. We have the experience and manpower to move heavy weight." Lake leaned forward in his eagerness.

"Well, I think we can do business, then, gentlemen. We have a shipment coming in just under two weeks– three kilos." Dante watched in disbelief as Lake's eyes grew almost comically large, and internally groaned. Fuck, they thought three kilos was a lot? That was child's play, in Dante's world.

"How much do you think you can move?" He sipped his scotch again, unfazed, as the two bikers glanced at each other. Surprisingly, Kane was the one who seemed to give the permission with the shrug of his bear-like shoulders.

"We can move at least a kilo a month," Lake answered.

Dante nodded. "Two keys, then?" His tone of voice was the same one he used to order an espresso in the mornings, utterly casual and detached.

"Two? At what price?"

And here came the negotiations. Dante wondered how much cash their club had available to make the deal.

His cartel family in Mexico sourced the heroin from Central America. In truth, Dante knew that its purity was almost unparalleled, and that meant he could get a premium price for it. The purer the source, the more their street dealers could cut it down, make a profit, and still have a happy clientele.

Dante's Southeast and East Coast clients paid $300,000 to $400,000 a kilo, but something told him these men couldn't afford that, not yet. He wanted their business, but he wasn't going to undercut his product, either. He had people to pay, as well.

"Two-seventy-five," he stated, and Kane choked on his beer. Dante chose to ignore his reaction.

"A kilo?" Lake's voice was an octave higher than before. Dante said nothing as the two men looked at each other again in silent conversation.

"That's more than double what we're used to paying for H," Lake answered at last.

"I doubt the H you're used to buying is 80% pure, either. In fact, I know it's not, because my family is the only source of H that pure coming into the United States." Dante ran his finger around the rim of his rocks glass and let that little tidbit of information soak in. "Can you get your hands on enough cash for two kilos, gentlemen? Yes or no?"

He was tiring of the hemming and hawing. They needed the heroin more than he needed to sell it to them. Why were they still talking? Dante decided to drop the price to move things along.

"Could you manage two-twenty-five a kilo?" Again, silence as they considered their options. Dante forged ahead. "But know that this is a one-time discount, gentlemen. I am not an unfair man, and I want to grow this relationship between our organizations, but that's the lowest I can go."

He drained the last of his scotch. He was done with this meeting. He was becoming bored. They were going to say yes. He knew it, and they knew it.

Once more, Lake looked at Kane, who with a shrug seemed to agree with the price.

"We can do that, Dante," Lake answered and extended his hand across the small table to seal the deal.

Dante shook it. "Then, gentlemen, we have a deal. I will expect payment in full in two weeks. We'll arrange for it to be transported to El Paso, but it will be up to your organization to take it from there to Arizona. Cross-state delivery is quite a bit more expensive, you understand, and I'm already giving you a deep introductory discount."

"Introductory?" Kane grunted his question and Dante sighed. He hated repeating himself and this monster of man either wasn't paying attention a few minutes earlier, or he was trying to manipulate him. Dante didn't appreciate either of those possibilities.

"Yes, if you're pleased with the product, you will not only make plenty of money to afford to pay what my H is worth, you will *want* to, to keep the supply lines open. We'll renegotiate the price when you're ready to buy more." Dante's tone was firm and allowed for no argument.

Lake was the first to nod his acceptance of Dante's words. He was an eager one, Lake was, but something told Dante the actual decision-making came from Kane, for whatever reason.

"We'll see if it's as good as you say," the large man finally relented.

Dante leaned back in his chair and crossed his leg over his knee. His posture reflected how he felt in the moment: confident, bored, and indifferent.

"Yes, the proof is in the pudding, as my *nonna* liked to say when I was a child." Dante stood. The other men did as well, understanding the motion as a wordless indication that the meeting was over. Dante would leave them to be Tony's problem for the night.

"Gentlemen, please enjoy the rest of your evening. I have matters elsewhere that require my attention, but Tony–"

Tony appeared from the shadows and smiled at the men.

"–will take care of you. Tony, make sure their drinks are on the house tonight." With one last set of eye contact between him and them, Dante took his leave. "Please enjoy."

Maribel and a couple of girls moved in to make sure Lake and Kane had a good night, and Dante made his way to the stairs. It was well past nine, and Cassie had not come down once. The prior night, she had crept downstairs and requested some dinner, but the club was much busier the present night. Dante would bet the contents of his bank account that she was too nervous to venture out of her safe little cave.

That was alright. He would go to her– that time.

But she'd be the one coming to him the next.

CHAPTER

FIVE

On Saturday, Cassie woke up mid-morning to her dog, in all her gray scruffy glory, whining.

"Sorry, Lucy, late night," Cassie said with a yawn as she stretched, then reached down and scratched the mutt behind her ears. She tossed back her covers and stood up, frowning to see the time on her phone. She was usually up hours before that and knew Lucy would be dying for her walk by that point.

Cassie slipped on some soft shorts; the long, baggy t-shirt she'd slept in covered most of her body and would do for a top. She shoved her feet into her sandals and grabbed Lucy's leash– and then her phone rang. It was Amber, again. Cassie swiped to ignore the call, then set the phone to 'silent' and left it on her nightstand.

Amber had called every day since arriving in Colorado, and spent each call begging to come home. It was a voluntary program and she could leave at any time, but she had no money to fly home, and Cassie refused to buy her a plane ticket until she completed the full sixty-day program. Listening to Amber cycle through pleading, then bargaining, then insults was exhausting, and Cassie felt no guilt in choosing not to answer her sister's call.

"Come on, Lucy, let's go potty, and then get some breakfast!"

Cassie said with determined cheerfulness, and bent to clip the leash on her collar.

Cassie spent the day resolutely ignoring Amber's calls. There had been so many when Amber had first begun her rehab that they concerned Cassie to the point of calling the clinic early on Friday, to make sure her sister was not truly in such a high level of distress, but one of the counselors explained that frequent calls were part of the process for many.

"We used to restrict phone calls in the first week, but we learned it was counterproductive and led to many of our clients feeling like they were in jail. We don't want that, but you need to know this isn't your sister calling you, this is the addict in her."

The counselor spent over an hour answering Cassie's questions and belaying her fears. It wasn't the first time someone Cassie loved had gone to rehab– their birth mother had been to one several times– but this was different. Cassie felt responsible for Amber in a way she hadn't for their mother. After the talk she felt better, more assured that it was best for Amber, but it was still hard to maintain her resolve. Amber was uniquely able to make Cassie feel weak.

At four in the afternoon, Cassie got ready to go to work at the club. Miranda had told her that the club filled up early on Saturdays, so Cassie was determined to get there by five and beat the crowd. She just couldn't handle all those eyes on her the way they had been the previous night.

Other than that, her first evening had been fine. She had begun combing through months and months of inventory reports, payroll, receipts, and it was all a jumbled mess. It would take her a while to get it all sorted in an organized manner, and then she could see where the shorts were coming from.

Cassie headed into the club right at five o'clock, relieved that the crowd was sparse and mellow, and pleased to see Miranda again. Meeting and talking with her yesterday had eased several of her fears... but not all of them. It was nice to have the start of a friendship, at least at the club.

"Cassie!" She turned her head to see Miranda making her way through the tables in her direction. When she arrived at Cassie's side, she leaned in for a hug.

"Hi, Miranda." Cassie returned the hug and couldn't help but feel boring next to the striking woman in little more than a silk and lace robe. Her insecurities weren't Miranda's fault, though, and the smile she gave the woman was genuine as she pulled out of the embrace.

"You're early tonight." Again, Miranda slipped her arm through Cassie's and guided her through the club, stopping to introduce her to a few people Cassie hadn't met the previous night, before taking her to the bar to say hello to Juan.

"Yeah, I wanted to get an early start on the books," Cassie answered and thanked Juan for the bottle of water he knew to give her by now. She blushed when he put a silly drink umbrella behind her ear. He seemed more friendly that evening than he had been the night before.

"Wanted to get an early start, or wanted to avoid the crowd?" Miranda asked, and Cassie ducked her head as they walked toward the stairs.

"Am I that obvious?"

Miranda shrugged one delicate shoulder and smiled. "Not really. I'm just good at reading people, is all. Is it the sex that makes you uncomfortable? Or is it the men?" Miranda prodded further and Cassie felt very much like a bug under a dissecting microscope. Her face must have shown her discomfort at the questions because Miranda hastened to apologize.

"Sorry, Cassie." She reached out and squeezed Cassie's arm. "Sometimes I can't turn off the psychologist even when it's rude. I hope you'll forgive me."

Cassie smiled a little at Miranda. In truth, while her questions were abrupt and uncomfortable, Cassie admired the other woman's honesty.

"It's okay, Miranda. I feel like I don't belong here, and it makes me uncomfortable. It's not the work you do or anything, I just really hate standing out. I've learned it's better to just blend in."

Miranda nodded and thankfully let the conversation drop. "Well, I don't know if I can help you blend in, but I'm here if you need anything else. I've got to dash back to my table, he's a regular– and a good regular, at that– but I wanted to say 'hi'. Pop down later, we can eat dinner together."

And she slipped away with a wave, disappearing into the growing crowd. Cassie unclipped the velvet rope that indicated none but employees were allowed beyond it and made her way upstairs to the small room she had claimed as her office.

She had been absorbed in numbers and pay logs and inventory receipts for a few hours when her phone rang. She pushed her reading glasses up onto her head, grabbing her phone from her purse, and sighed when she saw the number.

It was Amber... again. Cassie let the phone ring, the number for the rehab a stark reminder on her phone screen. The phone fell silent and then started ringing once more, right away: Amber again. Cassie took a deep breath and answered the phone.

"Hi, Amber–"

"Why aren't you answering when I call you?" her sister screeched, so loudly that Cassie actually checked to see if her phone was on speaker. It wasn't.

"Amber, I'm sorry. I've been busy–" she started, but Amber interrupted.

"Busy? Busy doing what? Don't lie, Cassie, I know you have no life."

Cassie flinched at her sister's angry words. She tried to tell herself it was just the withdrawal talking, and that once Amber worked through it, she wouldn't be so upset anymore. But a small part of Cassie didn't believe it; Amber had always lashed out when she didn't get her way, even in childhood, and Cassie was often the target of her rage.

Cassie closed her eyes and pinched the bridge of her nose,

"Amber, what do you need?"

"I need to come home. Tony called here, Cassie. They're going to hurt me if I don't pay them back. I need to leave and come back to Dallas." Amber was lying, of course, but what concerned Cassie wasn't the lie itself– addicts lie– but how easily Amber had told it.

"Amber, I know that's not true," Cassie replied in a steady voice.

"How would you know that? You don't know how to handle people like Tony. They will chew you up like the mouse you are, and not even blink."

The viciousness of Amber's words took Cassie by surprise. Her sister could be mean, especially when she didn't get what she wanted, but this seemed to be a new, worse level of mean, and not something Cassie was ready for or equipped to deal with.

"Amber, I know because I'm working at the club– for you. It would be counterproductive for them to threaten you when I'm already working here." Cassie's voice remained calm, a calm she didn't feel.

"You are not! I know you said you would talk to them. But I can't believe– what could you possibly be doing for them?" Amber's incredulous voice only rose in volume.

"Don't worry about it, Amber, please just focus on getting clean. Do the work. It will help."

Amber sighed. "I hate it here." Amber's voice became small and sad.

Cassie's heart hurt to hear her pain. "I know it's not fun–"

"Not *fun!*" Amber interrupted, angry again. The rapid-fire changing of her moods was giving Cassie emotional whiplash. "It's worse than *not fun*. They want to talk about everything. My childhood, my past, shit that's none of their business and shit that will not help me get clean."

Cassie sighed, because that was the crux of the problem. Amber's addiction was about avoidance. She wasn't ready to tackle things and really fix them, at least not yet, and if she came home before that, she would never be free.

"I know, sissy, and I'm sorry, but you need to stay and do the work."

Amber sighed, and an automated voice broke in declaring they had two minutes left before the call disconnected.

"Amber, stay. Get well. Next week starts some family therapy. I'll be video chatting with you and your doctors then. I will help you through this. I love you," she told her sister.

Amber took a deep breath. "I love you, too, Cassie. I'll try a little longer."

Cassie smiled at Amber's quiet words and hope bloomed anew in her chest. Maybe her sister could beat back this dragon after all. "Talk to you soon, okay?"

Amber mumbled a goodbye, and the line went dead. Cassie tossed her phone down and rested her face in her hands, elbows propped up on the desk. She felt wrung out and weary and so very alone. Sarah was supportive, but she didn't understand, not really. She had grown up so differently from Cassie, her parents still married, no one broken in her life. Not broken like Amber or like their mother had been.

"Are you okay, Cassie?" a deep voice asked her, and she jumped and flinched away at the feeling of a large warm hand rubbing comforting circles on her back. She never let anyone touch her back. She cringed to the side, turning to find that it was Dante in all his sexy, frightening glory, but the look in his eyes was softer than it had been on that first day.

Cassie had thought her reaction to him the first day a fluke, especially since she hadn't seen him at all the previous night. She had tried not to be disappointed, chalking up whatever she felt to simple attraction, something she might feel in the company of any handsome man, but looking up at him now, with his hand soothing her, she wasn't so sure.

She didn't know what it was, but she was drawn to him. There was a competence, a surety, to him that made her want to curl up into his embrace and let him fix everything for her. She felt certain a man like him could do it, too. He could protect her and handle all her worries and stress with ease, but he wouldn't want to. Men like him didn't want to care for little... What had her sister called her? A mouse? It was appropriate. Men like Dante crushed mice like Cassie; they didn't shelter them from the world.

"I'm fine," she said and leaned back in the chair in a desperate attempt to get his hand off her back. But he continued the contact, tucking a red curl behind her ear and only withdrawing his hand after his fingertips had caressed her cheek. It was a touch she didn't know how to process, so she pretended it hadn't happened at all.

Dante leaned against the desk and crossed his arms over his broad chest. Wearing another expensive suit, he looked as flawless and cold and hard as a diamond. Why was he there, in her office, invading her personal space? *Touching* her? What did he want from her?

"Was that your sister? On the phone?" Dante asked, his eyes intent on her and searching, and she wondered what he was looking for when he looked at her.

"It was," she said, nodding. She really didn't want to give him any more information than what was needed. She had the feeling that Dante collected information about people and saved it away, waiting to use it against them when it was needed, and she didn't want to hand him any ammunition.

Dante simply stared at her, for so long she couldn't help but fidget under his gaze, clasping and unclasping her hands in her lap. It was a habit her foster mother had tried to rid her of, but one she fell back on when she was anxious or nervous or stressed. In that moment, between Amber's anger and desperate pleas and Dante's formidable stare, she was all three.

Her fidgeting stopped though when Dante placed one of his hands, large and warm, over hers, engulfing them in a reassuring squeeze.

"She sounded upset," he commented gently, and Cassie paled.

"How much did you hear?" she asked, her voice small, and looked at a spot on the wall behind him, not at his face.

Shame burned through her. Not shame at her sister's addiction or the plethora of other problems that plagued her baby sister. No, it was shame that she couldn't fix it, couldn't fix Amber. It was an old shame, one she had carried since childhood, but it was always there, like the tide. It rushed forward and receded, but it was always there, inside her.

"Enough," he answered softly, and his hand moved from hers in her lap to her chin, tilting her face until she was forced to meet his gaze. His eyes were soft, but still there was something very calculating in his gaze. Like she was a problem he couldn't quite solve, but which he meant to, or die trying.

"Eat dinner with me," Dante said, a light demand, but Cassie shook her head.

"I can't–" she started.

But Dante moved his hand to cup her cheek and pressed his thumb against her lips, silencing her refusal. "I won't take no for an answer."

"I have so much work–" she tried again to dissuade him. Cassie wasn't sure what to make of the interest Dante seemed to have taken in her, but it scared as much as it thrilled her.

"Don't worry about it, for now," he said with a tiny, playful smile and stood upright, holding out his hand. "I happen to know the boss."

Cassie looked at his hand and then up at his face and back down at his hand. She knew she should say no, should do the safe thing. There was something growing between them, somehow, and keeping it from taking root would be the wise choice. Safe. And boring.

A mouse, Amber had called her, and she was, a safe, boring mouse.

She slipped her hand into his and let him pull her from her chair. He was still smiling as he led her from the tiny office, almost as if he knew her choice before she did. As they entered his office, his dark eyes were as calculating as ever, and she realized that he had known her choice before she had, because he never really gave her a choice at all.

CHAPTER

SIX

"What would you like to eat?" Dante asked as he guided Cassie to the same table and chairs in his office where they had shared lunch together earlier in the week. He tried again to lay his hand on her back, but she danced out of his reach.

"I have no idea. I'm not sure what the kitchen serves at night." She'd resumed her fidgeting, so nervous in his presence, and Dante wasn't sure why. She seemed intimidated; was it because he was, in a way, her employer? The fact that he was a strong presence in the criminal underworld of Dallas? Or could it be because she was attracted to him? He wasn't sure which... but he was determined to find out.

Dante left her seated at the little table by the window and fished a menu for the kitchen out of his desk drawer, handing it to her.

"Order anything you like, or if nothing looks appetizing, we could order from somewhere else. Though..." Dante checked his watch "–it *is* almost ten, so our options could be limited."

He smiled, trying to put her at ease. He wanted Cassie, at the very least her body, but maybe more. She was such a contradiction. Fierce and loyal one moment, and then shy and unassuming the next.

All goodness and sweetness and smiles, but then sometimes her gaze would shutter like it had when he'd touched her cheek, and he saw something deep and dark. A darkness he recognized, and he wondered what part of her was true: the good, sweet older sister, or the heat of a woman attracted to a dangerous man. He needed to know about her, learn what made her tick.

"Oh, no, this is– I'm sure it's fine. It all looks good," she hurried to say, perusing the menu.

She could be more than a brief physical diversion for him, he thought. He needed someone on his arm, but he also wanted someone to share things with. He'd grown up watching his mother and father, seeing how beneficial it was for a man in this life to have a true partner. It would have to be someone he could trust, and if Cassie could be as loyal to him as she was to her sister, she might be it. Plus her talent with numbers, if he could trust her fully, and her brilliance could be invaluable to the family.

And then there was the attraction they shared.

She may have shied away from his touch but her eyes told a different story. He just needed to delve beyond the walls she'd erected, get her to show herself to him, just enough that he could use to his advantage and her pleasure.

"I think I want to try the halibut," she said decisively at last, setting down the menu and pulling him from his thoughts.

"I think I'll have the same." Dante called down to the kitchen and ordered their meal, asking for a bottle of chilled white wine, too.

"I really shouldn't drink anything," Cassie hedged. "I'll have to go back into the books at some point tonight."

"You don't have to," said Dante, seating himself across from her. "Eat with me, and then go home. I have to come in early tomorrow and meet with my brother about one of the other clubs we run. You could come in then."

Not the complete truth, but not a total lie. He did need to speak with Matty. There were concerning happenings with some of their drug shipments and they needed to get a handle on it. Not that he would tell Cassie that.

Besides, now that he had her in his office, he was determined to get her to let her guard down and tell him some of her secrets.

"Oh, this isn't the only club you own?" she asked just as someone knocked on his office door.

Dante stood and opened it, permitting two of the club's waitresses to bring in their meal.

"Thank you, Yvonne, Alicia," Dante said to them as he sat back down.

"Yes, thank you," Cassie added, her smile genuine and warm.

He liked that she didn't look down on the wait staff, or anyone else. He saw a lot of people in the club, and many of them treated the employees with disdain or even contempt. They might be waitresses and strippers, but they were *Dante's* waitresses and strippers. They were part of the family, and he didn't tolerate that from anyone.

"You're welcome, Cassie," Alicia replied and then both women disappeared out of the office, the door closing with a quiet click.

"You seem to be making friends," Dante commented as he brought a mouthful of the flaky white fish to his lips. It was the perfect thing to eat so late at night, filling but not heavy. He added a point to his estimation of Cassie, for having the good taste to make such a fitting choice.

A faint blush bloomed on Cassie's face, and she took her own bite of food before responding to his words. "Yes, everyone has been very nice," she answered after swallowing.

"I saw you talking with Miranda earlier," he prodded.

"She's been nice," said Cassie. "I'm not sure why, actually. But she took the time to introduce me to a few other people that work here,"

"Do you like it so far?"

She shrugged. "I don't like *why* I'm here, but the job itself? The people I've met are fine."

He watched her sip her wine and thought carefully about his next words. She had relaxed a bit but he didn't want to make her tense up once more.

"Is this your sister's first stay at a rehab?" he inquired at last, with the same tone he would use to ask her to pass him the salt, attention on his plate as he loaded his fork with his next mouthful. The question was met with total silence. He didn't even hear her utensils scraping against her plate and when he looked up at her, she looked both angry and shocked.

"Did I upset you?" Dante asked, but he already knew the answer.

"Yes!" she almost shouted before swallowing hard, then cleared her throat and took a deep breath, obviously trying to reign in her emotions. "No," she corrected in a softer tone after a moment. "You didn't upset me. Shocked, maybe."

Dante toyed with the stem of his wine glass, observing her, waiting for her to continue.

"Most people don't ask," she said at last. "It scares people, I think." Letting out a breath, she resumed her meal.

"So, it's not her first stay?" Dante persisted, though gently.

Cassie shook her head. "Yes, it is, actually. But she's had other problems we'd had to get through... and then there was our mom, who was in and out of treatment facilities most of our life."

And there it was, her soft underbelly, unwittingly revealed. That thing, that one thing that everyone had, the thing that wormed its way into the fabric of one's very being. Dante had been taught by his father, by his *nonno*, by his *abuelo*, to find everyone's soft spot... and never fear using it when he needed to.

Despite his pressing for it, Dante was a little surprised she had told him. He'd expected hemming and hawing, dancing around the topic; or perhaps for her to be angry, as she had been moments earlier, but without calming and relenting and giving him what he had pushed for. He'd half expected her to throw down her fork and storm from his office. Yes, he was surprised.

Pleasantly surprised. Once again, she had surpassed his expectations of her.

"Is your mother still an addict?" he asked, so quietly it was almost a whisper, and Cassie's soft brown eyes filled with hurt.

"No, she's dead." Cassie set her fork down and leaned back into her chair, staring past him, lost in the past.

"How long has she been gone?"

"A little over ten years, now." She laughed, a sad and hollow sound. "That's hard to believe. I was sixteen and Amber was twelve. The police came to our foster home... she was found dead in a motel room." She started wringing her hands in her lap.

"Overdose?" Dante asked, and she nodded and bit her lip. "I'm sorry. That must've been difficult."

She took a hefty sip of her wine. "It was–" She paused and looked to the ceiling, as if the words had been written up there. "It wasn't unexpected. She hadn't been our mother, not really, in about five years, by then. But it was... " Her eyes found his again and the anguish he found there reminded him of how his youngest brother still looked when they spoke about their own mother, murdered not that long ago.

"It was difficult. It was painful, in an unusual way." She reached for her wine again, finishing off what was left in one large gulp.

"What do you mean, unusual?" Dante asked, and poured her some more wine.

"Have you ever lost someone close to you?" she asked, hesitant, understanding it was an invasive question but gaining confidence in how they were revealing themselves to each other.

Dante nodded. "I have," he answered, slow and soft. "My own mother. She was killed about seven years ago, now."

"Then you understand the grief, the trauma of losing someone. The guilt at not being able to stop it. But for me, there was also relief... which just compounded my guilt. At least, that's what my therapist said at the time." She shot him a sad little smile.

"A therapist? You must've been in a great foster home," he commented, thinking to make a light joke, but her smile disappeared and leveled a look at him that made him think he had been too clumsy about it, had overstepped, and she would retreat like a turtle into its shell.

"By then, we *were* in a great foster home," she replied, her tone much sharper than the softness she'd been speaking with just seconds earlier. "We were lucky, Amber especially."

Cassie took her napkin out of her lap and tossed it on her plate, her food only half eaten. She looked near to fleeing from a mixture of upset and offense and Dante knew he had to make haste in repairing the rift he'd just caused, even while feeling defensive. Talking with Cassie was like navigating a minefield; she would discuss something openly one moment, and the next, her eyes would flash like she was about to shout at him.

He would have been more annoyed by it than it was worth, with another woman. He was surprised to find that, with Cassie, it just made him more determined to get past her barricades, to smooth her ruffled feathers and create ease between them once more.

Standing, he grabbed their wine glasses in one hand, holding out his other for her to take.

"Come sit on the couch with me," he coaxed.

She glanced first at his hand and then up at his face. He could see her contemplate it and figured he had a fifty/fifty chance of her agreeing... or of leaving him there with two half-full plates cooling on the table. But she made up her mind to give him a chance, slipping her hand into his, letting him draw her to her feet.

He failed to step back for a second, remaining just a hair too near, so they had to breathe the same air, because he wanted to remind her that they were more than just words, more than her irritation at his prying at her private business. They were also bodies, primal, with blood running quick and hot. There was a physicality between them that Dante wanted– was beginning to *need*– to see realized.

Her breath hitched and he knew he had succeeded. The lesson delivered, he took that step back at last, leading her the few feet to the leather couch and sat, drawing her down beside him, a bit too close for the newness of their relationship. He was in the middle, with her in the corner; he gave her enough space to not feel trapped, but he could still feel the warmth from her body, could smell the faint scent of her perfume.

"Why was your foster family so good for Amber?" he ventured, taking a sip of his wine and leaned back into the deeply tufted black leather. Facing her, he bent his leg so that it just nudged her thigh. Then he stretched his left arm along the back of the couch, mere inches from the mass of wild red curls pinned up on her head. It was all very casual, completely unremarkable, and yet it was a definite encroachment upon her personal space. Just as he planned.

"Amber has always been... volatile," she answered, gaze averted, watching her fingers pick at invisible lint on her jeans. "She was constantly in trouble, even when she was very young and we still lived with our mother." She huffed a humorless laugh. "Not that living with Mom was a picnic."

Dante set his wine glass next to hers down on the low coffee table. He had to be more careful, now, what he asked and how he asked it. He didn't want to rile her up again. "How old were you two when you were placed in foster care?" he asked quietly.

It seemed to work; she released a slow breath and replied, "The first time? I was four and Amber was still a baby. We spent a year in foster care with a kind family... from what I can remember. They took us to the zoo, once." Her lips curved in a small smile that faded as quickly as it came.

"Mom got clean, and got us back, and things were okay for a couple of years. She worked in a diner. I remember eating dinner there often. But then she met Dale." She paused, pulling in a breath that shuddered. "Dale was everything mom loved in a man– abusive, never worked, loved his drugs. Drugs that she got back on, of course, and soon Amber and I were going to school in filthy rags and there was no food in the house. By the time I was thirteen and Amber was nine, Mom was in jail on drug charges and we were well-entrenched in the system and Amber had become a problem. She lashed out and became violent, so much that we got kicked out of two foster homes."

Dante reached out, slowly, to take one of her hands in his. He had consciously given her time enough to see his intention, to pull away, but she still seemed startled at the contact. Did she have anyone to comfort her, or was she always the one providing safety and comfort to others? He had a feeling he knew the answer; he suspected that her relationship with Amber was nothing near reciprocal, that Amber never provided any support to her sister, only taking, always taking.

"Both of you?" he asked.

She shrugged. "I wasn't going anywhere without Amber. If they weren't keeping her, I wasn't going to stay with them."

Dante nodded, understanding that feeling, that loyalty. Amber was her family. You do anything and everything for the family.

"Then, finally, the Garzas came into our lives, Carol and Mike. They hadn't been foster parents for very long, and when they agreed to take us, I was worried. They looked so *nice*. Their house was so pretty, and I knew Amber would destroy it. She had been diagnosed with ADD and a few other things, and needed so much help. Carol and Mike, at first, were a bit horrified. Here was this thirteen-year-old out-of-control child and her stubborn, quiet older sister. Soon, though, Carol in particular started fighting for us... for Amber, really."

Saying it seemed to take a lot out of Cassie; she slumped a bit, weary tension clear in her narrow shoulders. She leaned forward and grabbed her wine with the hand he wasn't holding, taking a deep drink.

"What did she do?" Dante rubbed tiny circles on her hand with the pad of his thumb.

"She got Amber real help. Psychologists, and medical doctors, and help at school. About six months into our stay, Amber got mad about something and attacked me. It had happened before, but it worried Carol. Carol got her in-patient help. The doctors figured out she was bi-polar and worked out medications. If Carol hadn't advocated for Amber, I don't know what would have happened. I was too young didn't know what to do, how to help." She leaned her head back on the couch and closed her eyes.

"You look tired," Dante murmured. She was so young, but had seen and endured so much. Such a little thing, and so strong, despite looking like a stiff wind would blow her over.

Cassie turned her head towards him and opened her eyes. They were soft and a bit hazy. He thought back to the multiple glasses of wine she'd consumed and realized she was probably a little tipsy, too.

"I *am* tired," she admitted. "Today has felt endless."

Dante grinned, teasing, "I think you may be a little drunk, Ms. Lockhart."

"Ugh, I am. I can't drive home. I'd better grab a rideshare." She paused, frowning as an idea struck her. "That's going to cost me a pretty penny," she grumbled in such an annoyed tone that Dante had to chuckle.

"Are you laughing at me?" Cassie looked up at him from under her lashes. Had she been any other woman, he would think she was flirting with him, but Cassie was utterly guileless. He didn't know her well, not yet– not as well as he wanted to– but he knew that much. He didn't understand her inherent goodness, but he was confident of its existence.

"I'm not laughing at you, per se," he hedged and then smiled when she narrowed her eyes at him.

"Sure, sure, I know when someone is laughing at me, Mr. Important Club Owner."

Dante stood, her hand still clasped in his, and pulled her up. "I'd better get you home before you become any sillier, Ms. Lockhart."

"I need to get my phone and order a car." She tried to tug her hand free, but he didn't release it.

"There's no need for you to order a car, Cassie. I'll take you home."

"Oh, no! That's–" She tried to argue, but Dante put a finger against her lips, stopping her words. He felt more than heard her gasp on his skin.

"Don't argue, Cassie." Dante bit back a smirk as her pupils dilated. "Come on, let's take you back to your office so you can grab your things, and I'll drive you home."

Cassie bit her lip as she pondered his words and finally nodded. Dante followed her out of his office and into hers, watching as she grabbed her small, practical purse and slipped the strap over her head. Nothing about Cassie was extra or practiced. She was completely without artifice, something Dante appreciated.

"Ready," Cassie said, smiling up at him. Dante took her hand again and led her from the office, then through the club, without severing the contact. He knew everyone would be watching them; their eyes were heavy on them the whole time. And it was exactly what he wanted. He was staking a claim. Cassie was his, she just didn't know it yet.

But she would soon.

"Which car is yours?" Dante asked as he pulled her forward to his black SUV.

"Over there. That's Betsy." She pointed to a blue compact car that had seen better days a decade earlier.

"Is Betsy old enough to vote yet?" Dante teased, and Cassie grinned as he pulled open the passenger door for her.

"Old enough to vote? Betsy is old enough to *drink!*"

Dante shook his head and climbed into the driver's seat. By the time he pulled onto the freeway, she was leaning back in her seat, eyes closed, dozing. She looked like a porcelain doll, all pretty and fragile and pale: one wrong move, and she would shatter into a million pieces.

He would have her. She was lovely, and loyal, and so, so decent. So *good*. He would corrupt that goodness, he knew, but he didn't feel regret or sorrow. It would make her better, to be a little more like him: stronger, more practical, and less sentimental, more aware of her worth, more protective of her time and resources. She wouldn't waste her energies, anymore, on lost causes like her beat-up car and her troubled sister.

She would be his, and together, they would have something extraordinary.

CHAPTER

SEVEN

CASSIE

Cassie knew she was dreaming. She and Lucy were in a park, with a large grassy area for dogs. There was a hazy glow around everything, and a feeling of wellbeing suffused the scene. She threw a ball and smiled as Lucy scrambled to run after it.

"I miss this."

Cassie turned to the woman sitting next to her, her greying hair pulled back into a ponytail.

"Carol," Cassie breathed, joy and relief filling her to overflowing. It had been years since Cassie had dreamed of Carol, but she was always so happy when it happened.

Carol smiled at Cassie and then looked back at Lucy, who had abandoned her pursuit of the ball in favor of sniffing a lone dandelion growing tall above the surrounding grass.

"I miss *you*," Cassie whispered, eyes still on Lucy, and Carol slipped her hand into Cassie's, threading their fingers together. "You loved me better– treated me better– in the short time you were in my life than the woman who gave birth to me. I should've told you I loved you."

"I knew you loved me," replied Carol warmly. "I knew it the first time you cooked supper for us 'just because you wanted to', and I knew it every time you hugged me, sweet girl."

Cassie smiled a little at the endearment. "I should've done it more. And I should've called you 'Mom'. But I never did."

"But you did, don't you remember?"

Suddenly they weren't at the dog park with Lucy anymore, but in the field on the fateful day. of Carol's death. The acrid stench of burning rubber was harsh in Cassie's nose, and broken glass and hard rocks dug into her feet, her sandals lost in the impact from the truck crashing their car.

"Cassie! Cassie!" Carol screamed, still pinned in the burning, upside-down vehicle. "Where are you?"

"Carol, I'm here!" Cassie cried, dropping to her hands and feet and crawling towards the burning wreckage. She couldn't feel her shoulders but her dress, the pretty one with the yellow flowers and puffy sleeves, was tight, constricting. On some distant level, she knew the fire had melted the synthetic material to her skin. But it didn't matter. She had to get to Carol.

The flames on the other side of the car– where her foster father was silent and still, already gone– were unbearably hot, searing against her face and hands as she fumbled around Carol to unbuckle her seat belt. Cassie's fingertips sizzled and burned when she finally reached the belt release and she pushed and pushed but nothing happened, it wouldn't release, and Carol was still suspended in the burning car.

Cassie wrapped her hands around Carol's upper arms and pulled, trying to pull her free both from the seat belt and the burning car, but no matter how hard she pulled she couldn't pull her foster mother free.

"Cassie. Cassie, baby." Carol's voice, eerily calm, broke through Cassie's increasingly frantic and desperate pulls on her body. "Stop, Cassie, it's no use."

"No!" Cassie cried, her voice hoarse and her throat burning from her tears and the fumes. She could hear the sirens, weak and far away, but help was coming... if she could just get Carol out of the car. "No, I can get you out!"

She was yelling over the crackling of the flames, the groaning of the car's metal warping and twisting from the heat. The heat was even worse, now, when Cassie leaned back through the broken passenger side window to once again reach for Carol, to try to pull her free.

But Carol stopped her, grabbing her hands and threading her fingers through hers for what would be the last time.

"Cassie, my sweet girl, stop. The fire, it's... it's too much. You need to get away from it," Carol said, her voice still calm. The flames began licking at the ends of her long hair.

"No—" Cassie argued, but Carol let out a painful moan.

"Cassie, baby, I love you. I love you and your sister so much. Tell her, please? Tell her she is loved, that you are both loved." Carol let go of Cassie's hands to push her away. "Go, Cassandra. Get away from the car."

"No! Carol– *Mom*, please, I can hear the sirens. I can get you–" Cassie tried to reach back in the car but the flames were now in Carol's lap and Cassie yanked her hand away, the heat too much, her body's sense of self-preservation kicking in.

"Cassie, you can't. Get away from the car." Carol's voice was more forceful, a thread of panic in it... but not for herself. For Cassie. "Go up to the road and wait for help."

"It's okay to let go, baby. I love you and I know you love me. Save yourself. Move away, Cassie," Carol's calm voice sounded oddly eerie against the roaring sound of the fire around them.

Cassie sobbed harder and fell back into the churned dirt of the field. The sirens grew louder as she cried, unable to block out Carol's moans and cries turning into screams... until they stopped altogether, all at once.

The sirens were loud now, shrill, but thudding somehow, like a heartbeat, and Cassie covered her ears to block them out—

She sat up with a gasp, panting, drenched in sweat and Lucy whining at her with concerned eyes from the foot of the bed.

"I'm okay, girl," Cassie said breathlessly, and reached down to scratch the dog's ears when she heard the knock again: louder this time, almost a pounding on her door.

Lucy yipped, satisfied that Cassie wasn't in distress anymore.

"Hush, girl," Cassie said. She stood, rolling her tight shoulders, and caught a glimpse of her scarred skin in the mirror. It had been years, and compared to her foster parents' deaths, she had been lucky, but at times the sight of the ropey, thickened flesh that covered her shoulders and upper back still shocked her.

She hadn't had enough wine for a hangover, but the wine coupled with the lack of sleep from the stress of the last week was enough to knock her out. She thought back to the dream– so vivid, so real.

When they had first died, she had dreamed of Carol, and some-times Mike, often– especially during those six weeks she'd spent in the hospital, recovering from her burns. Grief, the doctors had told her it was, grief and stress. The dreams were wonderful... and heart-breaking. Wonderful to see them, to talk to them, touch and hold them, and heartbreaking to wake and know they were gone forever.

She pulled her threadbare pink robe over her tank top and shorts and went to the door. Who on earth was knocking on her door at– Cassie peered blearily at the clock that hung on her living room wall– nine a.m. on a Sunday morning?

"Yes?" Cassie said, pulling her front door open with one hand, the other on Lucy's collar holding back her excitable dog. Before her stood a man in dark blue coveralls, the kind mechanics typically wore, a clipboard in his hands.

"Are you Cassandra Lockhart?" asked the man, his tone impatient.

"I am." Cassie's eyebrows drew together in confusion. What was it to him?

The man thrust the clipboard and a pen in her direction. "Will you please sign here, to take possession of the car?"

"Car?" she asked, bewildered, and took the clipboard, scanning the page. It was from a local car dealership.

"Yes, ma'am. If you could hurry... I never work on Sundays, and my wife is going to be right pissed at me, if we're late to church," the man prodded.

"I don't know anything about a car," Cassie mumbled. There was nothing on the receipt of delivery that shed any light on the reason this man could be there, trying to... give her a car?

The man sighed and reached to peel back the topmost page in the clipboard, revealing an official-looking document underneath.

"This is the title," he said wearily. "It's got Cassandra Lockhart's name on it. If you're her, this car is yours."

Cassie looked at the paperwork like it like it might bite her. "Are you sure?"

The man sighed again, impatience plain on his face. "Yes, ma'am, I'm sure. If you have any further issues, just call the dealership on Monday, but this car is yours."

Cassie nodded, still confused and doubtful, but signed the paper anyway.

"Here ya go." He took back the clipboard and handed her a set of car keys and an envelope, and started to walk away.

"Excuse me," she called after him, and he turned, an impatient scowl on his face yet again.

"Um, what kind of car is it? What color?"

He glanced down at the paperwork. "It's a black Audi A6, ma'am. It's parked right in front of your building's leasing office," He rushed off, then, probably to prevent her from stopping him again.

Cassie shut the door and stumbled back into her living room. She sat on the couch in a daze and pulled a folded piece of paper from the plain envelope.

Cassie,

I have arranged for your dear Betsy to have the retirement she deserves. Please accept this car as a humble replacement.

Yours,

Dante

Cassie fell back into the soft, worn cushions of her couch and ran a trembling hand through her messy curls. Lucy whined and put her head in her owner's lap, concerned at her distress.

"It's okay, girl," Cassie mumbled and passed her fingers through the dog's wiry fur, staring at the keys she'd dropped on the coffee table. Who in the world gives a near-stranger a car? A fancy luxury car, at that! And why? What was he doing? Was he toying with her? What did he hope to gain by it?

Cassie didn't trust presents. Before Mike and Carol, very little had been given to her without an ulterior motive or out of pity. Cassie could still remember those impersonal charity gifts the kids would get in the group homes. Well-meaning people donated items, which were sorted based on gender and age. They weren't terrible gifts, and logically, Cassie knew the people had donated them out of the kindness of their hearts, but as nice as fuzzy socks and bath wash were, it still couldn't compare to getting a gift someone picked out specifically for you.

Her first Christmas with Carol and Mike had been amazing, unlike anything she'd experienced before. In her stocking was a gift card to a used bookstore, for an amount that had made her eyes open wide.

"Look, Amber, we can get some new books." Cassie had turned to her younger sister, who was opening her own gift: a beginner makeup set, exactly what she had wanted.

"Cassie, sweetheart, that gift card is all for you," Carol corrected, gently, with a smile. "I know how much you love the library, and I thought maybe you'd like some new books... or new-to-you books. Start filling that shelf in your room."

Cassie could still remember with perfect clarity how Carol's long, elegant fingers were wrapped around her coffee mug, how rumpled she looked from sleep in her red and green pajamas, Mike sitting close with his arm around her shoulders.

"Really? I can fill the shelf?" Cassie had asked. She had never lived anywhere, even with her mother, that felt like home, like a place she could make her own, and here were these almost-strangers encouraging her to do just that. Carol and Mike had nodded, Carol's eyes suspiciously wet, and Cassie had thrown her arms around her. The very next day Carol had taken her to the bookstore. She had still bought a book for Amber, but all the other books had been hers. They, and the shelf itself, were in her apartment to that very day.

This gift? It was too much. Cassie wondered at the strings that might come with it and why such a man, handsome and powerful, would give her something so extravagant.

What does he want?

Her phone rang, the sound shrill and jarring in the silence that had fallen as she contemplated the car. Cassie jumped, then groaned as she reached for it, Sarah's face smiling at her from the lock screen. "Hello?"

"Oh, good you're awake! Wanna get brunch?" Sarah asked without preamble and Cassie's eyes darted to the keys once again.

"Yeah, brunch sounds good. The usual? An hour?" Cassie asked, and Sarah agreed and then hung up.

Cassie looked at the keys once again and then at Lucy.

"Well, girl, let's go for a walk. I've got to get my day started, and you probably need to potty."

Lucy sat up and barked her agreement. Cassie scratched her head, smiling, and went to get the leash.

Brunch with Sarah was interesting, especially when her best friend saw the new car.

"Betsy in the shop?" Sarah asked as they entered the restaurant.

"No, ah, this thing," Cassie gestured vaguely toward the ostentatious sedan, "seems to be a gift."

"A *gift?*" Sarah screeched. The hostess, leading them to their table, turned back and shot Sarah a frown. "A gift?" Sarah asked again, a bit softer, as a server arrived with complimentary mimosas, but the disbelief was still entrenched on her face.

Cassie just shrugged and sipped her mimosa while trying to decide between eggs benedict and French toast.

"Oh, no, you don't." Sarah pulled the menu right out of Cassie's hands, demanding her full attention.

"Who gave you a car? A $40,000 car, at that." Sarah glanced around and then leaned forward across the table to whisper, "Are some old dude's sugar baby?"

Cassie laughed. "No, Sarah, I'm not a sugar baby."

Sarah leaned back into the booth, visibly disappointed. "Damn. I was hoping he had friends."

Cassie grinned, then took a moment to order the eggs benedict. As soon as the server had departed, Sarah kicked her under the table.

"Details, Cassandra Lockheart. I need details," she hissed

Cassie sighed. "My new boss bought me a car."

"Is it, like, a work vehicle?" Sarah asked and Cassie shook her head.

"It's not. Last night he gave me a ride home because I got a little tipsy at dinner–"

"You had *dinner?* I thought you were working? Cassie, I need the complete story now."

So Cassie told her everything, from the beginning. Sarah wasn't new to Amber's problems, and she didn't judge her for them.

"Wow," Sarah finally said as Cassie's account of the last week came to an end at the same time their meal did.

"Yeah," Cassie agreed ruefully.

"Well, I think your boss has the hots for you," Sarah said, grinning, but Cassie shook her head.

"No, there's no way. He's so..." Cassie trailed off as her mind drifted to Dante.

He was handsome, sure, but it was more than that. He was powerful and commanding, but also steady and calm. When he entered a room, Cassie didn't just see him; she *felt* him. His presence was larger, more confident than anyone else's. There was no way a man like him was interested in her.

Right?

"Oh, and you have the hots for him, too," Sarah added casually, her eyes flashing with humor.

Cassie opened her mouth to argue and then thought back to the night before, how his touches had seemed to send little shocks through her. *Did* she have the hots for him?

She knew the answer was yes. She was drawn to him, wanted to expose all of herself to him. He was addictive and for the first time in her life, she understood why her sister and her mother would go to such lengths for the drugs they craved; the more time she spent with Dante, the more she wanted to hear his voice, to watch the way his mouth moved as he spoke and how he gestured with his hands. She wanted to know him, all of him, in the most primal way there was.

It was terrifying, but in a way that made her crave, too. Dante was a drug made especially for her, and she wanted more of him.

Did she dare open herself to the temptation he presented?

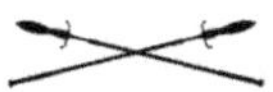

Cassie pulled her new car into the parking lot of the club at five p.m. on the dot. On Sundays, the club didn't open before five, and Cassie hoped Dante was there, because she wanted Betsy back. The gift of the Audi, whatever it meant, was definitely not appropriate.

"Good afternoon, Cassie," said James, that day's doorman. He smiled as he held the door open for her.

"Hello, James."

Inside, the club was mostly empty, with only a handful of

customers and one dancer on the stage. Cassie looked around for Miranda, but she didn't seem to be in the club. Dante was, however; he was speaking to Tony at the bar. Cassie took a deep breath and made her way to them.

"Excuse me," Cassie said.

Dante turned to her, and she had to remind herself how to breathe. "Ahh, Ms. Lockhart," Dante said with a smile. "How's the car?"

"I was hoping I could speak to you about that." She clenched and unclenched her hand around her purse strap, at her shoulder.

"Of course," he said at once, with a look at Tony. Tony picked up his glass and left the bar area, leaving her and Dante alone.

"I want to thank you, but–"

"If you want to thank me, there shouldn't be a but in the sentence," Dante interrupted, smirking, and Cassie rolled her eyes. "Did you just roll your eyes at me?" There was something akin to wonder in his tone.

"Maybe," Cassie hedged. "But that's neither here nor there. I need Betsy back," she rushed to say.

"Absolutely not." Dante crossed his arms and leaned his hip against the bar.

"Yes, your gift was very kind, but I can't accept it."

"Why not?"

"Because it's a *car*, Dante," she answered, incredulous, and he chuckled.

"So it's a car. I'm a wealthy man, Cassie. That's nothing for me. It's not even an expensive car."

Cassie's head swam. She couldn't imagine being so wealthy that a car, a luxury car at that, wasn't a big deal. "Give me Betsy back, and wipe out Amber's debt instead."

He shook his head. "No."

"Why not?" To her dismay, her voice was dangerously close to pleading.

"Because I enjoy having you in my club, Cassie. Now why don't you head upstairs and start working, and I'll get you around eight for some dinner."

"Dante–" she started and his grin only deepened.

"What, Cassie?"

"I am not comfortable accepting such a gift– any gift, really– from you," she persisted.

It was true; gifts were very rarely ever just gifts, and this one especially felt like it had some major strings attached. She was not blind to the fact that Dante di Ruggiero had his finger in some very dangerous pies. The idea of owing him, not just Amber's debt but anything she might incur on her own, was daunting.

"Well, Cassandra, you're not really in a position to refuse the car, are you?" His words were as pleasant, as bland, as his smile, despite how ominous his words were.. "You want to erase Amber's debt by working here. My agreeing to it comes with the stipulation that you accept this car."

There was something else in his look, something almost predatory, and she knew then she would never win against him, not in this, not in anything. She was the mouse under the tiger's paw.

So why did that send a shiver up her back that was more fascination, more arousal, than fear?

His smile became broader as he stood there, waiting, patient, for her to arrive at the conclusion he had dictated. It was clear he knew the paths her mind had gone down, and that she'd come to understand the futility of protesting, of fighting him. Cassie's realization at her predicament settled deep, into her bones, as did the new comprehension that there was something between them that went beyond that of an employee and her boss.

She was a fly caught in a web, helpless, as a spider took his time choosing his moment to pounce... a spider named Dante.

And yet, shouldn't she be more upset about this? Why was she... *pleased* at the outcome?

She had struggled and fought for so long, to take care of herself and Amber, and it was just so good to not have to make a decision for herself. Or, rather, to have a choice taken from her, to not have to struggle between what she wanted to do and what she should do.

She wanted the new car. It was beautiful, and comfortable, and she wouldn't have to suffer the Texas heat without air conditioning. She shouldn't accept it, but she wanted it. And Dante was giving her permission to do as she wanted, to not deprive herself because it was 'the right thing' to do. To indulge herself, for no other reason than because she could.

"Alright, then," she said, her voice almost steady. From somewhere, she found a bit of spunk and shot him a half-smile. "Thanks, boss," she told him with a jaunty, mocking salute before turning on her heel and making for the stairs.

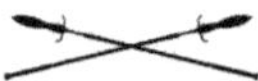

A few hours later, a little past eight o'clock, Cassie ventured out of her office in search of Dante. If she couldn't find him, she would order something from the kitchen by herself. The music was thumping downstairs, rhythmic and powerful, but over it she could hear raised voices from Dante's office.

The door to his office was cracked and from beyond it came Dante's voice, harsh and almost cold.

"Why were the police at your house last night?" Dante demanded.

"Sir, I, you don't understand my old lady, she–"

Cassie heard a meaty thud, and then a groan. Alarmed at the idea that Dante might be hurt, she pushed the door to his office a little wider. Dante was standing in front of one of the bartenders– Jay, her memory supplied– who was hunched over, arms wrapped protectively around his middle. Dante had punched him in the stomach, then. Tony and another man she didn't recognize stood by, observant and ready to act on command.

"I understand plenty," Dante said. "You like to beat your wife while your children watch." He hit him again, this time squarely on the chin. Jay fell backward in a slow, agonized arch and landed on the floor in an awkward sprawl.

"You do not lay a hand on someone you have sworn to protect. I will not have it, do you understand?" Dante told him, voice so low it was almost a hiss, but Jay was too busy moaning to reply. "Get up."

When Jay didn't move, Tony and the other man roughly hauled him to his feet.

"Do you understand?" Dante demanded again, his voice low and full of venom.

"Yes, boss," Jay blubbered, staring down at the floor, not daring to raise his head.

"Matty, get him out of my sight. He can work at one of your clubs, but not here. And if I ever hear about you raising a hand to your wife or kids, you will never work in this town again. Am I clear?"

"Yes, boss," Jay repeated. The man, Matty dragged him to the door and pulled the door wide, making Cassie peep in surprise. She'd been so caught up in the scene that she'd forgotten she wasn't supposed to be there, seeing it.

"Hey, Dante, you have a visitor," Matty said, laughing. Full-on, she could see that he looked like a younger, more carefree version of Dante, with dancing blue eyes and a smile on his lips.

"Cassie, come inside. I'm sorry this little meeting took longer than expected," Dante said coolly, gesturing for her to enter his office.

"Tony, please see if Jay's wife needs anything. Assure her that if she wants to leave, you will help her. And if she chooses to stay, and Jay touches her again, we will handle it," Dante said and Tony nodded, then nodded again at Cassie in greeting as he passed her, shutting the door with a click.

"I didn't mean to interrupt," Cassie started, but Dante moved forward and took her hand. His knuckles were reddened, but otherwise he was unmarked by the violence he had just perpetrated.

"How much did you see?" he inquired softly.

"Enough," she admitted, and smiled a little at the mirror of their conversation from yesterday.

"Did that frighten you?" Dante asked, his eyes keen upon her. Unlike most people, who glanced over her, if they noticed her at all, she knew Dante was actually *seeing* her, who she was, right to her core.

Did he scare her, this powerful and obviously dangerous man, whose world differed so vastly from the one she inhabited? Or did she feel a bit more powerful, herself, to have snared the interest of such a man?

"Why did you do it? Why does it matter to you if one of your employees beats his wife?" she asked instead of answering his question.

He tilted his head, considering. "Do you want the short answer or the long one?"

She frowned. "I want the truth."

He stared at her, and finally nodded. "For one, it's bad for my clubs. He'll eventually be arrested for it, and I prefer not to have employees in jail. Even more than that, it's about who they are. If they'll hurt the people they are supposed to protect, how can I trust them? How will I know they will be loyal to me, if they can't even be loyal to their own families?"

It was as if a string had been plucked within Cassie, deep in her heart, and comprehension flowered there. She understood, then, why she was so drawn to Dante. It wasn't his wealth or his good looks, but because Dante's comprehension of loyalty was absolute, in the same way that Cassie's was. Except where Dante demanded that loyalty returned, Cassie had not yet acquired the ability to command that reciprocity. She loved Amber, would do anything to protect her, but she also understood that Amber didn't share that bone-deep conviction... though she knew how to exploit it.

"Have dinner with me?" Dante asked, breaking the silence that fell as the ripples of understanding settled and smoothed, around Cassie's mind.

"That's why I'm here," she said lightly.

Dante shook his head. "No, I mean a proper meal. In an actual restaurant."

"That sounds good," she said, a little surprised at how appealing the idea was, especially since it would take a woman even more determined to downplay her attractions than Cassie to still believe Dante could not be attracted to her. No, this would be an actual *date*.

"Great. Tomorrow evening? I know Mondays aren't exactly an ideal date night, but it's my day off." Dante looked almost boyish in his pleasure, and she couldn't help but smile at it.

She watched him, as he called downstairs for their dinner. He exuded an air of sensuality and power, a suggestion of passion seething under a tightly-wrapped veneer of control. She should be afraid of him, should get the hell out of there and leave Amber to her own devices, should protect herself– her heart– but... no.

No, she was intrigued enough, compelled enough, by him that she wanted to see whatever was between them to the end, bitter or otherwise. Being wanted by him was heady stuff, intoxicating, and the temptation of peeling back a few of his layers, of exploring the reality of him, was irresistible.

Could it be possible? Could regular, normal, unexceptional Cassie Lockhart manage the feat? She actually felt like she could do it, like maybe she had a key to Dante di Ruggiero that few others had grasped.

She just had to find the courage to turn it, to open him up, to peer inside.

As he turned back to her, smiling, she thought she might just be up to the challenge.

CHAPTER

EIGHT

onday morning dawned early, if not bright– it was pissing down rain and the sky was a dark, gloomy gray... but still hot in a way only a rainy Texas summer day could be.

Dante had had a phone call scheduled with his grandfather, little more than a few pleasantries and one heavily coded sentence buried in questions about his brothers and the weather. If you observed it from the outside, you would think Esteban Garza was just a semi-retired politician quietly living out his twilight years on his hacienda.

In reality, he ran and kept a tight leash on one of the largest, most deadly cartels in Mexico. He had strategically placed his sons in the government on both sides of the border, and one of his daughters had married into the di Ruggiero family, giving him grandsons that ran their business north of the border.

Dante's *abuelo*, or more informally *Welo*, was a shrewd and cunning businessman. He was also the man who had taught Dante and his brothers to ride a horse in the deserts of Chihuahua... and how to smuggle drugs. *Welo*, more than his Italian grandfather, had taught him how disposable people really were. If the old *don* had imparted lessons about loyalty and family, *Welo* had taught him how to be fearless... and how to be feared.

"Good morning, big brother."

Dante looked up from the club's liquor order to see his youngest brother, Matty, stride into his office, his smile far too bright for a drenched Monday morning.

"Matty," Dante acknowledged and went back to the liquor order as Matty flopped into one of the chairs in front of the desk. Cassie would have to look over the orders for the last few months, he decided, because they were ordering more than usual but somehow making less profit.

"Dude, aren't you going to tell me about her?"

Dante looked up from his paperwork only to glower at his youngest and his most bothersome brother.

Sure, Elias was a disappointment, a waste of talent, and the life he had chosen to lead was unremarkable in the worst way possible, but he wasn't a constant thorn in his side like Matty was. Between his cars and his girls, Matty was almost constantly in trouble, and it was always up to Dante to smooth it over.

Today, though? It was his mouth and shit-eating grin that were going to get Matty in trouble.

"I promise you, I have no idea what or who you're talking about," Dante lied smoothly and resumed reviewing the liquor order.

"That's cute, bro," Matty said with a grin. "You know I'm talking about the tiny redhead that watched you punish Jay last night." He leaned back in the chair and placed one booted foot over his opposite knee.

Matty had gone to school out in College Station at Texas A&M University, swearing he was going to be a large animal veterinarian and instead majoring in beer and cheerleaders. All that had come of his college years was an enduring love for those stupid cowboy boots. City cowboy, the *vaqueros* on their *Welo's* hacienda would've called him, all swagger and no saddle: that was Matteo di Ruggerio in a nutshell.

"You know, most girls would've been scared, seeing the big bad *don* discipline one of his men. She seemed intrigued, though. Almost... entranced."

He was right. When Dante had looked up and found Cassie's wide brown eyes taking in the scene, he had been worried for a split second. Most women didn't respond well to violence, he had learned from experience, but Cassie hadn't looked scared, she had looked... awed. As if it hadn't occurred to her before, how respect could be commanded with the threat of pain, but that she liked the idea. And that respect in her eyes had only grown when he explained why he had physically disciplined his man as he had.

Dante wasn't stupid enough to think she would be comfortable watching his father or his brother Marco complete a hit, but she wasn't one to shy away from the violence completely. It pleased him, to make that discovery, to find a piece of her puzzle and fit it into place, but also to know that he could rely on her not to become squeamish at some of the uglier things in the world.

A Cassie-shaped slot was growing in his life, slowly but steadily, giving him ideas for how neatly she could solve a variety of his problems, could fill a variety of roles currently awaiting occupants. She was wasted as a mere bookkeeper, he was coming to see. She could accomplish so much more for him.

"It's nothing," he said dismissively. "Cassie is doing our books for the club. I've told you how much of a mess they've become."

But Matty was like a dog with a bone, impossible to deflect. "Oh, well, if that's all... think she'd go out with me? I've developed a weakness for redheads, lately."

Dante leveled a look at his brother that would make most men piss themselves, but Matty simply smiled angelically and waited for Dante to respond.

"No, Matteo. She's off-limits," Dante replied tightly, having to work at maintaining his patience.

"Why? You don't care how many of the dancers I fuck. How is she different?" Matty pressed, trying to get a rise out of him.

But no one got a rise out of Dante di Ruggiero, not even annoying brothers.

"She's different because I say she is," Dante answered simply. "I have plans for her." The specific scope of those plans were nobody's business but his own.

"She's not your usual type," Matty commented, studying his big brother, his gaze keen.

Dante shrugged. Matty was wrong about that. He couldn't see beyond Cassie's wide, innocent eyes and baggy clothing, but Dante did. Matty could drink the finest wine in the world and declare that it tasted like nothing but grapes, but Dante could detect the notes of plum and oak hiding behind those grapes. He knew to look beyond surfaces for substance. He had peered past those innocent eyes and baggy clothes to the beauty behind them, the intelligence and shrewdness and loyalty.

Cassandra Lockheart was *exactly* his type.

"I disagree, baby brother," Dante leaned back into his chair, the leather creaking. "She may be more my type than anyone who came before her."

Dante didn't expect Matty to understand. He was still too young, too full of himself, to realize that life wasn't about supermodels, strippers, and fast cars.

"I get that," Matty murmured, and Dante wondered about the melancholy in his brother's voice. But he wouldn't ask; even family was entitled to their privacy, and unless Matty was doing something that could hurt the family, Dante didn't particularly care.

"Anyway." Matty cleared his throat and sat up straighter.

Dante took the opportunity to bring up about the real reason he had called Matty in: to talk to him, and not about either of their love lives. "I spoke to *Welo* this morning."

Matty nodded. "I figured, it's been a bit since we got a shipment."

Dante pulled a small black book from the inside pocket of his jacket. It was a coded journal of each shipment of drugs that came or went across the border. He kept them for six months and then burned the little book and started a new one. He wished he had a photographic memory like his *nonno*, the old *don*, but he didn't. So he had come up with something that helped keep track of shipments and didn't leave much evidence.

"There have been complications," Dante said. Since graduating college, Matty had become his eyes and ears on the ground with most shipments. There were very few he would trust for it, and none outside of the family.

Matty nodded again. "Is there something going on with *Welo's* supplier?"

"No, but he's been dealing with a leak."

The shock on Matty's face mirrored his own, when he had spoken with their grandfather earlier.

"Did he find the leak?"

"He thinks he has. His last shipments have made it from Columbia in just the last six weeks, so he feels confident it's safe to resume transport across the border to us."

Matty chewed at his lip, contemplating the situation. "When?"

Dante consulted his little book. "The first will come across in Piedras Negras. Your team will meet them outside Crystal City in three weeks. The sacrifice shipment will come in through Nuevo Laredo."

Matty wrote nothing down, but Dante knew he was committing it to memory.

"Then in two weeks, the opposite will happen, and your team will meet the shipment in Encinal," Dante continued. It was part of the business to send a lighter shipment through and tip off either border patrol or the county sheriff, as a kind of bait-and-switch. It kept law enforcement busy, so the larger load got across undetected.

"Got it, boss!" Matty saluted and Dante rolled his eyes, interrupted when there was a knock at his door.

Miranda peeked her head in. "Sorry, Dante, but I have a lecture at noon. If you still want to talk to me, it has to be now."

Dante slipped his little black book back into the inside pocket of his suit jacket, then motioned for her to enter. Matty stood, stretching, clearly eager to get out of the office and do something physical. Their business was at an end, anyway.

"Miranda!" Matty treated her to a comical leer. "Woah, you look like a sexy professor."

"Matty, I *am* a hot professor," Miranda informed him sweetly, utterly confident in her appeal. "I teach freshman psychology three times a week, as part of my PhD program."

"None of my professors were ever as hot as you," Matty grumbled, but his pretend sulk was quickly gone, replaced with a dazzling smile as he took his leave, the door closing with a soft click.

"So, Dante, why on earth am I here on a Monday at 10 a.m.?" Miranda asked, smirking as if she already knew the answer.

"You're here because I need a favor," he said. "I have a date with Cassie tonight."

Miranda's green eyes lit up at his words. "Oh, really? Am I to be your chaperone?" she teased and then held up her hands in surrender at his glower.

Dante ignored her impertinent question. "I want to take her to *Toulouse*, but something tells me she doesn't have an appropriate dress for such an upscale place."

Toulouse was the best, most exclusive French restaurant in Dallas, and Dante's favorite. It was probably sacrilege for a French, not Italian, restaurant to be his favorite, but... oh, well.

Her grin was pure glee. "What's my spending limit?"

Dante took his black card from his wallet and pushed it across his desk towards her.

"No limit. Get her anything you think she might need. Do you know her size?"

Miranda looked at him like he was an idiot. "Dante, I'm a woman, who works around other women, all of us naked, four days a week. I can tell a woman's size at a glance, by now."

Dante nodded. He should've guessed as much.

"What I don't know is how to give her the dress after I buy it," Miranda continued.

Dante quickly jotted down both Cassie's work and home addresses on a scrap of paper and handed it to her. "Do you need her number?"

Miranda shook her head, standing. "Nope, I have that. We exchanged numbers that first night."

She turned to depart but Dante called her back. "Oh, Miranda!"

"Yes?" She paused and turned back to face him.

"Buy yourself something nice, as well, as my thanks," Dante said, and Miranda grinned.

"I was already planning on it, boss!" She tossed him a wink on her way out the door. "Thanks!"

Dante sat at the bar at *Toulouse*, sipping his twelve-year-old scotch, and surveyed the room.

He was early; he had arranged for his driver, Manny, to pick up Cassie at her apartment at eight, the time Miranda had told him she would be ready.

Miranda had sent him a few texts throughout the afternoon, including a picture of the dress, a daring black silk that he was dying to see against Cassie's pale, luminescent skin. Then, later, another text arrived, telling him she had arranged for a hair stylist and a make-up artist to pamper Cassie.

"She deserves it," was all Miranda's text had said, and he hadn't argued. Why shouldn't she enjoy all the benefits of a connection with the di Ruggieros? It would be good for her to have a taste of the privileges that would be hers when she officially became part of *la famiglia*.

"Dante?" a melodic voice broke into his thoughts and he turned and stood, smiling.

"I thought I recognized the back of your head," Grace said as she gave him a perfumed hug.

He had dated Grace for two years when they were both in their early twenties. She was lovely, intelligent, a refined beauty from old Dallas society. He had once thought she would have been his perfect partner, with her father a wealthy personal injury attorney and her mother a retired beauty queen. She was shrewd and gave him much needed legitimacy. He had proposed, but she had refused, crying, then moved out of his penthouse the following day. He still didn't know why she'd turned him down.

"Grace, how are you?" he asked, and she smiled, her long auburn hair falling in waves down her back, her shapely figure showcased to perfection in a sexy but understated dark blue dress. She was still stunning, even eight years later.

"I'm doing well," she replied, slipping onto the bar stool beside his as he resumed his seat. "I was so sorry to hear about your mother. I hope you got my flowers."

Dante nodded, but in truth he didn't know. There had been so many flowers, so many condolence cards, that he had left it up to office assistants to handle.

"Of course, thank you. You know Mama loved you," he said honestly, and she blushed sweetly. "Can I get you a drink?"

She shook her head. "No, thank you, I'm headed back to my table. My husband will be here soon; he was held up at the hospital."

"Oh, yes, I heard you had married. A surgeon, correct?"

She nodded, beaming, clearly overjoyed with the turn her life had taken. "Yes, we married a few years ago."

Dante cocked his head and looked at her.

"What? Is there something on my face?" Grace laughed and brushed at her perfectly made-up face.

"No, no, beautiful as ever. I was just wondering... why didn't we work out? Why did you turn me down?"

She blinked at the abrupt shift to a delicate topic. "Because you didn't love me," she said at last, her tone matter-of-fact.

"That's something you need?" Dante asked, surprised. Of course he hadn't loved her. He didn't love anyone. Love was a superfluous and unnecessary emotion.

"Of course, Dante. Most people need love, but I knew that wasn't something you were capable of." She reached over to pluck his high-ball glass from the bar before him, taking a delicate sip. "Though I do miss your taste in scotch," she said, sighing in bliss.

"I would've been faithful to you," Dante said. Had she worried his lack of affection meant he'd cheat on her?

Grace shook her head. "I know, and that is a lot, but for me it wasn't enough. To live in your dangerous world... I needed more than just loyalty, to make it worthwhile."

"What more could you possibly need?" Dante asked, genuinely confused, and Grace sighed.

"Love, to me, is putting that other person ahead of all others, and I knew I would always come second to your family. And that that fact would never change."

Something behind him snagged Grace's attention; she waved, her face lighting up at the sight of the new arrival.

"You left and found a surgeon," he teased.

Grace slid elegantly from the bar stool. "And found a man that loved me," she reminded him. She placed her cool, long-fingered hand against his cheek and kissed the opposite one.

But instead of pulling back right away, she leaned in closer and whispered, "Dante, if you asked me this because you've decided you need a partner, you need to realize that she'll need more than fidelity. Or... she'll need to be alright with knowing that she comes after your family."

Dante reached for her hand and kissed the back of her fingers in farewell. Grace was lovely, but she needed more than he could provide. It pleased him she had found what she needed, if it wasn't him.

"Thank you, Grace. It was wonderful to see you again."

She smiled. "Tell your brothers and father I said hello." She threaded her way through the tables to where a tall, handsome man awaited her with the expression of a person receiving his greatest wish.

Was she right? Would Cassie need more than loyalty? If it came to it, could Dante give it to her? It would take compromise on his part, and compromise was not something he had much practice doing. Was she worth it? Was he capable of it? If he really wanted her, he would have to figure out what she needed, and provide it.

Even if it wasn't, couldn't be, love.

CHAPTER

NINE

"Hey, how is the Cruz audit coming?" Cassie's boss, Tiffany, popped her head into her cubicle right before lunch.

Tiffany was just a few years older than Cassie and already running a moderate-sized accounting firm. She was smart, a great boss, and an overall wonderful person. Cassie had lucked out when Tiffany had hired her straight out of college and then paid for her to take her licensing exam.

"It's coming along," Cassie said, sighing, and rubbed her temples. The Cruz audit was a court-ordered audit of a chain of seven RV dealerships. Mr. and Mrs. Cruz had built quite the empire in their twenty year marriage but now they were divorcing, and Tiffany's firm had been hired to do an accurate accounting for the court.

"In truth, it's a mess, a jumble of business and personal accounts, and I don't think Mr. Cruz is going to like my findings." Cassie thought about the monthly debits to a leasing company for an apartment that was not inhabited by either Mr. or Mrs. Cruz.

"Isn't that usually the case?" Tiffany winked and Cassie nodded. "Do you need help? I could get you an assistant, if you're afraid you won't make the deadline."

Cassie shook her head. "Nah, I have a handle on it. I should have it done well in time for the court date."

"If you're sure?" Cassie's boss asked again, her face pinched with worry.

Another thing that made Tiffany such a great boss: she cared if she overworked her employees, and was always willing to help if someone were overwhelmed. It was something Cassie made sure not to take advantage of, so she would only accept help if she really needed it.

"I'm totally sure." Cassie smiled just as her phone dinged, signaling a message.

"Well, let me know if it changes, or if you find anything really juicy." Tiffany grinned and stepped out of the cubical with a wave that Cassie returned.

"Sure, thing, boss!" Cassie called after her and checked her phone.

–Hey what time can you get out of work? – Miranda

–Hey Miranda! I work until 5 but I have plans tonight.

–I know, silly! That's why I'm texting. I'm going to need you to duck out of work before 5, more like 4. – Miranda

–Why?

–Because I have been tasked with helping you get ready, something I agreed to wholeheartedly – Miranda

Cassie chewed on her lip, worried. She liked Miranda, but she didn't show many people her scars. She hated the look of revulsion or pity or, even worse, a mixture of both when they saw them.

–Thank you, but I can handle it.

–Nonsense! Are you a size 6 or 4? – Miranda

–Why?

–Because I'm bringing you some dress options. Don't worry about it, I'll bring some in each size. See you at your apartment at 4:30! – Miranda

Cassie didn't bother to respond, nor to ask how she knew where she lived. Cassie knew Dante would've told her. It was probably Dante who asked Miranda to buy her a dress. It was like something out of a movie, but Cassie wasn't exactly Julia Roberts.

In truth, she had thought little about what she would wear that night, or where he was taking her. He hadn't mentioned where, and now she was nervous. No, not nervous– terrified. Cassie doubted whatever dress Miranda purchased would cover her shoulders and upper back. Oh, she didn't think Miranda would get her anything distasteful; no, what was distasteful was her burned skin.

Cassie looked at her phone: 11:45am. If she worked through lunch, she could leave early. She stood and headed to Tiffany's office.

"Tiffany?" Cassie knocked on Tiffany's open office door.

"Did you find something juicy already?" her boss teased.

"No, I, uh, I have this date tonight–"

That caught Tiffany's attention, because in the three years she had worked there, Cassie had never mentioned a man. And that was because she hadn't dated, not once since that fateful night in her junior year of college, when her world had changed irrevocably.

"Really?" Tiffany blinked at her. She looked a bit like a surprised fish at the moment, her chocolate-brown eyes wide, mouth open in shock.

"I was hoping if I worked through lunch, I could leave an hour early. I know it's last minute–"

"Absolutely not," Tiffany interrupted her and now it was Cassie's turn to gape in shock, but Tiffany smiled.

"You will not miss lunch, and you will leave at 3:30, not 4:00. I don't want any traffic mishap to keep you from your date. But I demand details soon."

Cassie thanked her and returned to her cubicle. She had brought her lunch today because she was still trying to pinch every penny to pay back Amber's debt. But Cassie didn't reach for her lunch, because no matter what Tiffany said, she wasn't going to skip out on her work. Besides, now she was too nervous to eat.

Cassie put her nose to the grindstone and worked through the afternoon. Numbers had always soothed her. They were always black and white, unlike her life, which was a constant mess of confused, muddled gray.

At 3:30, Cassie shut down her computer and gathered up her things. With a wave to Tiffany through her open office door, she left the office. As she drove home in her fancy new car, her mind was a jumble of worry and nerves.

The drive took her only twenty minutes, not the normal forty-five, because of the earliness of the hour, and she blew out a relieved breath as she pushed open her door. She would have plenty of time for a quick shower and to take Lucy for a walk before Miranda showed up.

The dog was absolutely delighted her favorite human was home from work early. She danced around Cassie's feet, brushing her cold, wet nose against her hand.

"Yes, baby, I'm home early. Want to go for a walk?" Cassie teased, grabbing up Lucy's leash. Outside was sweltering, but Cassie wouldn't remove her sweater, because all she wore underneath the light cardigan was a tank top. She sat on a bench in the shade, watching as the dog sniffed the perfect spot to do her business, and laughed when Lucy chased a squirrel up a tree.

Her life had been so simple before Hurricane Amber sent it all to hell and she'd had to step into Dante's world. It was just her and Lucy, really. Oh, she had Sarah and even Tiffany: occasional drinks at the bar around the corner from work, a hole in the wall with great fries and an owner who had a crush on Tiffany.

But even those nights were few and far between, because though they were her friends, she didn't trust them, not completely. Not with all her secrets, her wants, her hopes, her desires. The last time she had, the ones who had promised to love her and take care of her had died. Everyone else had hurt her in some way, even her own sister.

And here she was, about to get ready for a date with a man who she knew was dangerous, was cruel, even, but something about him soothed her, soothed her the way numbers did. For all his complexity, Dante seemed simple, too.

No, not simple, that wasn't right. There was a... a regularity to him, something that made her know what to expect from him. There was darkness to him, an ominous cloud over his character, but beneath that cloud was a code he followed and did not deviate from. Just like numbers, Dante always added up to the same thing.

Cassie stood and called Lucy, who happily trotted over with her tongue lolling out of her mouth, so they could go home. Whatever she had with Dante could very well end before it began, because he might see her scars and go running for the hills. Hell, *she* would run from the ghastly reminder of the worst day of her life, if she could, but she was stuck with them.

Cassie went into her apartment and was in her shower before she could give it any more thought. She spent more time than normal, shaving parts of her body she normally ignored, moisturizing more thoroughly, and before she knew it, the time was ten minutes to five and there was a knock on her apartment door. Cassie wrapped her wet hair up in a fluffy towel and pulled on her robe to answer the door.

"Finally," Miranda huffed and pushed into Cassie's tiny apartment, her arms full of shopping and garment bags.

"Miranda, how much did you buy?" Cassie exclaimed, peering into the bag full of fancy shoe boxes.

"I brought four different dress styles in two different sizes, and the shoes– I hope you're a size 7 or 8, because I forgot to ask, so there are several pairs in those sizes."

"I wear a seven, mostly," Cassie said, grasping numbly for the arm of the couch and lowering herself down.

"Gosh, look at your face, you look terrified," Miranda said, laughing. She grabbed one of Cassie's hands and pulled her back up on her shaking legs. "Come on." She scooped up the bags and pulled Cassie through her open bedroom door. "Let's get you into some of these dresses! I think you'll like them."

Cassie tried to swallow the knot rising in her throat and sank down onto her bed as Miranda started pulling the dresses from the garment bags.

"So, these two are my favorites." Miranda removed a black silk dress with long sleeves and a V-neck that plunged so low it would go almost to her navel. Cassie brightened. Her back was a horror, but the skin on her front was flawless.

"I know this looks boring–" boring? with that neckline? "–but it's backless!" Miranda turned the dress, holding it out toward Cassie so she could feel the silk and reveal a V in the back that dipped just as far as the bodice.

Cassie's reaction was immediate and powerful; she flinched back, as if the dress might cut her if she touched it.

"Cassie?" Miranda frowned, a crease of puzzlement forming between her elegantly arched brows. "Is something wrong with the dress?"

"I can't wear it," Cassie replied, her voice strangled. A cold thrill of alarm barreled through her at the very idea of walking through a crowded restaurant with the wreckage of her back on display for everyone– for Dante– to see. "I won't wear it."

Miranda stared at her, eyes wide. Then she gave a nod and made quick work of stuffing the offending dress back in its garment bag. "Alright," she agreed pleasantly. "That's a definite 'no'."

Cassie's panic receded the moment the dress was completely hidden within its bag. She let out a breath and as the tension left her, so too did her strength; she let her head droop, glad when her hair fell to curtain her face. Only then did she let the tears come, just one quick rush of moisture before she blinked them back, angry at her weakness, at her lack of control over her reaction, over her fear.

"Cassie," said Miranda, her tone the kind of careful you used when someone was about to lose their shit, "you don't have to tell me what just happened, but if you want to... no judgment, you know?"

Cassie used the cuffs of her robe to dab her face, ensuring it was dry when she raised her head once more. "Thank you," she said with a watery smile. She didn't want Miranda to report back to Dante that his new accountant– and possible... girlfriend? romantic partner?– was a basket case. "I appreciate that. I'm okay now."

Miranda watched her a moment longer, waiting, giving Cassie

the chance to speak, but Cassie did not elaborate. Her scars were her own. She would not share them with the other woman, no matter how kind she was.

Miranda got the message, because she turned to the next dress in the pile. The next contender was a maxi-style wrap dress, also in black. The silk chiffon flowed like water from the hanger, and even better: it had sleeves! Just little ones, multi-layered cap sleeves in the same chiffon, but they were long enough for Cassie to be happy.

"With this dress, you may have to wear the five inch stiletos I brought on a whim, because it's a little long," she proclaimed.

Cassie gulped at that; even with her short stature, she never wore much more than a kitten heel.

"Now, these sleeves do have a slit," Miranda said, moving the fabric to show how the sleeves would flutter and move much like the long skirt did. "But if you don't like that, and have a needle and black thread, I could stitch them together while Julio and Steven do your hair and make-up."

It was a delicate offer, a sensitive one, and it meant more to Cassie than anything had in a long time. She offered a genuine smile to the other woman.

"That's not necessary," she told her, "but thanks." Then she sat up straighter, squaring her shoulders. "So, who are Steven and Julio?"

Steven and Julio turned out to be Miranda's favorite hairdresser and makeup artist, respectively, and the best of either that Cassie had ever experienced (not that she had experienced that many).

Steven tamed her wild red curls and put her hair up in a low chignon at the base of her head, a few wispy tendrils framing her face, and Julio had somehow made her skin look flawless– but not pale– and her boring brown eyes luminous and velvety. Cassie gave herself one last look in the mirror and wasn't sure who was looking back. The woman reflected was lovely, poised and sophisticated, not plain or boring or uncomfortable with herself.

Miranda helped her navigate down the stairs of her apartment in the steep, terrifying five-inch heels and into the car Dante had sent for her.

"Thank you," Cassie said for probably the hundredth time and gave Miranda a shaky smile.

"No thanks needed," Miranda declared. "I had fun with it. Now *you* have fun! And try to convince Dante to have some fun, too." She grinned and slammed the door shut.

Now Cassie was being led by the maître d' through the most exclusive restaurant in Dallas to where Dante sat at a table with a view of the entire city. Not for the first time in the last several days, Miranda wondered if she were in a coma and all of this was a dream. None of it seemed remotely possible, not for her.

He stood as Cassie neared the table, the smile on his face pleased. If she hadn't already come to the realization that Dante didn't really do 'happy', his lack of enthusiasm might have crushed her. Dante was either pleased or not pleased, and tonight, in that moment, he looked more pleased than she had ever seen him during their brief acquaintance. That she'd been able to bring him to that level of expression sent a zap of pride through her.

"Sir." The maître d' nodded to Dante and pulled out the chair opposite him for Cassie to sit. "The server will be with you shortly."

He left and Dante leaned forward an inch. "Cassie, you look stunning."

Cassie felt her face flush at his words. "Thank you, so do you."

And he did, wearing a black suit with a deep wine-red shirt open at the collar. He wore no tie, and some of his tattoos were visible. Cassie swallowed a sudden flood of saliva; he was literally mouth-watering and the confidence that had buoyed her to that point flagged a bit. He was *so* much more than she was used to.

She opened her menu. It was written in French, of which she spoke exactly none. She would have to have his help to order. Giving up on choosing any of the mystery meals, she decided to spend the time studying him from under her lashes.

The candlelight made his skin gleam like golden pearl, and not for the first time, Cassie wondered what it would taste like. But also like a pearl, his façade was blank, polished, *hard*. Did his control ever falter? Or did he remain in perfect control, even when making love? Was it possible for a woman to peer beyond the glossy shell into the many-layered secret heart of him? Was it possible for *Cassie* to manage it?

She sipped her water, trying in vain to rein in her thoughts, but they were unruly, slipping any leash she tried to place on them. She was in deep, so deep it would be hell getting back out again.

If she even wanted to.

CHAPTER

TEN

Dante hoped Miranda had gotten herself a very expensive thank-you present.

Cassie was spectacular as she approached his table. Gone was the frumpy mouse who had begged to pay back her sister's debt. In her place was a woman in full possession of her beauty, sophisticated and elegant, head held high and shoulders back.

Her dress was still more conservative than most women would wear, falling to her ankles, but the filmy chiffon moved around her like fluid, undulating and sinuous, and the sleeves kept fluttering open to permit tantalizing glimpses of her pale, slim arms. He wasn't the only man whose eyes followed her through the restaurant. But judging by the heated look of appreciation in her eyes when she spotted him, he was the only man she would be spending any time with.

He'd make sure of it.

Once she was seated, the maître d' disappeared and Cassie put her menu down. "I don't speak French," she whispered, her expression conspiratorial.

Dante smiled and leaned across the table. "Neither do I, but I know what's good here. Do you trust me?" He watched, waiting for her to comprehend that he meant more than just his trusting him about the food.

She sucked in a quick, surprised breath, eyes wide for a moment. But then she let it out again, determination replacing the surprise.

"Yes," she said, swallowing. She understood. She agreed. Satisfaction curled, thick and hot, in his belly alongside his hunger– for food, for her– and Dante picked up his menu.

"Do you like duck?" he asked.

"I don't know, I've never had it," Cassie admitted.

"Well, how adventurous are you?" Dante teased, and she looked up at him through her lashes. If she were a practiced flirt, he would've described it as coy, but Cassie *wasn't* a practiced flirt. That was why she was so compelling to him. There was no artifice to her interest in him.

"With the right person... or the right incentive?" she asked, and he could feel his smile growing, a rare genuine one.

"Either. Both."

"*Very* adventurous, then." She licked her bottom lip, and he wondered if she'd done it on purpose, trying to tempt him beyond bearing.

"Welcome to *Toulouse*," the server said, popping the little bubble encapsulating them. Dante bit back a laugh when Cassie jumped at the man's sudden appearance. "I'm David, and I'll be your server for the evening. Would you like to hear the specials?"

"No, thank you. We'll both start with the lobster bisque and then have the duck. And bring us a bottle of your best chardonnay," Dante answered, handing the man both their menus.

"Wonderful, sir," the server said and departed.

Dante leaned back in his plush chair and observed Cassie. She was glancing around the restaurant, a look of appreciation on her pretty face, and he couldn't blame her. *Toulouse* was as beautiful as its view of downtown Dallas, decorated in a timeless but current style that hinted of Hollywood regency by way of Europe, both classy enough for older diners and trendy enough for the younger ones. She studied the other patrons, each of them as well-appointed as the restaurant itself, and then gasped.

"Dante," she whispered and leaned across the table, granting him an enticing view of cleavage. He could tell she wasn't wearing a bra and her movement caused her breasts to shift in the most delightful way.

"Yes?" He shifted focus from her chest to her face, no less compelling to his libido.

"Is that the mayor?" She gestured with a flick of her eyes behind him. Dante turned slightly to see the mayor of Dallas and his wife enjoying a meal with another couple.

"Yes." He smiled at her wide eyes, pleased to be able to give her this experience. He'd expected to be amused by her excitement at meeting minor celebrities, but he found it charmed him instead. "And behind you is one of the star running backs for the Dallas Cowboys."

Cassie swung her head around so fast he actually worried she might get whiplash.

"Don't be so obvious," he said gently, but with a thread of command underlying it. Her appearance wouldn't embarrass him, but if she kept gawking at their fellow guests, her presentation of poise and elegance would be revealed as a farce. Dante was not interested in having to mend his image because he'd taken out a woman who stared at everyone like a child experiencing snow for the first time.

"Oh." Cassie said, seeming surprised at her own behavior. "I don't usually– I'm usually better behaved than this." She gave him a weak smile. "I'll do better."

He nodded as the server arrived with their lobster bisque and a bottle of wine.

"Try the bisque," he told her, and was pleased when she picked up the spoon without an argument.

"Oh, this is so good," she said after a mouthful of the soup, and followed it with an indecent-sounding moan that had Dante shifting in his seat to alleviate the tightening in his pants.

"I'm happy you're pleased with it," he murmured. He barely noticed his own bowl; he was more interested in learning how she tasted than the soup.

"I don't think *pleased* is the right word," she replied, her tone marveling, "more like *obsessed* or *addicted*. If they sell it to-go, I'll probably go broke buying it everyday, now."

He smiled at her little joke. She would never go broke ordering soup or anything else, not when she had him to buy her whatever she wanted.

"There are worse ways to go broke," he said instead.

"Yes, like shoes or plastic surgery," she said, and he nodded.

"I agree, what a waste of money."

"So sayeth the man whose shoes are probably Gucci or Prada," she teased.

He quirked a haughty eyebrow. "Testoni, actually,"

"See, that's such a fancy brand, I don't even know it," she said, laughing.

"You weren't raised by wealthy Italian men like my grandfather, so I forgive your ignorance."

"I appreciate your benevolence," she said with mock gratitude, then turned serious. "I made Miranda promise to return the dress that I didn't wear tonight, but she wouldn't take back the shoes, just left them in my apartment. I'll bring them with me to the club on Thursday night."

Dante waited as the server smoothly cleared their now-empty bowls before answering. Dante topped off each of their wine glasses and nodded to David's murmured "another?"

"There is no need," he said when they were alone again. "If you like them, keep them."

"Oh, I couldn't, they're way too expensive. Too fancy for me," she protested.

"If you can accept a car, Cassandra, you can keep a few pairs of shoes." Irritation flared; was she going to fight him on every gift he wanted to give her?

She shook her head as the server deposited their duck done two ways, pan-seared and confit, with a wild mushroom ragu and dauphinoise potatoes.

"I shouldn't accept that, either," she muttered, but didn't continue in that obstinate vein; instead, she cut into her duck breast. He waited while she tried it, hoping for the same reaction as she'd had for the bisque, and was not disappointed.

Her eyes rolled up into the back of her head, and this time the moan that escaped her was downright pornographic. He could cause her to make the same noise, would bring her to the point of abandoning herself to the same point. *Soon.* It would happen soon.

"Good?" he asked unnecessarily, but he wanted her attention back on him, wanted to remind her that he was the reason for the symphony of flavor taking place in her mouth at that moment.

She nodded, her eyes aglow like the finest brandy with pleasure, and for the first time he understood Elias had boarded a plane in the middle of night to come to the rescue of a woman. How their father had nearly started a war to be with their mother. The desire to bring a woman pleasure, to make her happy, feel safe, appreciated... it was a powerful thing, growing to monstrous size almost before he knew it.

Dante might not be able to love, but he could *want*. And he wanted Cassie as he had never wanted anyone or anything else.

Dinner passed like the other meals they had shared prior to that one, full of lively conversation... and this time, some heavy flirtation. Every moment spent with Cassie was better than the last. He coaxed her further and further from her shell and the more he learned, the more he saw, the more certain he was that she would fit into his life.

Not just in a practical way; not only could her steel-trap mind work numbers like a magician, but just as she'd said she trusted him... he was coming to see that he could trust her, as well. With his regular secrets– the clubs, the drugs– but perhaps even with the darkest, most hidden parts of himself.

As they departed the restaurant, he slid his hand into hers.

"This has been a lovely evening," Cassie said as they waited for Dante's driver to pull up. Even in the towering heels Miranda had put her in, her head barely reached his shoulder. He tucked a loose red curl behind her ear, delighting in the flush it brought to her cheeks.

"It has been," he agreed. "But it doesn't need to end, *cara mia.*" He cupped her cheek, her skin like satin against his palm. She was so warm, so soft, and he knew she would feel like heaven under him, while he drove himself inside her.

"It doesn't?" she whispered back, her eyes falling shut as his thumb caressed the stubborn, rounded jut of her chin.

"It doesn't," he confirmed as the black town car slunk to a stop before them. "Not if you come home with me."

"I don't think–" she began to refuse, but he silenced her protest with a kiss. Quick and deep, his tongue slipped into her mouth for a fleeting taste, a taste that only left him– and, he hoped, her– wanting more.

"Cassie, come home with me," he breathed, eyes closed and forehead pressed against hers.

"Yes, Dante," she whispered, and he pulled away to look at her face, into her eyes, to gauge precisely how poised she was to flee. He'd have to precisely manage and time everything to keep her from taking flight like a startled doe. She was so lovely, and so innocent, for a woman her age. Part of him, a dark part, a part that he kept under iron control, jumped at the chance to corrupt that innocence.

Dante waved away the pimple-faced valet and opened the door of the car for Cassie himself. Once they were both enclosed within its sumptuous leather interior, he slid an arm around her shoulders and pulled her body against his.

"My penthouse, Manny," Dante told the driver.

"You got it, boss."

The car pulled away from the restaurant and into the crowded streets of downtown Dallas. Dante didn't live far from the restaurant, but it would still take a good fifteen or twenty minutes before they arrived.

"You are so handsome," Cassie said after a few minutes, her voice somewhat dazed.

"Am I?" He asked, smiling, and leaned forward to nuzzle his nose against hers.

"Ugh, you know you are." She threaded her fingers through his hair as he peppered tiny kisses over along her jaw.

"Well, you're beautiful." He mouthed the shell of her ear, tugging on her earlobe with his teeth. Cassie rewarded him with a low moan, so he tugged a little harder. She moaned louder, fingers tightening in her hair.

"Do you like that?" he whispered.

She shuddered at his words. Slowly, Dante moved his hand up over her silk-covered midriff, until his hand clasped her breast. Its weight fit very pleasantly in the cup of his hand and this time, when he tugged on her earlobe with his teeth, he also pinched lightly at her already rigid nipple.

Cassie groaned. Dante smiled against her skin as she wriggled against him, burrowing deeper into his embrace. He understood that pressing need to be closer, closer, *closer*. The same compulsion was riding him, too, harder and harder as the seconds of touching and kissing passed.

She moaned her appreciation of everything he did to her; likewise, hee wholeheartedly approved of each of her caresses, the way she stroked his shoulders and raked fingers through his hair. It seemed like they were going to get along just as well in bed as they did out of it. Dante sealed his lips over hers and pressed his tongue into her mouth, exultant when she greedily accepted it, met with her own for a sensual battle.

He pushed her back into the seat, his body encroaching into her space without shame. She dragged him closer still, one hand in his hair, the other crumpling the lapel of his suit without care.

A crumpled suit was of no consequence; honestly, it only seemed right, that a passion such as what had risen between them would result in a bit of destruction. It didn't seem possible that there would be no consequences to the world around them in the wake of such a powerful force. When it was all over, when they lay in his bed, sated and sweaty and replete, he fully expected the curtains to be shredded, perhaps a window or two broken. Would be disappointed, perhaps, if that were not the case.

With that destructive force, or perhaps because of it, came corruption. His family was so thoroughly corrupted that there was no force in heaven or hell that could dig them free of it. And contact with him would only taint Cassie, as well, both in and out of his bed. If he were a different man, he would care. He would scruple that he was taking advantage of her naïveté, of her clear desire for guidance and instruction, her hunger for acceptance and appreciation.

But he wasn't a different man. He was the eldest of four sons, the heir to a legacy of wealth and power at the expense of the weak. He was the monarch of a kingdom fuelled by drugs and sex, and he ruled it with a heavy hand. He was a man who got what he wanted and damn the cost to himself or anyone else.

He was Dante di Ruggiero.

And she would be his, body and soul.

CHAPTER

ELEVEN

CASSIE

"We're here, boss."

Cassie could barely hear Manny's words over the beating of her heart and the daze Dante's touches had put her in. She tried to pull out of Dante's arms, worried that Manny had to have heard her enraptured moaning. The car was a luxury sedan, sure, with ample room, but it wasn't a limo with those privacy screens she had always heard about in movies.

Dante didn't let her, though. He gave her lips a gentle kiss and pulled away slowly, his dark, intense gaze heavy on hers.

"Thank you, Manny," he said, calm as ever, as if that hadn't been the hottest, most intense kiss of his life. And maybe it wasn't. He had probably kissed dozens of women, and all had probably been stunningly beautiful. It was probably nothing more than a regular night for him.

"Do you still want to come inside?" Dante asked, his hand cupping her cheek again, and she instinctively leaned into his touch. Her body knew what it wanted, even if her brain was conflicted. She decided to trust her body, for once, and nodded.

"Cassie, be very sure, *cara mia*," Dante whispered. "I do nothing lightly, least of all take a woman to my home. To my bed."

Cassie searched his handsome face. She knew so little about him, but she felt in her gut that he wouldn't lie to her about something this important. She was sure, with a certainty like a bolt of lightning, that if she followed him out of the car and into his penthouse, her life would never be the same.

She could refuse him, could go back to her tiny apartment and Lucy, continuing her boring life, doing little but working and waiting to bail Amber out of trouble yet again. Or she could take something she wanted, just for herself. He could hurt her, could probably *destroy* her, but the risk just made it all the more tempting. She stood to lose a lot, but she also stood to gain everything.

She wanted the thrill of gambling, of flinging herself headlong into betting the house, of hurtling into the unknown. She wanted all of it. She was all in.

"I'm sure," she answered, and leaned forward and kissed him. "Take me inside, Dante."

Dante swiftly brought the kiss to an end, pulling back so he could open the car door and help her out into the humid summer night air.

"Thank you, Manny. I won't need you any longer tonight," Dante told his driver over his shoulder as he guided Cassie into the building. It was one of those outrageously expensive high-rise apartment complexes, the kind she had only ever seen on TV.

"Mr. di Ruggerio." A doorman tipped his hat as his white-gloved hand pulled open the tall glass door to the lobby.

"Sam," Dante acknowledged. Cassie tried to smile, but the interior of the building was more luxurious than the black slats of glass would ever give away, and she was more than a bit breathless from its grandeur.

Cassie's own apartment wasn't exactly the pinnacle of architecture, but it was decent. It had been nicely remodeled a few years earlier and there were no vermin or bugs, but this place was a palace, a modern day Taj Mahal. A modern sculpture installation dominated the lobby floor and more art graced the walls. It was like a boutique hotel, or a museum, or both, and it was all too much for Cassie to take, in her state of heightened senses.

The front desk was staffed by a woman in a sleek black suit. As they approached, she stood and smiled in a simpering way at Dante, a look Cassie didn't care for, and which Dante seemed to ignore, anyway. Dante led her past the woman to a bank of gleaming brass elevators. He paused at the last one on the end and, withdrawing a key from his breast pocket, slipped it into the panel. He punched in a number and the doors parted immediately.

"Is this a private elevator?" Cassie asked as they stepped inside and the doors closed.

Dante nodded. Without his touching any button, it began to rise of its own accord. "I own the top three floors. This private elevator is the only way, besides the emergency stairs, to access them."

Cassie's eyes widened. She was no idiot when it came to real estate. She had hopes of buying her own home one day, but like most other people, those hopes had been of a small, affordable place in the 'burbs. To own a penthouse in the middle of downtown, in an elegant, modern building? It was wealth Cassie couldn't imagine.

"*Aphrodite's* must do very well," she murmured in awe as the doors drew open with a quiet swish.

"Well, you would know," Dante teased and gestured for her to precede him out of the elevator car. Before them was a small hallway with only one door, glossy with black lacquer. He opened the door, pushing it open for her and flicking a switch which turned on all the lights at once, bathing the space in a golden ambient glow.

Cassie couldn't stop her jaw from dropping. Had she thought the building palatial already? What she'd seen so far was nothing in comparison to the luxurious beauty before her.

There was no foyer area; the door opened into a massive open-concept room that was entrance, living room, dining room, entertainment area, and bar all in one. The exterior walls were all glass, floor to ceiling, offering incredible, unimpeded views of the city's skyline in three directions.

The click of her stilettos on the gleaming marble floor seemed abnormally loud in her ears as she progressed deeper into Dante's lair, drawn to the windows and their view. The buildings of downtown Dallas, the cars and streetlights far below them– it all seemed to glitter like man-made stars.

When she had looked her fill, she turned to study the rest of her surroundings. The room was decorated in a way that was blatantly, unapologetically masculine. Everything was done in richly varying shades of warm gray; the woods were reddish, dark cherry and mahogany, and there was enough brass and crystal in the lamps and overhead lighting to keep everything sparkling and bright instead of gloomy. The room was like an exquisitely tailored gray business suit paired with a burgundy silk tie and the finest golden cufflinks, and it fit Dante to perfection, just like his actual clothing.

Through a wide opening in the wall to the right, beyond the dining area, she could see what looked to be a pro-level kitchen.

"Do you do a lot of cooking?" she asked, tilting her head to see more of it. An eight-burner stove and glass-fronted refrigerator were framed by tall cabinets in more of the glossy, warm-toned wood and black granite counters. Rows of bright-shining copper pots hung from overhead on a pot rack. If she were more of a chef, she imagined she'd have had an orgasm just from the sight of the room.

"None," Dante answered, taking her hand to lead her to a staircase she hadn't noticed.

"Then why–" She was rudely interrupted by her feet stumbling in their tall heels and tangling in the trailing hem of her long dress. Dante was immediately there to steady her, sweeping her skirt back and holding it so she could ascend to the next floor without further problem.

At the top was a long hallway stretching in their direction. Dante pushed open the nearest door and, rather than the bedroom Cassie had expected to find, there was an office. A study, more accurately: while the furniture was more modern than otherwise, it was still the same sort of dark, hushed place lined with floor-to-ceiling shelves stuffed with books, filled with deep leather sofas. At the far end was a wide desk with a manager's chair, tall and throne-like, behind it.

A raunchy image, of Dante seated in the chair and Cassie straddling him, head thrown back as she sank down on him, flashed into her mind's eye.

"Would you like a drink?" Dante asked, and she whipped around to stare at him.

"Drink?" she squeaked.

"It's just that you look thirsty, all of a sudden," he replied mildly. "Overheated." He raised a hand to her forehead, testing its temperature. "You were tipsy from the wine with dinner. You're sure you're fine?"

"I'm fine," she managed, making her way to one of the sofas and dropping– almost collapsing– into it. "Yes, I'd like something cool."

He nodded and went to a small bar cart in the corner. She was no longer tipsy from the wine, Dante's lust having burned it all away in the car with his kisses, but she had work the next day and she didn't want to have to nurse a hangover in the morning. Still, a little wouldn't hurt; she'd stop before it was too much, but she'd have enough to ease her nerves. She still had to tell him about her scars, had to reveal them to his gaze. She figured there was a good chance they'd repulse him and she'd end up going home far earlier than she expected.

Dante pulled off his suit jacket and tossed it over his immaculate desk, rolling up the sleeves of his wine-colored shirt. "Do you like scotch?"

She did. In fact, the previous year, she had splurged for Christmas and purchased herself a $200 bottle of single-malt that she had savored and enjoyed for months.

"I do," she answered. "On the rocks, please."

His smile at her words made his eyes crinkle, a sight that had something inside Cassie deciding to make him do it as often as possible.

The tinkling *plunk* of ice cubes in crystal sounded, then the splash of liquid tumbling, and soon Dante returned to the couch with a lowball glass in each hand. He sat beside her, just as close as he had in the car, and she couldn't decide if the warmth emanating from him was because of the sip of the smooth scotch she had just taken or the way his eyes, darkly intent upon her, seemed to burn.

She took another, larger, sip of her drink and tried to think of something charming to say to fill the silence.

"I love your books," was what she came up with instead. She suppressed a wince and kept her gaze on the shelves, absently cataloguing in her head the titles she could see.

His touch was light, warm, just a whisper of a sensation on her skin as he ran his fingers up her neck, around the shell of her ear, skimming the upswept strands of her hair. His touch was wondering, exploring, but at the same time greedy, possessive, as if he were writing the word 'mine' on her skin with his touch.

"Mmm, yes," he agreed. He bent closer and his lips joined his fingertips on the tender flesh of her throat.

"You– oh! You have a lot of them," she said, melting back into the butter-soft leather cushions as his warm mouth brushed her skin.

"I do," he agreed, pursuing her into the depths of the sofa. "Reading was very important to my mother."

"Really?" she moaned, her eyes falling shut at the feel of his lips, hot, damp, demanding, on her skin.

"Mmhmm." He mouthed the hollow behind her ear as his fingers danced up her arm, toying with the silky chiffon of her sleeve.

It should have been a seductive touch, lulling her deeper under his mesmerizing spell, but instead it sent alarm bells skittering across her nerves. She flinched out of his embrace, huddling back against the farthest reaches of the big sofa until its arm halted her progress.

"Cassie?" His voice was smoky with passion, the confusion an odd note within it. He shifted closer, trying to take her in his arms once more.

"I– I need to tell you something," she gasped, hands sliding up not to grasp his shirt, to pull him closer, but to prevent him from coming any nearer. She needed space, a barrier, for what she had to do. She couldn't think when he was so close, hot and hard and smelling so good.

He froze, then sat back, giving her all the space she needed. Cool air swirled between them, sudden, surprising a shiver out of her.

"Tell me," he commanded. He was taut with control, with patience, and knowing he would not pressure her to rush gave her the strength she needed.

"I– I, I have–" She fumbled for words and put a hand over her face, fear and shame and sadness making her want to hide, to flee, to do anything to avoid the revelation she was sure would disgust him.

But she wanted him, too, not just sexually, and with a force that made her feel that the danger was worth taking the chance. If she was going to be worthy of what Dante was offering her, she had to lay herself bare, figuratively and literally, body and soul. A man like Dante would demand no less. And if she were honest with herself, she wanted the same: she wanted to peel back the barriers she'd shielded herself behind, to present herself, naked and quivering, seen and accepted for her truest self.

"Cassie." Dante pulled her hand away from her face. "There's nothing you can say that will shock me. Just say it."

"It would be easier to show you." She rose from the sofa on unsteady legs, ungainly as a newborn colt, but she had more to worry about than momentary gracelessness. Her wobbly dismount had her scotch spilling over the rim of her glass. She placed it on a side table and rubbed her hand dry on her skirt.

Dante had not switched on all the lights, as he had done downstairs; there was just a single lamp on, a pool of light cast around it only a few feet, leaving the rest of the study cloaked in shadows. He wouldn't be able to see the true extent of her scarring, but he would be able to see enough to horrify.

She girded herself, mentally, even as she began to unfasten the dress. The wrap dress fastened with long ties that flowed down from her waist to flirt with her legs as she walked. She unknotted them and then unfastened the row of tiny hooks that held the bodice together.

Dante licked his lips, hunger naked in his eyes, dark, ravenous, but Cassie turned away from him, fingers trembling as she began to slip the dress from where it hung from her shoulders. With a last nervous twitch, she let the chiffon silk fall like a river of ink to her feet.

She stood with her back to him; though clad in only the smallest of black lacy panties and her stilettos, she was more bare even than that. No one– *no one*– had seen her scars since the accident except her doctors. Not friends, not lovers, not even Amber. She always wore tops that came up to the neck in back, always with shoft sleeves at the very least. She'd even layered her full-coverage swimsuits with caftans or cover-ups opaque enough to provide a barrier to curious eyes.

Cassie waited, biting her lip, harder and harder as the seconds ticked by in silence, until she could taste blood in her mouth. Leather creaked behind her and fabric whispered as Dante stood, close enough for his body heat to warm her bare skin.

"Does it hurt?" he asked, voice low, then a warm touch stoked across her back, right below the scars.

"Not– not anymore." The lump in her throat threatened to strangle her but she forced herself to stand there, awaiting his verdict.

His hand slid up, up... when it moved over her scars, the feel of it dulled almost to the point of disappearing. The nerves had been so damaged, when she was burned, that all she could feel was a faint suggestion of sensation and pressure.

"Why does it stop so suddenly at your neck?" he asked. His voice was cool, curious, almost clinically so, and she could have wept with relief. He didn't sound revolted, didn't sound as if he were on the verge of throwing her out because she was too repulsive for him.

Cassie took a deep breath. "My dress... the back of it caught fire. The top part was made of flammable fabric, some sort of synthetic." She paused, gathering the next words, forcing her mouth to spit them out. "It melted to my skin. The skirt was cotton or something, it just turned to ash right away, only left me with the same as a bad sunburn. It healed fine. But up here–"

She choked off, unable to finish, but what more need be said? There it all was, laid out at his feet, a miserable offering to a haughty god. Now she awaited his verdict.

He removed his hand from her back, leaving the warmed skin to chill with his absence, and took a step back. Cassie closed her eyes, stomach plunging to her feet. It was just as she'd predicted, as she'd feared; he was too tough to be disgusted by her scars, but they had broken whatever attraction for her had woven between them.

Material rustled and she prepared to take her dress from his grasp, to put it back on and be returned downstairs to the lobby to await Manny's arrival with the town car, ready to bring her home.

Instead, skin-warm, cologne-scented linen, redolent of sandalwood and moss and mint, was draped over her. Cassie stood there, trembling, as realization washed over her. He wasn't rejecting her; just the opposite. He was not only accepting her, he was covering her, taking her under his protection, shielding her. The promise of it was a welcome weight belied by the lightness of the fabric. Her hands shook as she slipped her arms into the shirt's sleeves, going slowly, giving him plenty of opportunity to stop her, to change his mind, to send her scurrying, shamed, into the night.

He did none of those things, only waited until she turned back to face him, then made short work of buttoning it up. It hung absurdly large over her, the cuffs falling far past her fingertips, but the cozy security of it was more comforting than the thickest quilt or warmest bathrobe. She watched him as he did it, admiring the way the light gilded his jaw and temple, how the fans of his eyelashes cast shadows on his angular cheeks. The impulse to carve a likeness of him struck her, making her hands flex around an imaginary hammer and chisel.

When he finished with the buttoning and glanced up at her, seeing how she was watching him, something seemed to ignite behind his eyes. But it wasn't sexual, or at least, not only. There was something else there, banked, ready to flare up. It looked almost... angry? No. Protective, possessive, determined. He looked like he had made the decision that nothing like that would ever happen to her again, not if he could help it.

A ripple of fear, delicious and thrilling, went through her at the idea of being sheltered by Dante, owned, made *his* in every sense of the word. Was she ready to relinquish herself to another so wholly? Her situation– her life, her fate– felt like they were rushing past her to a destination that she wasn't entirely certain she wanted to arrive at, but which was inevitable, inescapable.

If there were no escape, why waste time trying to free herself? Why not sink into it, diving into its lavish depths, drinking it in until she was full to bursting?

Dante returned to the sofa, his hands coaxing her to seat herself in his lap. She went easily, molding herself to him. "Tell me," he commanded, a soft urging that had her mouth opening to obey before the last syllable faded into the night air.

And she did, every last tragic, sordid, lonely, heartbreaking bit of it, how a vacation with her foster parents had been ended by a drunk truck driver with no insurance. In just moments, catastrophe had taken from her the only people who had truly loved her. The scars marring her back were the universe's way of kicking her while she was down. To her way of thinking, the trauma of the burns was a pale comparison to the loss of Carol and Mike.

When she was done, she slumped against him, cheek pressed to the cool leather of the sofa, exhausted to have purged herself of so much pain and fear. It was like a sore had been lanced within her, all that ugliness drained out, but instead of emptiness, she felt filled with light and surety. She was safe, she was– well, if not loved, cared for– and nothing could touch her, not while she was in Dante's arms.

CHAPTER

TWELVE

Dante had known about her burns, of course; he left nothing to chance. It had all been in the file Ricardo had given him.

He hadn't seen the burns. The accident report of that night and the arrest record of the drunk drive had mentioned them, but there were no photos. Seeing them, though, was different than just reading about them. Dante ran his fingers over the thick, ropey scars and pondered how, if the man were still alive, Dante would've arranged for a severe beating to befall him.

Unfortunately, he was dead– liver damage in prison, her file had reported– and that left Dante with no one to punish for what had been done to Cassie. He was forced to merely sit there, to endure it. The impotence of the situation was not one that he was familiar with. He did not enjoy it.

He had waited for her to reveal the scars, the accident, to want him enough to face her fears and find the courage to tell him, and she had. He found a curious sense of... pride, in this accomplishment of hers. That, too, was unfamiliar to him. His history was one more of fulfilling and demanding a high caliber of performance without contemplating his feelings about it.

She kissed him. It was the first time she had initiated it, and he was interested to see how she did it, where she took it. Her lips were sweet, her tongue nimble, but there was a hesitance to her that said she was holding back. Dante drew back and trailed a fingertip across the fine slant of her cheek.

"Come to bed with me," he said. It was not a question, but a test: after her upset of the night, would she obey?

She would. She nodded, rising from his lap. Besides his shirt, she wore only her panties and those sky-high heels that had been distracting him all evening. He clasped her hips, turning her to face him, drawing her to stand between his spread thighs.

Before rising from the couch himself, he turned her around to face him and pulled her between his legs. Dante nuzzled his face into her midriff and pressed tiny kisses to her through his shirt. He had to do this the right way or, no matter how well he had primed her to comply with his wishes, she would spook and run. She wasn't one of the top-shelf whores who he paid for their obedience and silence; nor was she like his sophisticated ex-girlfriends, who understood the deal with the devil that they had made.

No, Cassie was new to this world. There was a genuine, unpracticed softness, a gentleness, to her that had shined through even when she was threatening Tony. She would lose some of that softness in his world, it was inevitable, but he would make sure she kept enough for him, for when he needed it.

She could be her true self with him, and he… he would be his true self with her. Eventually. Not tonight; they were still too new to each other in this new dynamic, as lovers. She was too new to his ways. But once she acclimated, once he knew she could take it– take him– he would share all of himself with her. For tonight, though, he could keep his monster at bay: let it watch, but keep it in his cage.

The bars of that cage rattled, now, at the thought of helping Cassie shed some of that innocence, of debauching her. The thought excited him as much as her body did.

"Dante?" She tugged lightly on his hair.

"Yes?" he replied, not looking up at her but kissing further down her chest. He rucked up the shirt so his hands could clench her ass, fingertips sinking deep into the plush globes.

"You– ah..." she gasped as he passed his tongue along her panties' waistband. "You said something about a bed," she said, breathless.

He trailed his nose down, down, until it was pressed right against her lace-covered cleft. The smell of her arousal, fresh and hot, made him light-headed, awakening a hunger in him that was starting to make demands stronger than his ability to withstand. He knew if he slipped a finger inside her panties he would find her warm and wet, but yes, a bed was a much better place to bury his face between her thighs.

"So I did." Dante trailed his gaze, hot, lusting, up her body to her face. Her lips were plump, reddened from his kisses, and her eyes... he had never seen a better example of 'bedroom eyes'; half-lidded with ardor and sensuality, she looked as starved for him as he felt for her.

He stood, sliding his body against hers the whole way up. Her tits, soft and plush, felt heavenly against his bare chest. Hands on her hips, he turned her to face away from him, pushing lightly to indicate she should precede him out of the study.

"Next door on the left," he purred into her ear, enjoying how it raised goosebumps on her skin. His bedroom was huge, dominated by an enormous bed that faced another full wall of glass looking down over Dallas. He flicked on the lights, and the dark space lit up around them.

Dante had once read that men preferred high-rise buildings for offices and homes because it made them feel like kings. Dante didn't need to feel like a king; he was the *don*, and that was better. The penthouse, though, with its security and physical separation from the ground, gave him a place to distance himself from the chaos of life in general and that of his life in particular. Here, he could relax. Every-thing was tailored to his wants and needs.

Dante maneuvered Cassie closer to the bed and then drew her close for a deep, probing kiss that had her melting against him, exactly how he wanted her. He pulled away to look down into her face. "Cassie."

Her eyes fluttered open, her look both sweet and sexy, confused and curious. "Yes?"

He kissed her again quickly, her lips too tempting by half. "Cassie, I need you to understand that I'm different from the other men you've dated."

She just gazed at him. "Of course you are," she said, as if she were agreeing that the sky was blue, and he chuckled.

"No, *cara mia*, I mean it. What I enjoy may be a little..." Dante wracked his brain for a word to use that wouldn't scare her, but all he wanted to do was push his shirt from her shoulders and fuck her till her she was screaming his name. "...intense," he finally settled on.

"Dante." She put her hands on his bare chest, one right over the family crest tattooed onto his skin. "I want you, all of you." She shrugged a little. "I trust you. I probably shouldn't, but I do. And besides, haven't I shown you, tonight? I'm not so easily breakable."

It was true. She was tiny, physically, but she'd been through hell, between losing her foster parents, enduring the horrific pain of her burns, the tragedy of her mother, and all the stress had Amber caused her. She could handle it, being his, both in and out of the bedroom. If he hadn't known before that moment, he knew it then.

She was meant to be his.

Dante unbuttoned his shirt, then pushed it from her shoulders. "Get on the bed."

Cassie instantly complied, sitting prettily on the edge of his bed in her lacy panties and fuck-me heels, and he smiled in dark satisfaction.

"Lie back, Cassie." She moved to lay back but paused, starting to toe off her shoes. Dante put his hand on her ankle. "Leave them on."

She blinked up at him but then nodded. She pulled a long pin from her hair, making it tumble around her shoulders, a river of molten copper. With a kittenish wiggle, she scooted further back onto the bed and laid back against the pillows, never taking her eyes from him. She looked like a goddess, a Venus with skin like pearl, offered up on a cockle shell for him to worship.

"Fuck, you're beautiful," Dante breathed, climbing up the bed on hands and knees, prowling over her. When he reached her face, he dipped his head and kissed her in a voluptuous slide of lips and tongues, unhurried, unrushed, with all the time in the world.

He lowered himself onto her, relishing the press of her small breasts against his bare chest once more. He loved the way he fit so well between her legs, how they came around his waist, clinging in desperation for him, wrapping him up in the satin of her flesh.

If they had been naked, he would have slid inside her right then. Instead he pressed his hard cock, still trapped in his trousers, against the center of her. Even through the layers of fabric, he could feel her heat. But it wasn't enough; he had to know the taste of her, to make her come completely undone.

He kissed his way down, sucking and nibbling at the sensitive skin of her neck, probably leaving marks, but he couldn't make himself care. Fuck propriety. He wanted to mark her, brand her so thoroughly there would be no question about to whom she belonged.

"Dante," Cassie groaned when took one hard nipple into his mouth. He used his teeth lightly, and she gave a sharp gasp. He decided to reward her by pinching her other nipple while he sucked harder on the one in his mouth. "God!"

Dante reluctantly let her nipple slip from his mouth as he resumed his path down her body, her hips moving restlessly against the bed as he ran his lips over her, leaving a scorching trail from his tongue across her skin.

"Cassie." Dante looked up to find her head pressed back pressed back into the pillows, her normally pale skin flushed a pretty pink. "Cassie," he said again, louder, and this time her eyes fluttered open, fuzzy and unfocused from arousal. "Cassie, you need to keep still," he told her and slipped his fingers under the lace of her panties. Her hips rose from the bed, undulating, coaxing him to peel the undergarment away.

"Nuh, uh, uh," Dante scolded playfully and pulled his hand back.

Realization dawned on her face. "Sorry, sorry," Cassie said breathlessly.

Dante returned his hand to her panties. She relaxed against the mattress, a little too much, he felt, so he pulled out the waistband and let it snap back against her skin. She jumped in surprise, letting out a nervous giggle before settling back again, but this time the thread of tension in her remained taut.

Dante decided he'd teased her enough– for the moment– and at last pulled the scrap of lace down her hips and off her body. He knelt between her open thighs, sitting back on his heels, running his palms over the soft skin of her thighs.

"Alright, Cassie–" Her eyes, dazed with passion, fluttered open and met his again. "–I want you to grab onto the headboard." He took her hands and placed them around the small metal slats over her head. "I don't want you to let go. If you do, I'll stop what I'm doing... and I don't want to stop. We'll both be unhappy, if that happens. Do you understand?" He brushed a fiery curl from her cheek, watching her face, her eyes completely blown black with desire.

"Yes, Dante," she whispered. The surrender in her voice flooded him with exultation. He had to pause, head thrown back and eyes closed, as it raced through him. Once the euphoria of domination had settled– never gone, only banked– he opened his eyes once more. "Good," he breathed.

Ducking down, he took her mouth in a deep, luscious kiss, pulling suddenly back so she was left bereft as he slid down between her thighs. He enjoyed few things as much as he enjoyed the act of pleasuring a woman with his mouth. He alone controlled how hard, how fast or slow, they came. It was all within his power– her ecstasy, her joy, her abandon.

"You're doing so well," Dante said softly, running his fingers over Cassie's soft, plump outer lips. She wasn't shaved completely bare like most of the women he had been with, but the wiry auburn curls were neatly trimmed, instead. She was trembling, muscles leaping under her skin, and he could tell she was fighting the urge to move her hips, her grip on the headboard so tight he thought her hands might hurt tomorrow.

Good, he thought fiercely. Let her have something to remember him by, every time she moved a finger.

"Don't worry, *cara mia*, I'm going to put you out of your misery right now." He blew a cool breath against her wet, needing flesh and then spread her open. She was so pink, here, soft and satiny, and he leaned in to put his tongue against her, tasting her for the first time. The flavor of her burst over his tongue, salt and musk in alluring concert.

She moaned loud and long, thighs tense to either side of him. He used his tongue to tease her clit, flicking it, teasing her and then pressing against it hard.

"Oh, god!" She shuddered under his mouth. Her hips flexed in aborted, jerky motions as she tried in desperation to keep still in the face of so much sensation. She grew wetter against his mouth, giving him more delicious nectar to lap at, and he probed between her silken lips until he found her entrance and could slip in a finger.

Inside she was scorching, a living flame, the heat suggested by her hair color borne out by how she scalded him. And she was tight, gripping his finger, sucking at it, greedy, reluctant for him to leave her. He eased his finger in and out, slowly, gently, while his tongue tormented her clit.

"Dante, I– please!" she begged above him, incoherent with desire, but Dante continued his torturous teasing between her thighs. He judged her ready for more and slipped another finger inside. She groaned as her body stretched, accommodating the increase in width. Dante moved his fingers just a little faster, fucking her just a little harder, giving her more of what her body needed.

When the rippling flex of her settled into a smoother rhythm around him, he increased the pace of his fingers, suddenly. Instead of teasing her clit, he sucked on it, tongue rubbing against the underside in counterpoint to the suction. Her slick inner muscles gripped his fingers even harder. The moans that burst from her gained in volume and urgency, became words that became pleas, pleas for Dante to let her come.

"Dante, please, let me– please– I'll– I'll do anything, just let me–"

Oh, she begged so prettily. She deserved a reward. On the next upward stroke of his fingers, he crooked them just right, searching for that spot of softness that, if he could just find it—

"Dante! Oh! Yes!" Cassie screamed, her entire body arching, jerking in his grasp, and then she was coming all over his fingers, soaking his tongue.

More, he thought with fierce satisfaction. *I want more.* More of her taste, of her lust, of her submission and devotion. He wanted her screams of passion to ring through his bedroom, making the windows rattle, over and over.

Her whimpers faded in volume and desperation; accordingly, he slowed the motion of his tongue, prolonging her orgasm but aware of her sensitivity. When she finally went limp against the pillows, Dante slid his fingers from her body and sat back on his heels. She was panting, her entire body flushed red, hips twitching from the aftershocks... and her hands were still gripping the headboard.

She'd done well. It was time to reward her.

Dante shucked his pants and boxer briefs, dumping them without care onto the floor, eager to run his hands over the curves of her calves, up the long muscles of her thighs, admiring how fucking lewd she looked splayed out on his bed, her feet still in those impractical, erotic shoes.

He couldn't resist any longer. Dante slid his body against hers, covering her, cock pressing insistently against the heated flesh of her mound. He kissed her, deeply, thoroughly, his tongue branding her as his, writing *Dante* like a tattoo marking her as his possession. Her whimpered surrender threatened to set him on fire, made him groan and press into her, the tip of his cock slipping inside her.

"Please tell me you're on the pill," he groaned into her mouth, powered by the last of his failing control. His hips flexed, independent of his command, pressing further inside, drawn by the carnality of her snug, drenched heat.

"Mmmm, yes, the shot," she managed, her words sluggish, drugged by craving.

"Thank fucking god," he groaned. With a snap of his hips he buried himself inside her, moaning helplessly at the sleek, scalding pressure clasping him.

"Oh, *yes*," she whined, twisting against him, jerking her hips up to take him deeper.

And her hands were still on the headboard.

"You're so good, Cassie," he said, a note of exertion in his voice as he began to put earnest effort into fucking her. "You'er so fucking good."

He pulled back to watch her face. Her eyes were screwed shut in pleasure, her lips swollen and red from his kisses, her throat dotted with purpling marks from his mouth and teeth. She was wanton, craving the pleasure and completion only he could give her... she was his, and he was starting to think that maybe he was hers, as well.

He slid his arm under her leg, her knee in the bend of his elbow, opening her wider, gaining another inch of depth into her. She mewled, frantic, fingers fumbling their grasp around the headboard as he thrust against her even harder. The room around them, dimly lit, was silent except for the wet sound of impact as he stroked into her, fast and hard. Climax was hurtling toward him, the threat of it starting at the base of his spine and inching outward.

"Touch yourself, Cassie," he commanded. "Now." He pulled one of her hands free from the headboard and put it between her thighs, right where they were joined.

"What?" Her eyes sprang open, glazed with confusion.

He slowed his hips just a little, halting the climb of ecstasy for them both. "Don't question me. Do it."

Her eyes widened and she rippled around his cock at his words.

Oh, yes, she liked this, his Cassie, his mousey little bookkeeper. She liked being told what to do in bed. Fuck, she really was made for him.

"Be a good girl and touch yourself. Make yourself come while I fuck you." She bit her lip, her eyes wide, "unless you want me to punish you? Because that can be arranged Cassie, but then we won't come for a while and I—" He ground his hips into hers to get his point across, "–I really want come inside you." She nodded and her fingers began to rub her clit.

"That's my good girl." He started thrusting inside her, long and deep, but soon he was back to fucking her hard, his cock pounding into her over and over again. Pressure built in his lower back, his balls tightening, and he knew he would not last.

"Come for me, Cassie." He pressed sloppy, uncoordinated kisses to her mouth, her face and throat. "I need you to come."

She keened, arching hard against him. Her body tensed, pussy clenching on his cock so hard he started coming mid-stroke.

"Fuck!" He exploded deep inside her, body rigid as pleasure wracked him, and he was certain he blacked out, because he seemed to have lost a few seconds: one moment he was holding himself off her body on stiffened arms as his pelvis pummeled her, and the next he was collapsed over Cassie, who ran a hand through his hair, her other arm wrapped around his chest, clinging damply. He had never had such an intense orgasm with a woman before.

"You okay?" Cassie asked, her voice sweet and concerned and her touch soothing.

Dante managed a smile and brushed her wild red curls back from her face. "More than okay, *cara mia*." He rolled to the side and pulled her into his arms, her head resting on his chest.

"That was–" She faltered, but he kissed the crown of her head.

"Yes, it was." He yawned, a deep and sated exhaustion weighing down his libs. It was contagious and she quickly followed with a yawn of her own.

"Sleep, now." He reached to a nearby chair and pulled the blanket from it over their cooling bodies.

There was more to his world, and to him, that Cassie had not yet encountered. Doubtless it would startle and even alarm her. She would have to learn to deal with all of it, though, because she had sealed her deal with the devil that night, even if she didn't realize it yet. Dante was satisfied that she was exactly right for what he wanted in a woman.

He'd made his decision, had formed his conclusion, and now it was set in stone. There would be no others for either of them, from that moment forward.

CHAPTER

THIRTEEN

Cassie, stretching, came awake slowly. Her body still tingled and ached in places that hadn't any kind of action in years. What Dante had done to her, the ecstasy he'd drawn from her– well, none of the men she'd ever dated had made her feel even a fraction of what Dante had.

She yawned and turned to him, but when she opened her eyes, his side of the bed was empty. He had slept next to her; the pillow still held the indentation of his head, and the blankets were mussed. The wall of windows revealed a city on the cusp of sunrise. Sitting up, she looked around for her clothes, before remembering she'd left her dress in the study and all that she had in the bedroom were her sky-high pumps and black lace underpants. She definitely needed more than that.

Climbing from the bed, Cassie searched around for something to put on and found Dante's shirt from the night before, discarded on the floor next to her heels. That would do for now. Maybe she could get him to lend her some sweatpants to get home in. She slipped the shirt on but left the shoes on the carpet. They were sexy, for sure, but excruciating to wear for more than ten minutes at a time. Give her comfy ballet flats any day.

She pulled open the bedroom door and stuck her head into the hallway. "Dante?" she called out and waited, but heard nothing in response. Maybe he was in the office? She knocked before poking her head in. "Dante?" He wasn't in there, either, but a cup of coffee and an open book were on the table in front of the leather couch. She crept in and touched the cup, finding it was still warm, so surely he had just stepped out and would be back soon. Cassie decided to wait for him there.

She picked up her dress, now sadly crumpled from a night wadded up on the floor, and shook it out before folding it, enduring a pang of guilt for treating something so costly with such negligence. It hadn't felt like negligence when she'd removed it, though; more like a chrysalis she was emerging from into an exciting new world.

Laying the dress aside, Cassie took a seat on the sofa and studied her surroundings. The room was just as appealing in the early morning sun as it had been the night before, if in a different way: whereas it had been cozy and snug, inviting a long read with a glass of scotch in dim lighting, now it was flooded with the early morning light, and all the books created a sense of curiosity and even excitement– which to read? How to choose? It was an unlimited buffet for someone like Cassie, who loved reading.

Her gaze was drawn once again to the coffee table and the book opened on the table, wondering what a man like Dante would enjoy. Cassie picked it up and found it to be a book of poems by Percy Bysshe Shelley. She registered a moment's surprise; whatever she had expected, it was not romantic poetry from two hundred years earlier.

Well, she thought, *let's see what he likes about it.* Tucking her legs under her, she settled in to read. It was lovely, if written in a form of English that she had to think about to comprehend, and she became so immersed in it that she didn't hear the door open.

"Do you like it?" Dante's voice made her jump, and the book clattered to the floor.

"Dante!" Cassie sucked in a shocked breath. She fumbled for the book, replacing it where she'd found it on the table. Dante only smiled, handing her a steaming cup of coffee and settling next to her on the sofa. He had pulled on a loose t-shirt and gray sweatpants at some point, and looked just as attractive in the casual garments as he did in his superbly tailored suits.

"Are you a Shelley fan?" he asked, and she sipped her coffee. It was perfect; she could taste the rich brew through the hints of milk and sugar he'd added. Cassie wondered how he knew they way she took her coffee, as he'd never asked. But he seemed to know everything about her. This was just one more thing.

"I am now," she answered. "The imagery is beautiful." She took another drink of coffee. "Do you read poetry often?" she probed gently. It occurred to her how little she knew of Dante, besides that he was rich and powerful and handsome and very good in bed. She wanted to know more, but was wary that if she pushed too hard, too fast, he might retreat.

He looked at the book in his hands and the relaxed expression on his face turned closed and unreadable. "I do." He offered nothing else and Cassie mentally sighed.

So much for that, then. But she couldn't expect him to open up if she hadn't.

"I first started enjoying poetry in middle school," she told him. "We were living in a pretty crappy group home, at the time, and Amber was having a very hard time adjusting."

She warmed her hands around the hot mug and watched Dante covertly under her lashes, hoping he would give her some kind of reaction, but he just watched her as he drank his coffee, so she pressed on.

"I had– have always been a reader. It's lovely to escape into worlds, especially when mine sucked so much." Her voice trailed off at Dante's lack of reaction and she ended up staring down into her mug, wishing it held a few answers for how to interact with him. She was usually so good at concealing her history, her feelings, yet Dante could get her to reveal her innermost secrets simply by staring silently at her. It was more than a little daunting.

"My mother studied literature and reading in college," he said at last. "She loved it." Her gaze flew from the mug to his face, surprised he'd offered the detail. "Poetry, she always told me, 'is the window to the human soul'."

"I like that," Cassie said with a smile.

Dante did not reciprocate. "I've never understood, really," he said instead.

"Understood what?"

"The need for such unnecessary words. I've never understood the value in it. What's the point of so much work? They think so hard about exactly which words to choose, arrange them with painstaking effort, just to express some feeling they have." His tone was both confused and dismissive, his eyes on the book the entire time. "It's why I keep reading it. I'm trying to figure out why they matter. Why anyone would bother going to so much trouble to do it."

What an extraordinary thing for him to say, that he didn't understand the point of poetry. She'd have thought it self-evident to pretty much everyone. And even more strangely, that he would continue to read it, searching to understand what everyone else grasped instinctively.

"My– my creative writing teacher in high school," Cassie began, stumbling a little as she groped for a response. "He said that poetry was the most purely human pursuit he's ever witnessed. It doesn't have a moral or a lesson to teach, like we find in fiction. It's not a how-to manual or a historical recounting of past events, like nonfiction boils down to be. It just... is. It's pretty or dark or loving or sensual, but it has no ulterior motives. It just *is*."

She trailed off, feeling oddly exposed with how intently Dante's dark gaze was fixed on her, but suddenly Dante leaned forward and kissed her, his mouth hard on hers.

"Mr. Dante?" There was a knock on the study door.

"Yes, Sandra?" Dante answered, and the door squeaked open. Dante didn't remove his hand from her cheek but his gaze skimmed above her head to the voice at the door.

"Breakfast is ready. Should I bring it here, or do you want to eat at the table?" a woman asked.

His hand kept her from looking back over her shoulder, to see who was there. It was soft, cupping her face gently, but it was immoveable. Why would he keep her from turning? Cassie figured it mattered to him, somehow, so she relaxed, trusting him to know best why she should remain as he wanted her.

"Please bring it up here," he directed. "With more coffee. Water and orange juice, too. Thank you, Sandra." As the door clicked closed, his attention was fully upon her once more.

There was a challenge in his eyes– would she question him? A sense of defiance sparked in Cassie; did he think her so incapable of behaving herself? She glared back, daring him to say something, but his face shifted, from that goading expression to something like approval, and he leaned in to brush a light kiss across her lips.

"Sandra has worked for me for years," he said. "She's an excellent cook... and she's discreet. She'll tell no one about the beautiful redhead in my shirt, eating breakfast with me, if that's what you're worried about."

"No, I wasn't worried," she told him, and realized it was the truth: she hadn't been worried about Sandra seeing them, her in nothing but a shirt and Dante's embrace. It had been mere curiosity to see which person had free access to his home, and if he felt she didn't need to know, she must not need to know.

He rewarded her with a kiss, shallow playful caresses of lips and tongue, seeking nothing more than light pleasure to while away the time. When was the last time she'd kissed anyone without any certain purpose to it, like chasing an orgasm? She couldn't remember. It didn't matter.

Sandra returned after only a few minutes with plates of eggs and sausage and bowls of fruit. Dante didn't seem to need her focus only on him, this time, so Cassie turned to face the other woman, smiling and thanking her as she left the study.

Sandra was as good a cook as Dante had said; the food was delicious, everything done to perfection, and she was suddenly ravenous as the aroma of it wafted into her nose. She hoped Dante wouldn't want to chat while they ate, because she didn't think she'd be able to do anything but chew for the next ten minutes.

Fortunately, he was happy to eat in silence as well. They demolished their meal, side by side, and then the plates were bare but for a few crumbs, they sat back, bellies full.

"What time is it?" Cassie asked, her mind snapping to matters of practicality now that her hunger was sated.

"It's just past seven," he replied. "What time do you need to be at work?" As he spoke, he undid one of the top buttons of the shirt she was wearing– *his* shirt.

"I– mmm," she moaned, eyes closing when his warm palm curved around her breast, squeezing it lightly. "N– not until nine, but I have to walk Lucy first." She gasped when his fingers found her nipple, still a little tender from his attention the night before, and pinched it. Heat burst low in her belly, and a rush of arousal started to dampen her thighs.

"Oh? Who's Lucy?" His voice was surprisingly calm in the face of what his hand was doing. Cassie opened her eyes and searched his face, relieved to see that he wasn't as unaffected as his voice made him seem, his chocolate-brown eyes smoldering. Unable to resist, she glanced at his lap. His grey sweatpants did nothing to hide that he was the direct opposite of unaffected.

"Lucy is–" Her words caught in her throat when he pulled her across his lap, straddling his thighs. "Lucy is my dog," she finished in a rush.

He unbuttoned the rest of his shirt, and her hands found their way under his t-shirt.

Dante lifted his hips so he could pull the sweatpants down and his hard cock was like a red-hot iron bar between her legs when it sprang free.

"Then you best make this quick, so you can go home and let Lucy out." With one hand Dante steadied his cock, thick and ready, flushed with arousal, presenting it for her to seat herself upon.

"Make what quick?" Cassie asked, pretending to not understand what he wanted, slowly getting into the game Dante was playing.

"Fucking me. Making me come. It *is* your job, after all," he answered and cupped her face with the hand that wasn't holding his cock, his thumb rubbing her lips, dragging the lower one down.

"That's my job?" she breathed her question against his thumb, and he groaned when she sucked the tip of his thumb into her mouth.

"Yes, your job. Now be a good girl and fuck me." He rubbed his cock harder against her for emphasis, a thrilling caress right over her clit. "Make me come, Cassie. Unless you want me to punish you. Is that what you want? You want me to bend you over and spank you for being bad?"

For a moment, Cassie thought about defying him. She had never *ever* been with someone like this, who threatened to punish her during sex. It was like something out of those dirty romance books she'd borrowed from Sarah... and which she had enjoyed probably a little too much. The thought of being bent over and spanked, corrected because of disobedience, made her even wetter.

Suddenly Dante's hand was gone from her face. It connected, sharply, with her ass, the sound shocking in the quiet of the study. It took a second for her body to register the sting to her flesh... and the pleasant tingling left in its wake.

"Which is it going to be, baby?" Dante crooned, his hand now rubbing the spot on her ass that he had just smacked, and in response, Cassie lined up her body with his and sank down on his hard cock. "Ahhh," he sighed, sounding happier than she'd ever heard him.

She started slow, teasing them both, her hips rocking into his. Her hands pushed up his t-shirt so they could explore the hard planes of his chest. There were even more tattoos than she had realized, the images marking him in ways that reinforced how deadly and dangerous he was, and she moved faster, plunging up and down on his shaft.

"Yes, Cassie," Dante groaned, his hands on her waist moving her impossibly faster as he pounded into her from below, stealing away the scrap of illusion she might have had that she was the one running that encounter. She might be on top of him, but Dante held all the control, and all Cassie could do was hold on and trust him to bring her where she needed to go.

With every upward thrust, his cock hit an electric spot deep inside, stoking her arousal harder and higher. Then Dante's mouth found her nipple, sucking, worrying it with his teeth, and Cassie was gone. Her orgasm hit her like a train, her entire body stiffening, writhing on his cock.

"Dante!" she cried out, too far gone, too wracked with pleasure, to mind her words or volume. He hadn't said she should be silent, he wouldn't be upset with her for saying his name, and even if he were, she wouldn't mind a spanking, not really... the risk of it pushed her ever higher, had her biting her lip to keep from screaming.

The taste of copper filled her mouth: her teeth had drawn blood. Cassie swallowed it down, dazed, flexing and rocking, her body no longer her own. With shocking suddenness, Dante levered her off his lap, off his prick, rising to his knees and positioning her on her own over the arm of the couch. Almost before she could register the new shift in placement, his hand was on the back of her neck, pushing her down, as his arm wrapped around her waist to hoist up her hips. Without a word, he hilted himself inside her to the root.

Stretched beyond anything she had ever experienced, Cassie forgot to worry about being too loud and screamed. Oh, it was so good, so *good*, Dante was so thick in her, so long, stretching her, making her take him, all of him–

"Don't make a sound," Dante growled. His palm came down on her ass again. "I've wanted you just like this," he gritted out. "Since the moment I saw you."

The sting of the impact, the heat of it, spread between her legs. Cassie felt aroused almost beyond endurance, soaked, opened up, spread out, taken, used, and another orgasm was rising steadily, inescapable. She took her lip between her teeth again, worrying the sensitive little wound she'd created earlier, making it swell along with the tide of lust she was riding.

"Yes, Cassie, take it," he groaned and pulled her up from the arm of the couch, his arm holding her against his chest, his hand on her throat loose but confining as he pounded his cock into her. "You love this, you want it, anything I give you, you want all of it."

Cassie relinquished herself completely, let him take her weight as she leaned back, legs too weak to hold her any longer. There was no need for her to have balance, traction, anything– she could leave it all to Dante. She could just place herself in his hands. He knew what to do.

Her surrender seemed to be what did it, what snapped the last thread of tension in him. With a shout, he slammed himself into her, holding her motionless for the long seconds of his release. She had done that, had given that to him, only her, no one else could please him like Cassie could–

She keened as she came again, whimpers forcing themselves past her bitten lip, body arching into him, pressing back, wanting whatever more of him there might be. Sound and vision receded, slurring into a shapeless red mist of hunger at last fulfilled. It would never be enough. Dante had established himself inside her, body and soul, and she would never have enough of him.

When it finally ended, when Cassie had returned to herself once more, her senses came back with a vengeance. She throbbed between her legs, sore and tender from how hard Dante had worked her. Her vision seemed filled with light, as if the whole room were suffused with a glow, and her heartbeat pounded heavy in her ears. He was hard and hot, draped over her, and their flesh was stuck together with sweat. There was a wet trickle running, itching, down her thigh. The air was thick with the smell of salt, of semen, of pussy.

Cassie said nothing, only waited.

Slowly, Dante straightened from his slump over her and withdrew from her body. She couldn't repress a hiss at the sudden emptiness. The trickle turned into a cascade, reaching almost to her knee. If he cared about his sofa, he'd tell her what he wanted her to do, soon... or maybe he didn't care about the sofa. He could afford a new one, that was for sure.

"Here," he said, hoarse, handing her his t-shirt. Cassie used it to catch the flow of come down her leg just in time, swiping carefully when she passed it over her sore flesh. She was going to need a cold compress; her lady parts were worn *out*.

Sweat-drenched, come-stained, on the verge of pain from a harsh fucking, she'd never been happier.

Dante leaned in and kissed the side of her head. "Stay here," he said. "I'll get you another t-shirt and some shorts and take you home."

He was gone only moments. She was still wobbling to unsteady feet when he returned, dressed in his own t--shirt and shorts, handing her an almost-identical set: a much-washed, buttery-soft t-shirt and slippery pair of nylon running shorts. She had to roll the waistband a few times to keep it above her knees, but the shirt hung past them anyway. Her hair was a knotted disaster but she'd deal with it at home, where she had detangler and a big-toothed comb.

He escorted her from the penthouse and down the elevator, into the parking garage. It was fairly busy, being prime commuting time, but Dante behaved as if they were alone in the vast, echoing space, so Cassie took her cue from him and sailed past the other people as if they weren't there, head high.

"Do you have plans tonight?" Dante asked once they were in his car and he was backing out of the parking space.

"Other than a hot date with the books at *Aphrodite's*, you mean?" she replied wryly. Emerging from the garage into the bright light of day had her squinting against the glare and hurrying to fold down the visor.

"Yes, other than that hot date," he said, amused, guiding them with expert nonchalance up the entrance ramp to the freeway.

"No," she answered. With the sun no longer drilling pinholes in her retinas, she was free to slouch back into the plush leather. "I probably won't get to the club until six, though. I left work early yesterday, and I need to play a little catch up today."

"Not later than six," he told her. "I need you on my arm tonight."

"On your arm?"

"Yes, *cara mia*. Did you think I only meant you were mine in bed?" His tone was light, but the glance he flicked sideways at her was dead serious.

Her breath caught in her chest. No, she hadn't specifically thought their relationship was just physical, but to have it be assumed without any sort of discussion, any kind of turning it official... well, rituals like that were for regular people, she supposed. Dante was anything but regular. Of course he'd do it without asking permission or waiting for a reaction. Like everything else he did, he simply presented what was to be. Her choice was to accept, or not. In for a penny, in for a pound, Sarah would say.

"No," Cassie whispered, then decided to take a chance on what she thought he wanted from her. "I didn't think about it at all. I was just going to do what you told me."

Dante's answering smile was feral. "Good," was all he said, but there was a world of deep satisfaction in it. He pulled into the parking lot of her building, aiming the car into an empty spot and shifting to 'park' almost carelessly so he could take her in his arms, pressing her back against the seat, his kiss so fierce it stole her breath away.

Cassie's heart was thrumming when he finally released her, her bitten lip throbbing with the delicious reminder of his mouth.

"Go," he said, unbuckling her seatbelt and flicking it open. She was out of the car between one breath and the next, standing numbly beside it. It felt wrong to simply turn her back on him and leave him there, so she waited.

The window gave a low mechanical purr as it slid down.

"And Cassie?" he said, leaning so he could meet her eyes.

"Yes?"

"Wear something comfortable, but sexy." Dante winked, grinning. "Always sexy."

He flicked the car into gear, reversed, then drove away.

Cassie watched until he turned out of view before making her still-unsteady way to her apartment. She wasn't entirely sure what she had agreed too, but she also knew she didn't own anything remotely 'comfortable but sexy'.

Surprisingly, that was her greatest concern, at that moment.

Of Dante, she had no doubts.

CHAPTER

FOURTEEN

Upon returning home again, Dante wasted no time showering, dressing, and heading to the office. He drummed his fingers on the steering wheel as he contemplated the text from Matty that had woken him at five that morning.

–Donkeys sick, may have to change their feed– Matty.

Dante hadn't bothered responding. What he and Matty would have to discuss would be better discussed in person.

The text wasn't about a farm or ranch; Matty was referring to their mules, their very *human* mules. And the 'feed' would be the heroin they transported into and across the country. In fact, they had a large shipment that was headed to Europe, but if something was wrong with the product, they might not be able to make good on the buy. That would be... problematic. Those were not clients Dante wanted to cross; they were not just lucrative, but also dangerous.

After Matty's text had woken him, Dante remained awake. He watched Cassie sleep as the sun rose, slowly flooding his room in soft light, and thought about the night before. She lay face-down on the bed, the blanket bunched around her waist and her hair fallen to the side. Her scars were clearly visible in the growing daylight. They weren't attractive, for sure, but it didn't reduce his attraction for her.

If anything, it strengthened it, knowing the pain she had endured, never giving up.

Then there was the matter of how hard she'd tried to save her foster mother, even at the expense of her own safety. That level of loyalty was exactly what he'd been looking for. He'd struggled to find a woman he would be able to trust, who would put him and the family before everything else, and he had found her at last.

And then there was the question of whether he liked her, in addition to feeling she was a good fit for his needs. And the answer was a resounding *yes*. She was lovely, amusing, intelligent... and she'd responded beautifully to the small taste he had given her of his sexual appetite, matching him stroke for stroke. He was excited to show her more, as well, his mind buzzing with ideas for what to do with her next.

Grace's words lingered behind the hum of sexual satisfaction, however; he was no more able to love a woman at that moment than he had been when Grace broke up with him. Was that something Cassie would need, even if he gave her everything else? Security, prosperity, companionship, sexual satisfaction, perhaps even children, some day... could that be enough for her? He didn't want to invest time and effort into a relationship that was doomed to failure because she was unable to be in a match where there was no emotional connection, at least on his part.

Dante got out of bed at six a.m. on the dot. Sandra would be coming in soon to start breakfast and he needed to tell her to make enough for Cassie, as well. He pulled on sweats and a t-shirt and padded barefoot downstairs. He was fairly useless in the kitchen, but he could make coffee. He was in the middle of the task when Sandra entered his apartment.

"Good morning, Mr. Dante."

"Good morning, Sandra." He smiled at his housekeeper. He liked her. She was a hard worker and a wonderful cook, but she was getting older, and he knew some of the cleaning was getting harder on her body.

"You're up early," she commented, pleasant as always, donning an apron over her nondescript blue scrubs.

"No rest for the wicked," Dante teased the older woman, who laughed.

"You're not wicked, Mr. Dante," she chided, opening the refrigerator to gather items for his breakfast. Sandra thought he was a saint. He had given her nephew a job, a good one, as one of the family's regular truck drivers. It didn't matter to Sandra what her grandson transported, only that he earned enough money to support her great-grandchildren.

"The usual for breakfast, Mr. Dante?" she asked, cutting up some fruit.

"Yes, but please make enough for two. I have a guest."

"Is it one of your brothers? I can make Mr. Matteo his favorite omelet, if it's for him." Sandra doted on Matty as if he were her own son.

"No, Sandra, it's not Matty. It's... a new friend of mine, Cassie," Dante hedged. He didn't want to explain all the details of his romantic life to his housekeeper, but if things with Cassie went the way he planned on them going, Sandra would be seeing a lot more of her.

"Of course, Mr. Dante." Sandra didn't even try to hide her approving smile. Dante felt more like her son and less like her boss at that moment.

Dante went back upstairs and peeked in the bedroom. Cassie was still sleeping. It was still very early, though, so he decided to let her sleep and went into his study, needing a moment to think. The previous night had been better than he'd anticipated. The sex had been well beyond his expectations, and Cassie seemed to enjoy at least some of what he enjoyed– what he *needed*– from it.

Dante had long known that his sexual needs were not the norm. He had to be in control, dominant, in all things, including the bedroom. He could easily find a dynamic like that with paid professionals, but he didn't only want sexual gratification on his terms. He wanted an entire relationship with a woman, not merely an encounter a few times a week with someone he compensated.

He had had that with Grace and the woman he dated before her, but neither of them ever seemed to actually enjoy it, merely indulging him to make him happy. Cassie, though... Cassie appeared to be different, seemed like it could genuinely excite her, and it was a more-than-welcome change.

Still, the issue insisted on prodding him. As he always did when he couldn't get it out of his mind, Dante selected a volume of poetry from his shelf and sat, sipping his coffee as he paged through flowery, sentiment-filled language.

Love was not an emotion he understood; there'd been little time and less opportunity to learn or experience it. From an early age, Dante had been shown what was expected of him, while his brothers grew up in almost complete ignorance, reaping the benefits of the life provided to them by their father and grandfathers. His brothers thought that education had started when he was seventeen, breaking legs and rounding up payments for the family with their father, but it had begun much, much earlier.

He was probably nine or ten when *Nonno* had first told him about the family legacy, explained to him how they turned money into wealth, how they gained and kept the power needed to maintain that wealth. Dante had learned math better from Gino the bookie than any teacher at the fancy private school he and his brothers attended.

He wasn't just Dante, a regular boy from a normal family. He had been told from boyhood who he would become, the empire he would rule, and how important he was as the heir apparent. He didn't get to discover his own way, his own passion, like Elias did with the law. He didn't get to fuck up and be wild like Marco and Matty, the babies of the family. No, he would be the *don*, the choice made for him the moment of his birth.

It wasn't like he didn't *enjoy* his life. He was rich and could indulge any whim, with every single thing– women, cars, luxury beyond description– his at the snap of his fingers. He didn't lack for the power he craved, either; if he were going to be in the mob, being boss was best.

But even though he controlled the family and the business, it wasn't enough. He'd inherited those, been groomed for them from birth. A gnawing sense of pride goaded him to wanting to command that sort of obedience in all aspects of his life, personal as well as private, and he wanted to do it himself, on his terms, not as something he'd acquired as a birthright.

There was something chaotic about sex. The lack of predictability, the chance that something he didn't like or want could happen at any moment, made his interest and arousal flag. It needed some level of order, of control, for him to enjoy it. It had to unfold precisely as he wanted it... or he didn't want it. There was nothing, to him, like the satisfaction of directing a woman who submitted willingly, who trusted him to know what she needed and that he would give it to her. It was delicious: a ripe juicy peach, a decadent chocolate confection, a mouth-watering steak, all at the same time.

He was no sadist; in fact, the idea of hurting his partners offended him. He didn't need to control or confine them, to make them comply with his wishes. They did that because they *wanted* to, not because he compelled it. He didn't need to tie up his partners, though a little restraint was always nice. What he needed to know is that the woman under him would give herself to him completely.

Not easy to find, particularly because he also wanted them to be intelligent, head-strong women. It was so much more satisfying to have a stubborn person bow down, after all, to be even more forceful than they were. And they, in his experience, didn't tend to want to relinquish control– at least, not enough to really please him.

So, he learned to avail himself to some of the most expensive, talented, seductive call girls the world had to offer. Women who, for a price, not only gave themselves over completely but were also very discreet. He didn't care about his reputation so much, but if knowledge of his tastes got out, people might try to use it against him somehow. They'd be unsuccessful, of course. But the idea of having to cope with a parade of would-be blackmailers was a waste of time he wasn't interested in permitting.

No, it was better if it was not widely known. After the prior evening with Cassie, he had high hopes that she would not only be tolerant of his preferences, like Grace, but that she would enjoy it with him, come to desire it as much as he did. If so... she stood to become more to him than anyone else ever had.

Upon arrival at his office, Dante spent the morning working while he waited for Matty to arrive and explain to him exactly what was going on with the heroin that needed to be on a plane in just over twenty-four hours. By mid-morning, Dante was ready to strangle his little brother. What part of 'first thing in the morning' did he not understand?

"Good morning, big brother!" Matty strolled into the office smiling, as if they weren't about to renege on hundreds of thousands of dollars to some of their best clients.

"I'm glad you could make it," Dante snapped, glaring at Matty, and set his phone back down on his desk. "I told you to be here early."

"I *am* here early," Matty said with his trademark 'how can you be mad at this face?' grin that never failed to make Dante want to punch him.

Dante pointedly ignored that grin. "What's wrong with the shipment? Do we know?" He was pleased to see Matty's demeanor become serious right away.

"Yeah, I figured it out last night. I had our chemist run some purity tests." He paused for effect. "It's been cut with mineral oil."

"Mineral oil?" Dante had been in the drug business his entire adult– and even some years of his pre-adult– life, and that was not one of the normal cutting agents for black tar heroin.

"Yeah, and it's not really cut with it, it's more like each pellet of the heroin was rubbed in it and then packaged in the condoms."

"So it happened on our end?" Dante asked, and Matty shook his head.

"No, because the pellets came in the truck wrapped. All we did was split it up and put it in the condoms for the mules. If we hadn't had that celebrity who moved out to bumfuck Wyoming wanting some of our H, we wouldn't have known. We would've had ten mules o.d.'ing on their flights to Europe this whole week."

"Was it a fuck-up, or was it intentional?"

"I don't know, Dante." Matty rubbed the back of his neck and sighed. "It could have been an accident, but it's not an accident anyone has *ever* made before. Or even heard of being made before."

Dante stood, too restless to remain seated. He went to the window that provided him a view of the industrial sector of Dallas that had built up around the club in the last seventy or so years. *Nonno* had always told him the difference between a good *don* and a great one was his gut.

"Always trust your gut, Dante," *Nonno* had said. "Your gut will keep you alive and ahead of the cops." That had been his advice the first time Dante oversaw a drug bust, and it was the last advice he'd given during those final days in the hospital as his heart gave out.

And in Dante's gut, he knew something was very wrong. Something had been going wrong since his mother's murder. It had never sat right with him, that some man she had spurned thirty years earlier was still so angry that he waited decades to exact his revenge. No, the García cartel had used the old wound to take a shot at his mother's family– Dante's family in Mexico. He would never run the Ramirez cartel; that would fall to his uncle, and then his cousins, after their *abuelo* eventually passed.

But they were still *his* family, his to protect. The ensuing war that had taken place between the Ramirez and García cartels had been a bloody year that had shown his family the victor, but what if the storm hadn't fully passed? What if it had only been dormant, waiting for the right moment to reassert itself, to gain in money and power to ensure victory over the hated rival? He'd already lost his mother. Who else might be collateral damage in this battle?

Unbidden, a thought of Cassie surfaced in his mind. He imagined her in a scenario much like that of his mother: one minute enjoying the day, not a care in the world... and the next, riddled with bullets, her life flowing out of her. His body ran cold, a refusal rising within him in a howl that fought to break free. No, that wouldn't happen, not to Cassie; she was *his*. He was too selfish to protect her from himself, but he would protect her from every other foe. The only monster she would ever encounter would be him.

"Dante?" Matty's voice, hesitant and younger than it had sounded in years, broke into Dante's thoughts. He turned his gaze from the window to his baby brother, an adult now, a made man for the family.

"We need a family meeting," Dante said and returned to his desk.

"Dante, what's–" but Dante held up his hand. Thankfully, Matty took the hint and shut up.

"We need to meet with Papa and Marco and possibly even call Eli. Something big is coming, and we need to be prepared."

Matty's eyes flickered with apprehension, even a touch of fear. Dante watched with pride as he grappled with it, gained the upper hand, tamped it down, replaced it with comprehension and resolve and fury. "Want me to handle it?"

Dante shook his head. "No, I'll do it. I need you to deal with our drug supply. I have to meet with Alec tonight and confirm the final payment. Do we have H to ship him?"

Matty nodded. "We do. The black tar H we had set to go to dealers along the Gulf coast is fine, and because we use trucks and not mules to ship it, I'm just swapping supplies. The mules will go out as scheduled to Europe. The first one left this morning, actually." Matty smiled, obviously proud of his plan, and Dante found that he was, as well. There was substance under his brother's spoiled playboy ways.

"That's good, Matty. I knew I could rely on you." Dante briefly returned his brother's smile. "And the mule that did get the tainted supply?" Matty's face fell and Dante knew the answer. He knew the answer before he asked, but he needed to know how Matty had handled the situation.

"It's been taken care of. It was too late for the family doctor to help the girl, but I sent her payment on to her mother back in Mexico. It may be soft, but it was only right." Matty lifted his chin in defiance, as if he expected Dante to complain about the loss of five thousand dollars.

"It is, and it's a good call. Make a donation to the church wherever she was from, to handle the funeral, as well. There's no need to sow bad feelings among any of our workers, especially right now."

Who or whatever organization was targeting them was smart: organized, methodical, dangerous. The fewer unhappy members of their organization, the fewer opportunities for their enemy to hurt them.

"There's a storm brewing, Matty," Dante said cryptically. "We need to batten down the hatches."

Matty nodded and departed, no less determined to protect the family than Dante himself.

Dante sat there, contemplating his own next steps, and those of whoever was trying to thwart the di Ruggieros. It was an elaborate, complex game of mental chess, but he was up to the challenge. He meant to be prepared, not just to counter any further attacks on his family, but to defeat them. No other outcome was acceptable. It would end as he wanted, according to his plans, and no one else's.

CHAPTER

FIFTEEN

Miraculously, Cassie got through work with limited daydreaming. She focused on the numbers in front of her and resolutely kept her mind from wandering to Dante's intoxicating words or his addictive touch. At lunchtime, Cassie unpacked her turkey sandwich, grapes, and bottle of water and for the first time since Dante had dropped her off at her apartment, let her mind wander back to that morning.

The way he had fucked her, taking her so hard, commanding her... and how she probably shouldn't want it. How she should probably be scared of such a complicated, dangerous man, and contemplating why she wasn't. Instead, she was captivated by him, by his presence, and her body ached for his. No, not just ached, burned; she *burned* for what he was offering, to let go and give herself over to the fire he stoked in her.

A low whistle drew Cassie from her thoughts; Tiffany was leaning against the opening of her cubicle with a dirty grin on her face.

"I was gonna ask how the date went, but if your glazed eyes and pink cheeks are any indication, I'm gonna say it went well?" Cassie flushed hotter and Tiffany laughed. "Wanna have drinks at Cliff's after work and tell me about your date?"

"I can't." Cassie ducked her head and popped a grape in her mouth, trying not to smile.

"Oh, that's a 'I got lucky and have a second date' smile if I've ever seen one! Are you seeing him again tonight?"

"I am." Cassie gave up trying not to smile; it was impossible to keep her lips from curving at the anticipation she felt.

"Well, that's great." Tiffany squeezed her shoulder. "But I'm gonna need details soon!"

With a wave, her boss was out of her cubicle, and Cassie was left alone with her thoughts for the rest of her lunch break: thoughts about Dante, his hands, his lips, all of him.

The rest of work was uneventful, and Cassie was proud of herself for staying on task and not letting her mind wander. At five o'clock on the dot, she shut down her computer and gathered her belongings. She had just pulled out on the freeway when her phone rang. It was a number she didn't recognize, but she had a feeling she knew who it was.

"Hello?" she said.

"Cassie? It's Dante."

His voice alone made her shiver. How could she have such a reaction to one man?

"Yea–" Her voice came out squeaky and high-pitched. She cleared her throat and tried again. "Dante, yes, hi. It's me, Cassie." She scrunched her face up in embarrassment for sounding like a four-teen-year-old talking to her crush.

"Hello, *cara mia*," he said, with amusement in his voice, and she was glad there was no one in the car with her to witness the fiery blush that lit her cheeks.

"Hi," she breathed, not trusting herself to say anything else.

"Are we still on for tonight?"

Her heart rate trebled at his question. "Yes, I mean, if you still want—"

"I *want*, Cassie, so much." His words stroked over her skin like a tangible caress and a bolt of arousal hit her, lightning-bright. "But what I called for, was to check and make sure eight p.m. works for you. I want to take you for a quick bite beforehand."

"Yes, eight is fine," she replied. "Should I still dress comfortably?"

"I said comfortable *and sexy*, Cassie. What that means to me is, no fuck-me stilettos, but I still expect you to look good. Nothing prim or baggy. Something..." He paused, and Cassie bit her lip, apprehensive with growing excitement. "Something red."

She couldn't help sucking in a little gasp. "Red? With my hair? Dante, you can't be serious."

"Oh, I am," he purred. "Red. You can wear flats, or sandals, but I want you in something red. And short. You have beautiful legs, Cassie. I want to see them tonight."

"Dante..." She didn't even have anything red. She'd have to buy something last-minute, and it would clash with her hair, she'd be uncomfortable and self-conscious the whole time–

"Cassie?" he prompted, and she realized she'd been ruminating in silence for several seconds. There was something in his voice, some dark texture that had the silence pulling taut. She got the feeling that her response– her acceptance or refusal– would be instrumental in the future of their relationship.

She didn't know where things were headed with them, but the idea of it ending now, when it had just started, garnered an immediate reaction of *no*. It was too soon, she'd just found him, just revealed her scars to him, she'd never find another man like him again–

"I'll have to stop by a store," she blurted, and the rising tightness in chest began to melt away. "I might be a little late."

"That's okay." The satisfaction in his voice, the approval, promised deep, drugging pleasure by the end of the night. "Just text me when you're ready, *cara mia*. I'll pick you up." Without waiting for her to say goodbye, he hung up.

Cassie went to her favorite shop and decided a compromise was in order: a short red and gray color-blocked dress with cap sleeves long enough to keep her scars from being visible. The top was charcoal gray, and from the bust down, a brilliant crimson. With the red nowhere near her hair, the color and her auburn wouldn't clash. She glanced at the time on her phone as the clerk rang up the sale: 5:37 p.m. As soon as the bag was in her hand, she practically ran out to her car.

She was home in record time, rushing through feeding and walking poor Lucy so she could shower. Wrapped in a towel, hair dripping on her rug, she pawed through her shoes until she found another compromise: dark gray kitten heels. Then she rummaged around in her meager collection of jewelry until she settled on silver hoops, a little silver horseshoe pendant on a delicate chain, and a pair of chunky bangles that chimed whenever they clinked together.

But instead of putting them on, she sat on her bed and flopped back with a sigh, a move Lucy instantly took advantage of, jumping up and licking her face. Cassie threaded her fingers through the dog's gray fur and sighed.

"I'm starting to lose myself, a little," she whispered. The knowledge that she was doing things Dante wanted, but which *she* did not particularly want, had been a slight but persistent thread of awareness in her subconscious all day, even as she'd been preoccupied with memories of the deliciously filthy things they'd done the night before. "Will you still love me, no matter who I am?"

Lucy whined a little and laid her furry head on Cassie's chest with a satisfied doggy sigh. Cassie scratched Lucy's floppy ears one last time and stood back up. It was after six; Dante would be getting impatient if she took much longer. She smoothed lotion over her skin in a hurry, put her hair up but coaxed a few curls to fall smoothly around her face, and began to apply makeup. Sexy, she was supposed to be sexy... eyeliner, then, and mascara and blush and...

Struck by inspiration, Cassie dug through the drawer until she found the gold tube Amber had left behind months earlier.

...and red lipstick.

Dante wouldn't know what hit him. She grinned.

"Ready," she texted.

"Be there in fifteen," he texted back.

She donned the dress and jewelry, and stepped into the kitten heels. The lotion had made her legs gleam like pearl. Against the bright red, she had to admit that her paleness was intriguing, even... pretty. *Sexy.*

Cassie glanced at her phone: he'd be there in under five minutes. She transferred her driver's license, a credit card, $100 in cash, a tiny packet of tissues, and after applying a judicious coat, the lipstick into a tiny silver pleather bag. She was just dropping her phone into it when there was a knock on the door.

Lucy ran to it, barking much more ferociously than she really was, and Cassie went to the door.

"Lucy, quiet, sit." Cassie's voice was stern and Lucy, being the good girl she was, sat obediently on her haunches, tail wagging in excitement to receive a visitor. Cassie pulled open the door and her mouth went dry.

Dante stood in her doorway dressed as she had grown accustomed to seeing him, most nights at the club: he was in black, probably expensive, well-fitted trousers but no jacket. No tie, either, and a delectable slice of bronzed throat was visible in the open collar of his black dress shirt. Now that she knew what his skin tasted like, all she could think about was licking him there, over his Adam's apple, into the hollow between his collarbones.

"Fuck, Cassie, if I didn't have some business to attend to tonight I would want to know exactly what thought put that look on your face."

She blushed brightly at being caught ogling him so openly. She was glad she'd thought to keep the red away from her head, but then remembering she wore red lipstick. She probably looked like a tomato wearing wax lips.

"Oh, god," she groaned, and screwed her eyes shut.

"*Cara mia*, open your eyes." His voice, deep and inviting, coaxed her to do it but she was too embarrassed so just shook her head 'no'. "It's no secret, after last night and this morning, that you want me. Why be embarrassed?" He paused, leaning in closer, nosing behind her ear, inhaling the light perfume she'd thought to spritz on at some point. "I like it. I like knowing that you want me like I want you."

She drew in a shuddering breath and opened her eyes. His face was intent, his eyes avid. She opened her mouth to say... something, she wasn't sure what, but he took advantage and laid a scorching kiss upon her, his tongue slipping hotly into her mouth, making her knees dissolve. If not for his arm still wrapped around her waist, she might have melted into the floor.

"Woof!" Lucy barked. Cassie pulled out of the kiss to look down at her dog still sitting there, a confused look on her scruffy face.

"It's okay, Lucy girl, he's a friend," Cassie assured her dog, who seemed content that this strange man wasn't hurting her owner.

"Is she your guard dog?" Dante asked, a dubious look on his face.

"Hey, she may not look like much, but she saved me from a crazy squirrel just last weekend."

"As long as she's protecting you, that's all that matters to me." Dante held out his hand for Lucy to sniff and he must've passed the test because she pressed her nose into his hand, expecting– demanding?– a pet. Dante didn't dare disappoint; he gave Lucy a scritch behind her ears and was rewarded with a big doggy smile.

"Hey, now, don't be feeling up another girl with me in the room," Cassie teased.

"Never," Dante answered, and the intensity of it caught her breath, even scared her a bit, gave her that same feeling of losing herself. But even as it scared her, it made her burn, the idea of belonging to someone– to *Dante*– so completely.

"Are–" she took a steadying breath. "Are you ready?"

He smiled and pulled a little box from his pocket, handing it to her. "Yes, but I got you something."

She pulled the little ribbon, opening the velvet box. Laying on the black velvet was a pair of diamond stud earrings, brilliant-cut, throwing sparks of light when the sun hit them. They were big, *really* big. Her brain was stuttering; the only thing she could think to compare them to in size were croutons. Small croutons, but... yeah.

"Dante– I, these are–" Cassie floundered for a response. They were gorgeous. She wanted them. She shouldn't accept them, couldn't possibly–

"They're not half as beautiful as you are, but they'll do," he said smoothly, "and you'll wear them for me tonight. Won't you?"

Another choice that would decide their future, she could feel it in the air. It was easier, this time. She swallowed the little voice– her conscience, she suspected– telling her to refuse, and nodded. She removed her silver hoops, laying them on the foyer table, and plucked the diamonds from their velvet bed. She slipped them in and twin rainbows shot around them when a sunbeam hit her just right. She felt like a walking disco ball. In a good way.

"Ready?" Dante asked, holding out his hand and smiling like the cat who'd gotten the cream: pure satisfaction.

She smiled in return and threaded her fingers through his. "Ready."

"So where are we going tonight?" she asked once they were in the town car and Manny was guiding it out of the parking lot.

"A quick dinner, first. I hope you like tacos."

"Doesn't everyone?" she demanded in pretend shock.

He laughed. "Sorry I asked." He pressed a quick open-mouthed kiss to her throat and it took all of her willpower not to moan at the sensation.

"So– so just tacos?" Her voice sounded breathless, even to her, and thankfully Dante stopped his assault on her neck; after a day of reliving their sexual encounters in her mind, she was fully primed. It wouldn't take much more than a touch to set her off, even if Manny was only a few feet away.

"No, I need to meet with a client at a fight," Dante said absently, fingering the diamond at her ear.

"Fight?"

"Yeah, we're going to an MMA fight." He paused; when he spoke again, his voice was sly, almost taunting. "You're not squeamish, I hope?"

"Nope." Cassie shook her head. "The opposite, actually; I enjoy a good fight. I just didn't realize there was one tonight."

"It's more of an exhibition bout. I'm going to see if it might be something we can hold at one of the other clubs."

A few minutes later, Manny was pulling up to a food truck in... well, not the best area. It was a predominantly industrial zone, much like *Aphrodite's Palace*, but this was a rougher part of town.

"The usual, boss?" Manny asked, turning a little in his seat to face them.

"Do you trust me?" Dante asked her.

"Completely," she breathed, and suddenly the air was charged with something more than just planning their dinner.

"The usual, Manny... and two beers," Dante told his driver, his eyes never leaving hers.

Their dinner was the best birria tacos Cassie had ever had, eaten in the back seat of Dante's car. Manny delivered the food but didn't resume his seat behind the wheel so they were alone, nothing but good conversation passing between them.

Granted, it was mostly Dante asking her questions, things about her life, what she enjoyed, what she didn't, and never once did she feel on display or judged, as she often did when others pried into her life– even when they were well-meaning.

"Oh, this was good," Cassie groaned, popping the last bite of her taco into her mouth. Then her phone started ringing. "I wonder who that could be?" she mumbled and extracted her phone.

The screen flashed a number Cassie didn't recognize... but the area code was familiar. Her stomach clenched. Her first inclination was to ignore it, not wanting to ruin the evening being berated by her sister. But something could be wrong... "Hello?"

"Hello, Cassie? It's Maribel, director of Rocky Mountain Rehab."

"Maribel, hello, is everything okay?" The food Cassie had just eaten threatened to come right back up. Yvonne would not be calling her at nine o'clock on a Tuesday night if everything were fine.

"Well, no, it's not—"

Cassie sat up straight at those words. If she weren't stuck in the backseat of Dante's car, she would be up and pacing.

"Is Amber hurt?" Cassie asked and almost jumped when she felt Dante lay his hand on her back, trying to sooth her.

"No, Cassie, nothing like that." Maribel's voice slipped into a soothing cadence Cassie imagined she used a lot with her patients. "Amber left the facility, though. Sometime between dinner and bed check, she snuck out of her room and disappeared off the grounds. We have video of her climbing the fence. She must've gotten a ride, somehow, because we drove all the way into town and didn't see her. We've informed the authorities, but there isn't much they can do, since she's an adult and wasn't here on a court order."

Cassie's eyes closed as worry flowed over her, not only for Amber's safety but also the fact she hadn't completed the rehab program. "Did she take her belongings? Her phone?"

"She left a bag of clothing, but she has her phone and some of her things. She doesn't have the money that was on her when she checked in, though. For safety reasons, we don't let them keep that. Of course, I will mail you a check for it, Cassie," she hurried to add.

"That's fine," Cassie replied, distracted, unable to keep from imagining what her sister would do for money. Amber wouldn't call Cassie, not until she was in major trouble. The best Cassie could hope for was Amber getting arrested and needing to be bailed out. She'd call then, that was certain.

"Thank you for letting me know," Cassie whispered into the phone, her hands shaking with the strain of not letting herself cry, and hung up before Maribel's kind, sympathy-filled voice did bring her to tears. She instantly dialed Amber's number. It rang once and then went to voicemail, so Cassie dialed again. This time, it didn't even ring, just went straight to voicemail, telling Cassie all she needed to know. Her sister didn't want to talk to her.

"Amber?" Dante's voice broke through the fog of worry and sadness that had descended upon her.

Blindly, she shoved her phone back into her purse. "Yeah, she ran away from the rehab and isn't taking my calls." Cassie closed her eyes and took a deep, steadying breath. She didn't feel much steadier after it, though.

"Want to call her from my phone?" Dante offered and Cassie opened her eyes, surprised by his offer. She hadn't expected him to put himself out for Amber, not even in such a minor way.

"No, I don't," she said after a moment. Amber was an adult, and as much as Cassie wanted to save her, i twas clear that Amber didn't want to be saved. And Cassie was just so tired of the constant fear and worry that came from having a sister with Amber's issues.

"If she needs me, she'll call. She always does." She shrugged a little and tried to smile.

There was a slight rap on the driver's side window, and a second later, Manny opened the door. "Sorry, boss, but it's starting to fill up. The fight will be starting soon."

Dante nodded. "Well, come on, let me take your mind off Amber." Dante held out his hand.

And there was that crossroads once more. Old Cassie, the Cassie of just last week, would want to go home and climb the walls, waiting for Amber to call, or someone to call about her, stewing over the issue, increasingly upset at the lack of contact, until she fell asleep, worn-out from all the worry.

She was bone-tired of that Cassie. She wanted to be a new Cassie, who was building something with a handsome, powerful man, the Cassie who went to fancy restaurants and taco trucks and underground fights on his arm, the Cassie who reveled in the way he touched her. Cassie, for once, wanted something for herself.

"Yes, Dante, please," she said and placed her hand in his. For the first time in possibly ever, Cassie put her worry for her sister to the side and reached for something that was only hers.

CHAPTER

SIXTEEN

When they pulled up to the complex of three large warehouses grouped together, Dante wasn't surprised by Cassie's wide-eyed reaction. The music thumping from the rave taking place in the front building only hinted at the extent of what was occurring in the others.

Nothing going on in the area was legal: not the alcohol being sold without people showing IDs, not the gambling, not the fight to take place, and definitely none of the drugs being sold. This den of iniquity, called The Site and buried between trucking yards and steel recycling plants, had been around for years. A good number of palms had been greased to keep it open.

Oh, sure, it would be raided occasionally, but anyone of importance knew well ahead of any raids and stayed far away. It was beneficial, really; the cops would come in and make a few arrests, scare some minors straight, get some good press, and The Site would cool off for a few weeks. Then rumblings would start, people would want to dance and get high, and The Site would open back up.

That night was no different. It wasn't a scene Dante enjoyed; it was too loud, too messy. It was more Matty's scene, but Dante knew Alec would be there that night and he needed to see how much his best European customer knew about their recent troubles.

Hopefully, very little.

Dante led Cassie through the first warehouse where the EDM music was pumping and the lights were flashing. Bodies writhed in what some would call 'dancing' on the floor out back, where a courtyard of sorts opened up. There, people sat on broken and dirty couches drinking, laughing, even fucking. Dante wove through it all to the VIP area.

This smaller building had probably at one time been a mechanics bay of some kind, but now most nights it hosted a who's-who of various bad guys, from high-ranking street thugs to men like Dante himself who ran whole organizations. He nodded to the guy at the door that night, one of his own men. The family didn't run The Site exclusively, but he knew some of his men didn't mind the extra cash they made running the door, and it helped Dante keep apprised of who was in town and who was talking to who.

The vast room was dominated by an MMA-style fighting cage, with stands for seating around three-quarters of it, and an area with tables and chairs for VIPS. Dante scanned the crowd: it was early yet, but there was already quite a number of people milling about.

"Dante!"

He turned to see Matty walking towards him. Good; he had told Matty to come and it pleased him that his little brother was on time. He wanted Matty to watch and learn. He needed Matty to take more control of their already established drug routes, because Dante had ideas for expansion, ideas that wouldn't ever come to fruition if they didn't figure out what was going on first.

"Hey, Matty. You remember Cassie."

"Of course I do! Come here, give me a hug."

Dante clenched his jaw while Matty pulled Cassie into a hug. His little brother was doing it to annoy him, and it was working. Thankfully, Cassie didn't seem all that inclined to hug him back and was quick to step back, out of his arms.

"Hello, Matteo," Cassie said with a smile, and Dante wrapped a possessive arm around her waist.

"Call me Matty," he said, grinning.

A woman Dante vaguely recognized sauntered up and draped herself all over Matty. In a short, skin-tight red dress that hugged all her surgically-enhanced curves, discretion did not seem to be in her vocabulary.

"Hi, I'm Shanna," the woman said to Cassie, who offered her a smile and a quiet hello.

Shanna, Shanna... ah, Dante remembered her, now. She had danced at the club for a bit, and then decided getting naked in his office was the best way to advance her career. He had fired her, but she was clearly more determined than he'd thought, and now she had set her sights on Matty. That was not acceptable. She wasn't the kind of woman that Matty needed in his life, but as always, Matty seemed incapable of picking a woman that would suit him.

"Shanna," Dante acknowledged her briefly. Over her shoulder, he saw Alec enter the building with some of his own men.

"Matteo, why don't you get some drinks and then invite Alec to sit with us?" Dante suggested.

But before Matty could reply, Shanna scoffed and opened her mouth to say something. Matty, however, was smarter than she was; right away, he nodded and steered her away in the direction of the bar.

Dante and Cassie claimed a vacant table for their party. They hadn't been sitting long when Matty returned with Alec and, unfortunately for them all, Shanna still in tow.

"Dante." Alec held out his hand and they shook hands. Alec had been a business partner for years, and was one of few outside his own family he liked and respected.

"Alec! It's good to see you. Join us?"

"Of course, my friend! I'm glad to see you here tonight." Alec took a seat across from him.

"Yes, well, I wanted to see the fight, and spend some time with my girl," Dante only half-lied. He didn't give two shits about the fight.

He had more important things on his mind. "Cassie, this is Alec, my friend and sometime business partner."

"It's nice to meet you," Cassie said as they shook hands, her voice and posture very elegant and classy, unlike Matty's date, whose eyes seemed to follow every man like a tiger looking for her next meal.

Cassie, on the other hand, couldn't seem to care less about who Alec was. His exotic Greek accent and expensive clothes showed the world he was a wealthy man, but she had hardly spared him a glance before turning back to Dante. He didn't need to tell the world she was his. Cassie said it loud and clear with every gesture.

Shanna took a seat next to Cassie, and Matty on her other side. It wasn't opportune, as Dante wanted Matty to pay attention and learn, but that was another battle for another day, it seemed. Dante heaved an internal sigh for the lost time and opportunity.

A cheer went up in the crowd; the first match of the fighting had begun. Dante watched it with scant interest; the fighters had no finesse, barely above street brawling. It was boring.

"So, how long are you in the States for this trip?" Dante asked Alec, who he knew split time between there and Greece.

"I'm headed home in three days. My wife is due next month."

Dante raised his eyebrows. "I didn't even know you were married. Congratulations."

Alec nodded. "It's not something I enjoy having known by most people. Our life is dangerous and I try not to let it touch her."

Dante was reminded of his mother, her body cold in a graveyard only a few miles away.

"True, but that's the deal we make with the devil, is it not?" Dante asked and pretended to wince as one of the men in the ring landed a pretty hard uppercut to his opponent. Might as well look as if he gave a damn about things.

"It is, but it doesn't stop me from trying. Surely you understand." Alec nodded toward Cassie, who was giving Shanna a polite but tight smile as the other woman chattered at her nonstop.

"I'm beginning to," Dante replied and took a swig of his terrible scotch, struggling to hide a grimace.

"So I'm hearing rumblings," Alec said coolly after a few moments of silence, his eyes still on the fight.

"Rumblings?" Dante repeated, his tone amused even if he himself were decidedly not. "What kind of rumblings?"

"That you're having some troubles in your organization." Alec took a swig of his own scotch but did not keep from frowning at its poor taste.

"And where did you hear that?"

"I was contacted by someone who told me you wouldn't make your delivery to me in Europe." Alec placed his glass down on the table and pushed it away with a finger. "Matty has already assured me that is not the case, however. That the first mule landed in England a few hours ago. So either it was a complete lie, or you fixed the problem."

Dante felt Alec's eyes on him but he continued to watch the fight. One of the fighters had just delivered a devastating uppercut and it was clear his opponent was unconscious on the floor. Most of the warehouse's patrons jumped to their feet, cheering and clapping, but not Alec or Dante.

"If you get what you were promised, it hardly matters either way, does it not?" Dante asked. He was not about to admit to weakness, not even to a man he almost considered a friend.

Alec's expression shifted to one of wry understanding. "You have a leak in your organization," he said. "I don't know who it is, though. I was sent this information anonymously, with instructions to wait, that they would contact me in a week when you didn't deliver."

He went instinctively for his glass but remembered why he'd pushed it away and relaxed back in his seat. "I would assume that, since the shipment actually did go through, I won't hear from them after all. But if I do, I will tell you."

"I appreciate that," said Dante noncommittally.

"I appreciate our partnership. It's very profitable for me. And I like working with reliable suppliers." Alec paused, clearly measuring his words, picking his next ones carefully. "I want to continue working with you, Dante, but if your organization is further compromised, I'll have to take my business elsewhere."

"Business over friendship," Dante murmured, trailing a fingertip through a ring of condensation on the tabletop. "I understand."

"I hope it won't come to that." And damn if Alec didn't look like he meant it. Dante wasn't used to seeing such... sincerity on the other man's face. Marriage and impending fatherhood had softened him. Foolish.

"It won't come to that," he told Alex. "I'll see to it personally."

Alec nodded once and turned back to the ring, where new fighters had taken stance inside the cage. The two men circled each other, hopping from foot to foot, each waiting for an opening. It was what Dante felt like he was doing with this unknown foe, dancing around them and waiting for a soft spot to reveal itself.

Except Dante's adversary already had a leg up. They knew who he was, while Dante was shadowboxing, throwing punches in the dark.

"So, where are you from?" Dante heard Cassie ask Alec, obviously more interested in a conversation with Alec than with Shanna, who had the depth of a puddle, from what Dante remembered of her.

"I'm originally from Greece. Santorini, to be exact. I live in Mykonos, now, with my wife."

"That sounds wonderful. Greece has always been one place I would love to see. So much history and beauty." Her face lit up as she spoke. Animated, eyes bright, she was a woman who appreciated the beauty of the world, probably because she had experienced so much of its ugliness.

"You should tell your man here," Alec tipped his head toward Dante, who raised his glass in acknowledgment, "to bring you over for a visit. I think my wife would enjoy your company."

"We might take you up on that," Dante said, his gaze on her instead of Alec. Her wide eyes met his in clear astonishment but also delight and hope, if he weren't wrong... and he was never wrong. "After your wife has the baby, maybe," Dante added, and Alec smiled.

"We could all go!" Shanna interrupted. Her voice– no, her everything, from her shrillness to her oblivious intrusion in what should be obvious was a private meeting– was swiftly making her a person Dante wanted gone.

"Wouldn't that be great, baby?" she prodded Matty, who was ignoring her to talk to another girl. "Matteo!" Shanna called louder, finally getting his brother's attention.

"What?" The irritation in his little brother's voice would've amused Dante, but he could tell a scene was building between the two of them, a scene Dante had no patience for.

"We're all going to Greece," she informed him. "Alec, here, just invited us."

"Bitch, I'm not taking you anywhere," Matty muttered into his glass, sucking down a mouthful of the scotch as if it didn't taste like twice-used dishwater.

"What was that, babe?" Shanna asked. She was still smiling so she must not have heard his brother's sweet nothings.

"I said, a trip to Greece is always nice."

Shanna seemed satisfied with his agreement, because she shut up, for which Dante was very grateful.

Alec stood. "Gentlemen, as much as I would like to see the last fight, I've already lost enough money this evening, and I have an early video call with my wife and her doctor tomorrow." Alec shook both Dante and Matty's hands, then kissed Cassie on both cheeks in that touchy-feely European way Dante did not care for. He ignored Shanna. With a last grinning flash of teeth, he left.

Dante snagged Alec's chair by the back, pushing it toward the next table, then pulled Cassie's chair closer to him in the spot Alec had just vacated.

"Are you ready to leave?" Dante whispered, leaning closer than he had to in order to whisper in her ear; he wanted to catch a sniff of her perfume, so deliciously innocent and simple when she was nothing of either. Now that his business with Alec had concluded, he was itching to get Cassie home and out of her lovely dress. It wasn't entirely red, as he'd directed, but he found he was more amused by her subtle show of defiance than irritated. He wanted her submissive, not spineless.

"Can we stay for the last fight? I actually bet fifty bucks on the underdog," she answered with a sheepish smile.

"Just who am I dating?" Dante asked in mock outrage. "Who replaced my mousy accountant with a gambling, brutality-loving vixen?"

"I don't know. I hardly recognize her, myself." Cassie slanted him an impish grin. "It must be the company I'm keeping."

"Must be," he agreed and dropped a quick kiss on her tempting lips. "Okay, we'll stay and see if your underdog can pull out the win, but then I'm taking you home."

There was a world of things left unsaid in that vague statement, but the way her pupils dilated told him she understood every implication.

"Oh, yeah? Taking me home to–" she began, but was cut off when Dante's phone rang.

"Just a second, cara mia." Dante pulled his phone out and glanced at the name on the caller ID: it was Tony, who knew not to call him unless it was very important. He thumbed the button to accept the call.

"What's wrong?" he demanded without preamble.

"Our shipment coming in from Laredo just got seized. And not the dummy shipment, though they got that one, too," came Tony's angry voice over the line.

"Fuck," Dante growled.

Matty's attention instantly shifted to him, his playful expression fading to one that was deadly serious. "What happened?"

Dante shook his head and held up a finger for him to wait. Beside him, Cassie had gone still, watchful, her eyes on him.

"Arrests?" Dante let his arm fall away from her, needing to pay attention. Her soft curves in that brief dress were not conducive to paying attention.

"Four of our best guys, including the driver," said Tony grimly.

Dante's eyes slipped closed. They did not need that right now. "Get them bonded out as fast as possible. Call our lawyers."

"I'm on it, boss," Tony said, and Dante disconnected the call.

"What happened?" Matty asked again, more urgently.

Dante opened his mouth to respond and then closed it again, peering around the room. He knew he could trust Cassie. She knew he was a drug dealer, even if she didn't yet know the scope of what it entailed in his business. But Shanna was watching their conversation with entirely too much interest, and he didn't trust her as far as he could throw her.

Dante was just about to suggest he and Matty go outside to speak privately when Cassie stood and grabbed Shanna's hand.

"Shanna, I really need to pee, will you come with me?" she asked, sliding Dante a quick glance that told him she understood his dilemma and was doing her part to solve it. Yes, he thought. Exactly what I need. He wasn't only referring to the matter at hand.

"Oh, I don't–" Shanna protested, tugging unsuccessfully on her hand, but Cassie was clinging to her like a barnacle.

"Yes, Shanna, go," Matty cut in. "I don't want either of you going to the bathroom alone, and I know my brother agrees."

His tone brooked no argument; for all that he could be an airheaded playboy, Matty was capable of pulling a 360 and growing deadly serious in the blink of an eye. His demeanor had shifted, just then, and the face he turned to Shanna could have been carved from granite.

She seemed to recognize that any hope she had of remaining was doomed, and nodded, whether she knew she was being dismissed or was hoping she was gaining favor with Dante he couldn't tell, nor did he care.

"Okay. Yeah, you're right. I need to pee, too, anyway." Shanna stood and let Cassie pull her through the crowd.

The moment they were out of sight, Matty turned to him, eyebrows raised.

"Both of the shipments, the decoy and the real one, were seized in Laredo," Dante told him.

"Fuuuuuck," Matty said, slumping back in his chair.

Dante nodded. " 'Fuck' is right. We have a mole, one high up enough to know the trade routes."

Matty closed his eyes and rubbed his forehead. "How many people is that? Eight? Ten, including us?"

"That sounds about right," Dante said. "We need to figure out who it is– what their motivation is– and we need to do it soon."

A flash of auburn appeared in his peripheral vision: Cassie and Shanna were making their way back through the crowd.

"I'm moving up the meeting for Thursday night," he told Matty, his eyes on the women as they approached. Cassie had an expression that suggested he wasn't the only one irritated by Shanna. She glanced to the side, saw the other woman wasn't paying attention, and rolled her eyes the slightest bit at Dante, grinning.

"For the love of God, find someone better to date," Dante muttered.

Matty laughed. "Hey, not all of us can get as lucky as you have." He gestured to Cassie, warm appreciation in his eyes.

"It's not luck, baby brother, it's knowing what you want, and recognizing those qualities in a woman." Dante watched Cassie smile politely at something Shanna said, his own lips curving at the sight.

"Maybe I should just let you pick who I should date, next time," Matty commented.

"Do better, or I will," Dante replied, the humor leaching from his voice in a heartbeat. That was a great idea and he just might do it; he couldn't possibly do worse, that was certain.

Matty stared at him, wide-eyed, shocked, with dismay dawning slowly on his face.

"Your actions reflect the family," Dante continued. "If you take up with trash, people will view you as trash. And, Matteo–" he leaned closer to his brother, ensuring uninterrupted eye contact "–di Ruggieros are not trash. Remember it."

Matty gave him a shaky nod as he drew back. Dante held out a hand and smiled up at Cassie as she reached their table.

"Cassie, I'm sorry, but I need to leave. I know you wanted to stay for the last fight..."

"Oh, no, it's fine if we need to go." She looked more relieved than disappointed. Dante felt sure Shanna was responsible for that.

They bid Matty and Shanna goodnight and departed. The night air, though on the verge of unpleasantly warm, was welcome; inside the warehouse, it was muggy and redolent of sweat, spilled booze, and the faint tinge of blood. He much preferred to be outside in the moonlight, with Cassie's perfume wafting to him on the breeze.

He needed to get her home. Whatever was happening, whoever was coming for his family, was making him feel like control was slipping through his fingers. It made something feral want to claw its way out of his belly, the surging need to protect, to vanquish, to avenge.

But there was one place he knew he could get some of it back: in bed, with Cassie.

"Manny," he said to the driver once they were inside the car, "take us home." He slid a glance to Cassie, saw the eager, excited gleam in her brown eyes. "And step on it."

CHAPTER

SEVENTEEN

CASSIE

After the shock of learning Amber had run away from the rehab, a very old, deep-seated anger set into Cassie. Once again, Amber had taken something good, something that Cassie had gone out of her way to provide for her, and shit all over it.

But something had shifted within Cassie, had changed and altered her. A month earlier, she might have spent the evening crying over her own inadequacies as well as the persistence of Amber's addiction, wracking her brain for yet another solution to her sister's self-made problems, but now...

...now, Cassie gave herself ten minutes to think and worry before putting the matter resolutely out of mind. Amber might be hell-bent on ruining her life, and a-okay with ruining Cassie's, too, but Cassie had no intention of letting that happen. Just because Amber's life was unhappy didn't mean Cassie's had to be, as well.

And she would start right away: she was going to enjoy that night as much as possible, and not let her sister's usual drama interfere.

Cassie tried not to gawk at the dancers as Dante led her through the gigantic warehouse, but she couldn't help it. She had never in her life been to an underground dance club, and it was looking like something out of a movie, with the laser lights and the pulsating music and writhing bodies. Much too quickly for her liking, they were exiting the loud warehouse into some kind of open yard, all concrete, littered with broken couches and chairs. The humid air was thick with cigarette smoke and the not-so-faint pong of urine. Everywhere she looked, couples were making out... or more.

She wasn't sorry to leave that section, relieved when they entered another, smaller warehouse. With a knowing nod from Dante, the man at the door let them inside. There was nothing spectacular about the interior, really; it was open space dominated by a makeshift MMA-style fighting cage. Rows of cheap metal bleachers ran along three of the sides, and a few tables were set up with prime viewing of the cage.

And then there was a bar. It was nothing like the beautiful and ornate bar at Aphrodite's Palace. No, this was just a humble horizontal surface that seemed cobbled together from whatever wood they could find– plywood, two-by-fours– and a scant few bottles of liquor on a rickety shelf behind the gruff man pouring drinks with absolutely no flair or style whatsoever.

Dozens of men loitered about, from men in fine suits, like Dante, to those who wore baggy jeans and Dallas Cowboy jerseys. Cassie could almost feel the power coming off who she was sure were probably some of the most dangerous people in Dallas– and maybe the entire state of Texas.

Part of it excited her, the same part that Dante aroused in bed, the dangerous part of herself she tried not to engage, but which still called to her. She was coming to realize, more and more, that safe, boring Cassie only existed because she needed her to, needed to be the type of person who could keep Amber calm, or make them more likeable in group homes. It had always been a role that had been comfortable to fall into; Amber was wild and beautiful and Cassie was her opposite, staid and boring.

Then Dante had burst into her life, releasing something inside her that had long been ignored, and she was beginning to believe that she shouldn't ever go back.

Dante was introducing her to his business associate; she shook hands with Alec and sat next to Dante as he and the other man began their professional discussion. Cassie didn't strain to overhear them; it wasn't her concern and she had a gut feeling she didn't really want to know what they were talking about.

"Doesn't it drive you crazy?" came a female voice, almost in her ear, and Cassie jumped.

Shanna, Matty's date, was leaning in close to be heard over the ambient noise. She sat sideways on her chair, legs crossed and lipsticked mouth wrapped around a straw as she sucked down half her drink. Her heavy perfume was the sort of sickly-sweet scent favored by teenaged girls but, if the crêpey skin under her eyes were any indication, she hadn't had a one as the first digit of her age in a long time.

Or maybe she was just tired; God knew Cassie was no supermodel when sleep-deprived. She shouldn't be so catty right off. There was plenty of time, yet, for Shanna to prove herself worthy of cattiness.

"I'm sorry, what?" Cassie tried to both turn to face Shanna while scooting closer to Dante, eager to put distance between herself and the cloying thickness of the other woman's perfume.

"When they talk business, but don't include you. Matty and I have hung out a few times now, and he's always doing that to me." Shanna rolled her eyes. She was done up to perfection: her makeup looked like something off a beauty influencer's page, her figure was slim, her skin bronze, and her bosom plentiful. Her dress was minuscule– when she uncrossed and recrossed her legs, she flashed Cassie a glimpse of bright white panties.

Blinking against the unwelcome sight, Cassie replied, "Oh, well, no, it doesn't bother me. Dante's business dealings aren't anything to me." She turned to face the fight, trying to indicate her lack of interest in the topic, but Shanna was on a roll.

"I guess," she admitted grudgingly, "but I don't just want to be arm candy, you know? I want to be involved."

Involved... what, precisely, did that mean? Involved in Dante's business? She knew it was something illegal and probably nothing to do with the clubs, maybe a drug deal. But Cassie was interested in Dante, wanted Dante, not his business. She didn't care if he ran clubs or suddenly decided he wanted to open a grocery store. It wouldn't change her feelings for him.

Not that she had a strong antipathy to discussing his professional matters. She didn't mind if he failed to share the details of his business with her, but she wanted him to know that he could, if it could help him in some way. She wanted him to know she could be someone he trusted, but she wasn't sure how. He was such a cautious and private person, always drawing a line between his family and the rest of the world.

Shanna had scooted her chair even more into Cassie's personal space, so near that her body heat was radiating against Cassie in a way she didn't care for, with how warm and close the air was in the warehouse. And she got the distinct feeling Shanna wasn't trying to be her pal, but instead was trying to eavesdrop on Dante and Alec. Cassie braced herself, not letting Shanna get any closer, even if her perfume was killing the oxygen all around them in a six-foot radius. Cassie couldn't do much to help or protect Dante, but she could do this.

A man appeared in front of them. "Would you ladies like to make a bet on the final fight?"

"No," Shanna answered, her voice clipped and impatient. He started to walk away, but Cassie seized the opportunity to provide even more of a buffer for Dante.

"Oh, I would like to," she said, and he ambled back to them. "What are the odds? Do you know their stats?" Cassie didn't care one way or the other, but the sound of a conversation with the guy would muffle and distract from the one Dante was having with Alec.

It worked; not long after Cassie and the man began discussing the odds of which fighters were likely to win or lose, Shanna sat back in her chair, pouting as she sucked up more of her drink.

"Give me fifty dollars on the underdog, then," Cassie said finally, and pulled the cash out of her purse.

"Sure thing," the bookie said, writing down her wager, taking her money and moving on.

As the night progressed Cassie relaxed in the atmosphere, though that might have had something to do with the drinks Matty kept pushing into her hand, with a playful wink each time. Cassie had had little interaction with Dante's youngest brother, but he seemed to be fun and free-spirited in a way she could never imagine Dante being.

"Baby, I'm bored," Shanna whined for what had to have been the fifth time just in the last hour. It clearly grated on Matty; his mouth, where there usually seemed to be a permanent smile, was pressed into an irritated line.

"I told you you would be, Shanna," he said through gritted teeth.

"Can't we just go home?" Shanna ran her hand, tipped with impossibly long nails, down his arm in a way that, had Matty not been annoyed, Cassie bet he might have enjoyed. But as it stood now, it only seemed to only anger him further. So much so, that he plucked her hand from his arm and stood.

"No, we can't go home, but you can, Shanna. I'm staying. I didn't come here just to leave early." He strode away, irritation clear in every line of his body.

Shanna crossed her arms under her round, barely-covered breasts, eyes narrow as she watched Matty leave them. With a burst of sudden energy, she launched herself from her chair and followed him into the crowd, her backside twitching like she meant business. Cassie began to laugh. The bloodier fight may have been on the mat, but the most entertaining fight of the night went to Shanna and Matty.

"I'd love to know what's so funny." Alec's voice broke into her thoughts.

She turned to share her amusement with Dante, but found him staring at the fight, but without focus or interest, lost in thought. She decided not to interrupt him.

"I was thinking how Shanna and Matteo's little spat was better than the three fights we've watched tonight," she answered honestly, Alec gave a huff of laughter. He was probably a few years older than Dante, his inky black hair beginning to grey at the temples. He was not as attractive as Dante, not to Cassie, but still handsome, with charm to spare.

"Did I miss a good fight?" Alec leaned in conspiratorially.

Cassie shrugged. "Shanna seems to be... dramatic."

"She does seem like that. My own Anna can be prone to dramatics, as well." Then he grinned. "But I like that about her. Keeps things exciting. It seems Matteo doesn't share the opinion."

He nodded toward the crowd, where Matty was talking to another girl.

"I've never had a flair for drama myself," Cassie told him, then decided to try sparing a little charm of her own. "In fact, some have called me boring."

"That can't be true," Alec protested, hand on his chest in exaggerated shock. He had no small talent at theatrics, himself.

"Oh, I promise it is," she said as Matty returned to the table, his face set in a fearsome scowl. He plopped heavily down into his chair. Cassie bit her lip to keep from smiling and when she looked at Alec, found he had pressed his lips tightly together for the same reason. Eyes dancing in shared humor, they were about to resume their conversation when Dante came back. He took the empty chair on the far side of Matty and began speaking to his brother in low tones.

Shanna stomped back to the table, surveying her seating choices with a glare: there was a single seat empty between Cassie and Dante, but Matty was safely fenced in by the other men. With an audible huff, she took the seat by Cassie and snatched up her unfinished drink.

"So where are you from?" Cassie asked, watching as the next bout commenced. The new pair, at least, seemed a little better trained than the first six fighters on the card.

"I'm from Greece. Santorini to be exact. I live in Mykonos, now, with my wife," Alec answered.

"That sounds wonderful," Cassie said wistfully. "Greece has always been one place I would love to see. So much history and beauty."

She had dreamed of visiting many exotic or historical places, especially in her youth; travel books and magazines had been one of her favorite ways to escape while living in group homes.

"You should tell your man, here–" Alec turned his head and tipped it toward Dante, "–to bring you over for a visit. I think my wife would enjoy your company."

"We might just take you up on that," Dante said, his tone casual, but Cassie's breath seized in her chest. That declaration spoke of intent for more than just a brief fling; it hinted as a relationship, of something long-term.

She hadn't dared to consider, to wonder, to hope that he might want to turn what they had into anything more than what it was: her repaying her sister's debt, and them enjoying sex together, without commitments or promises of a lengthy future together.

She made herself glance at Dante, wanting to see if something in his expression gave away his thoughts, and found him watching her, not Alec. His expression was bland, as usual, but there was a flame flickering behind his eyes, a kindled emotion she couldn't bear to put a name on. Not yet.

"After your wife has the baby, maybe," Dante added.

"We could all go!" Shanna's voice broke in. "Wouldn't that be great, baby?" she cooed louder when no one, especially Matty, as he was too busy talking to another woman, acknowledged.

The empty moment stretched, awkward and uncomfortable, and Cassie was about to say something, probably lame and trite, to fill the silence. She didn't like Shanna, but it seemed cruel to let the woman hang there, ignored by everyone.

But before Cassie could say anything, Shanna shouted, "Matteo!"

"What?" It was painfully obvious Matty was fed up with Shanna's antics tonight.

"We're all going to Greece," she told him with a wide smile. "Alec, here, just invited us."

He hadn't, but that little fact didn't seem to bother Shanna overmuch. Matty muttered something Cassie couldn't quite catch, but which she was sure wasn't complimentary.

"What was that, babe?" Shanna asked, her smile tightening. It seemed she was sure it wasn't complimentary, too.

"I said, a trip to Greece is always nice," he answered.

Shanna sat back, waving her empty glass over her head to signal that she wanted a refill, happy with her tiny victory, even if Cassie was positive Matty wouldn't even be taking Shanna to the movies after tonight, much less to Greece.

"Gentlemen, as much as I would like to see the last fight, I've already lost enough money this evening, and I have an early video call with my wife and her doctor tomorrow." With a flurry of handshakes (Dante, Matty) and kisses on cheeks (Cassie, not Shanna), Alec departed.

Dante wasted no time pulling her closer, his arm again possessively around her waist.

"Are you ready to leave?" Dante whispered in her ear, his warm breath making her shiver. She did want to go home, truthfully. The night had been fun, but Shanna's perfume had given her a faint headache and all the drama was tiring. But Matty was still flirting with another girl while Shanna glared, and Cassie had a feeling that if they left, Shanna would make a scene.

"Can we stay for the last fight? I actually bet fifty bucks on the underdog."

That wasn't entirely true– she would've left in a heartbeat to get Dante alone– but she didn't like what seemed to be brewing between Shanna and Matteo. She worried if she didn't stay as a buffer something would pop off between them, a scene that would embarrass and anger Dante.

"Just who am I dating?" Dante teased. "Who replaced my mousy accountant with a brutality-loving gambling vixen?"

He was right, it wasn't her scene, but playing peacekeeper? That was completely her. He just hadn't caught on with what she was doing, yet. She decided to play it cute.

"I don't know. I hardly recognize her, myself," Cassie replied, smiling flirtatiously. "It must be the company I'm keeping."

"Must be." He made to kiss her and she leaned in, eager to accept it. "Okay, we'll stay and see if your underdog can pull out the win, but then I'm taking you home."

All she'd wanted, all night, was his searing touch, his tempting kisses, caresses on heated skin, the pull of his mouth on her nipples–

"Oh, yeah?" she breathed. "Taking me home to–"

Dante's phone rang. "Just a second, cara mia." He took the call, his tone brusque. "What's wrong?" A dark look overtook his features as the other person spoke. "Fuck," he muttered.

"What happened?" Matty asked, but Dante silenced him with a look.

"Arrests?" Dante sat up straighter and Cassie did as well.

She didn't want to eavesdrop, so she scooted away to give him some privacy. She focused her attention on the fight in front of her until she felt Shanna leaning into her personal space yet again, obviously trying to hear whatever Dante and Matteo were discussing, trying once more to butt in where she had no place.

Cassie shot to her feet and took Shanna's bony hand in hers. "Shanna, I really need to pee, will you come with me?"

She shot Dante a look, trying to communicate her intent. Awareness in his eyes said he understood.

"Oh, I don't–" Shanna began to argue, obviously dying to know what was being discussed between the two men.

"Yes, Shanna, go," Matty told her firmly. "I don't want either of you going to the bathroom alone, and I know my brother agrees."

Shoulders slumping in defeat, Shanna nodded. "Okay. Yeah,

you're right, I need to pee, too, anyway." Shanna stood and let Cassie drag her from the table.

The bathroom was disgusting. The stalls– though calling them that was a disgrace to proper bathroom stalls– were made from cheap plywood poorly painted black, with plastic shower curtains for doors. Cassie hadn't really considered using them, but somehow between leaving Dante and Matty, and arriving in the bathroom, her ruse of having to pee had become a reality. She didn't know how much longer Dante would want to remain, but if it were longer than ten minutes, Cassie wouldn't last the wait. Resigned, she drew aside one of the shower curtains and stepped inside.

The interior of the stall was no less a horror show than the exterior, but the pressure on her bladder was increasing with every second. With a sigh, Cassie hitched up her dress.

"Ugh, these stalls never have toilet paper," Shanna groused from the stall next to her.

Cassie paused in the act of pushing down her panties to look around; sure enough, there was no toilet paper. She sighed again.

"I've got some tissues in my purse. Hang on a sec." Cassie dug through her little purse, pulling out the travel-sized container of tissues and pulling out a couple to see to her own needs before reaching under the stall and passing the packet to Shanna.

"Thanks, girl."

"No problem," Cassie replied. She did what she needed to do and exited the stall, washing her hands at the sink when Shanna joined her.

"Thanks again," Shanna handed her back the little packet of tissues with a grateful smile, one Cassie returned. "You know, you're lucky," Shanna told her as she lathered up her hands in the dingy sink.

Cassie met her eyes in the cracked mirror. "What do you mean?" She reached for a paper towel, only to find that empty as well. She settled for flapping her hands back and forth to dry them, instead.

"I mean, Dante seems to really like you, and you fit the role of mobster girlfriend well."

Huh?

"Mobster?" Cassie repeated.

"Yeah, mobster." Shanna didn't bother flapping, just ran her hands down her tiny dress. It was the size of a paper towel, anyway, so it was fitting. When she saw Cassie gaping at her, she rolled her eyes. "Oh, come on. You can't be that naïve."

"No– I mean, no, I know Dante's businesses aren't all legitimate, my sister bought drugs from his people, that's how we met. I just–" Cassie stammered, but Shanna took pity on her and interrupted.

"He's not some middle level drug dealer that owns a few clubs, girl, he runs one of the largest mafia organizations in Texas. Hell, probably in the whole country."

Cassie swallowed as shock coursed through her, seeming to rattle her very bones. She hadn't realized how powerful Dante really was. Or how dangerous. "Okay, well, that's–"

Shanna only rolled her eyes again and left the bathroom, leading the way back to their table while Cassie trailed behind her, feeling a little numb. The crowd was boisterous, jostling them as they wove through it, but she barely noticed.

She was shaken from her daze when they approached the table, where it was clear the di Ruggiero men were having an intense conversation.

"Cassie, I'm sorry but I need to leave. I know you wanted to stay for the last fight..."

"Oh, no, it's fine if we need to go," she hurried to say. If she'd been willing to leave, earlier, now she was positively eager to go.

They said their goodbyes to Shanna and Matty, and they retraced their steps through the warehouses and courtyard. The fresher air outside, and the lack of noise, cleared her head. By the time they were comfortably in the car, she'd processed the news she'd just heard.

Shanna was right. The respect, the deference, that Dante garnered from his men– his wealth– the power that he exuded– it was just like what a king commanded. She waited to feel alarmed by it, or repelled. Contemptuous. Turned off. But it never came, not any of it. She couldn't imagine a situation with Dante that could turn her off. He seemed able to make any act, any sin, acceptable– desirable– as long as he was the one doing it. And instead of being disgusted by it, she just found it all the more arousing.

"Manny," Dante addressed his driver, "take us home." He looked at Cassie and whatever he saw on her face turned the little every-present flame of attraction in his eyes into a roaring bonfire. "And step on it."

As they sped through the humid Dallas night, Cassie knew she was giving up her soul, piece by piece, for Dante. But as he lay a trail of burning kisses down her throat, as his hand slid up her thigh and plucked the edge of her panties, pulling it tight so it rubbed where she wanted contact the most, she thought it was a worthy price to pay.

One soul, only slightly used, barely dented, in exchange for long nights of blinding ecstasy.

It was a bargain.

CHAPTER

EIGHTEEN

DANTE

The car ride home was quiet, which suited Dante just fine. The news Alec had imparted would cause a cascade failure of event after event spiralling out of control if they couldn't find out who was responsible for this interference with his family. How much of it was connected with his mother's death? The lack of answers, the many dangers lurking in the unknown, had his stomach in a knot.

"Dante? We're here." Cassie's hand, warm on his cheek, broke him out of his thoughts and he blinked, finding the car had indeed stopped in front of his building.

Manny was holding open the car door and Dante hadn't even heard him exit the driver's seat. Cassie slid out of the car quickly and thanked Manny with a smile. Dante took a breath to settle himself before exiting the vehicle himself.

"Yes, Manny, thank you."

"Of course, boss."

Dante was striding through the quiet lobby of his building before Manny had even gotten back in the car. The knot in his stomach had tightened, and it felt close to alarm, to fear. Except Dante didn't get afraid. *Ever.* Any time he came close, he... well, he had his ways of beating it back, of regaining the calm and confidence he needed to run the family.

The moment the elevator arrived, he pulled Cassie into it. He had her pressed against the wall, pinned by his body, his mouth slanted over hers, before the doors shut. His hands were rough as they roamed her body, squeezing, rubbing, and in her hair as his fingers thrust through its fiery mass, tugging her head back so he could get at that beautiful throat of hers with his mouth. And she didn't protest at all, his little Cassie, only made soft moans that went straight to his cock.

"I would turn you around and take you in this elevator if I didn't know for a fact there was a camera," he growled hotly in her ear and then swallowed her whimper with another searing kiss, only stopping when the elevator doors opened on his floor.

Inside his apartment, he pressed her up against the closest wall and plunged his tongue back into her mouth, snatching her moans right out of her mouth. Her hands, soft and warm, ran down his chest, over his shoulders. It was a calming gesture, soothing, but he didn't want to be soothed. He wanted to take, to own, to possess. To control. To know exactly where something was going and that he was the one getting it there. Gentle wasn't in the cards for them that night.

Taking both her wrists in one of his, he lifted them over her head, holding them against the wall. The action made her back arch in the prettiest way, like she was offering herself to him, her small plump breasts pressed into his chest. He drew back and feasted his eyes on her: lips red and swollen and wet, chest heaving... she was entrancing, a goddess.

But it was her eyes, velvety brown with tiny flecks of gold, that made him stop breathing for a moment. In their fathomless depths was desire, but also so much more. If he were a different man, he would probably feel guilt for sullying her with his touch, his very presence. But guilt, like fear, was not something Dante experienced. Instead, there was nothing but the raging fire of his lust, and his determination to slake it inside her soft, enticing body.

"I want you, Cassie," he whispered, so close that his lips brushed hers as he spoke.

"I want you too–" she began, but he pressed his finger against her mouth, silencing her.

"No, baby, let me explain." Eyes wide, she nodded, and he pressed another kiss to her lips to reward her for obeying before he continued. "I know I gave you a taste, last night, of what I like, what I need, but tonight…"

She leaned forward and pressed her lips to his as he searched for a way to explain it. He had never explained it to a woman; he hadn't needed to. The professionals he'd paid in the past were well-acquainted with the practices, and experts in responding to the various cues their clients might give to indicate what they wanted.

With his previous girlfriends, if he had felt like he did at that moment, with the need to exorcise a demon or two, he would go to an escort, keep the monster at bay. The idea of doing that just then, of making excuses to Cassie and phoning an escort, left him cold. Only Cassie could properly feed the monster inside him.

"I understand, I think," she whispered, saving him from having to explain. "I can be what you need, just tell me. I won't say no, Dante."

Her words hardened him to steel, driving his need to a fever pitch. He pressed his forehead into her shoulder, breathing deeply of her scent, trying to regain some control. She didn't know how close he was to ripping that dress from her body, pushing her to the floor, and taking her right there in his entryway. But he knew she'd let him, and she'd even enjoy it.

He took a few breaths and looked back into her eyes.

"If I do anything you don't like, say the word 'red', and I will stop immediately," he told her. They would need a longer discussion in the near future about what all of it entailed, but not that night. Tonight, he needed to fuck her. "Do you understand?"

She nodded. "I do. If I don't like anything you do, I'll say 'red'. But, Dante," and here she gave him a dirty little smirk that made his head spin, "I think I'm going to like it."

In one motion, he picked her up and kissed her. She wrapped her legs around his waist as his tongue invaded her mouth. His hands cupped her ass as he climbed the stairs, squeezing the luscious globes hard and drinking down the little sob of pleasure she gave. He needed to get her naked, needed to bury his cock in her, more than he needed oxygen.

When he finally made it to his room, he set her on her feet and stripped her clothes from her body. Then he froze, instead of going with his plan of pushing her onto the bed and fucking her raw, because the sight of her stole his breath.

Her creamy skin wore a pink flush that started at her face and spread down to the upper curves of her gorgeous little tits. She wasn't bombshell-gorgeous, with big breasts and curvy hips and a round ass, but she was lovely despite her slightness. She was slender and soft, graceful in the way she moved, her skin like silk running through his fingers, her rosy nipples made for his lips.

When his scrutiny went on too long for her liking, she fidgeted under his gaze, crossing her arms over her chest, wanting to hide.

"Oh, no, Cassie." Dante braceleted her wrists with his fingers and tugged them down. She let them fall back down to her sides, but she still wasn't comfortable under his gaze, clenching her fists. "I love looking at you, knowing I caused this flush–" he ran his fingers over the tops of her breasts, "–and knowing no one else gets to see it." Dante leaned in and took one of her nipples in his mouth, sucking. "Because it's mine, Cassie. Did you know that?"

His teeth worried the tender flesh, pulling it until she exclaimed. Then he went to his knees. It was funny; for all his talk about being in control, of dominating her, he was spending a lot of time at her feet.

He pulled the scrap of fabric covering her cunt to the side, baring her to his hungry gaze. The smell of her, hot and fresh, made him lick his lips in anticipation. He nudged her open with his thumbs and dove in, wetting his face in her, mouth and tongue slicked by the juices he made pour down. He eased in one finger, then another. She was searing-hot around them, tight, slippery. He gritted his teeth, once more, against the urge to simply skip everything else and fuck her.

And then he pulled back, gazing up the pale expanse of her body to her face.

"Cassie," he prompted, "Did you know that?"

Her hips twitched and pulsed, seeking more of the brutally good sensation he'd taken away. "Dante, please," she whispered, her hands in his hair, trying to press his face back between her legs. Around his fingers, her sleek interior flexed and clenched in frustration.

He sat back on his haunches, ignoring her dismayed moan. "Please what?"

"Oh, god, *please* make me come," she pleaded. There were patches of pink high on each cheekbone, and that red lipstick was gone, kissed away. Her hair looked rumpled as only a passionate clinch could effect. She looked positively debauched, and he loved that he was the one who had debauched her.

But he couldn't deny her, not when she begged so prettily. He put his mouth back on her, his fingers moving with more purpose instead of the lazy, uncoordinated caresses he'd been lavishing upon her. Sealing his lips around her clit, nose buried in the neat little auburn patch above her pussy, he sucked it into his mouth.

Dante had to tighten his hold on her hip to her from falling down as she flung her head back and screamed. It snapped the last tether of his restraint. Before she'd finished the last throes of her orgasm, he was on his feet, kissing her, ravenous, tongue as deep in her mouth as it had been in her cunt.

He was panting when he pulled back. "On the bed," he rasped, and she scrambled to obey. But she laid back, staring up at him with those trusting eyes, and it wasn't what he wanted.

"No," he said. "On your knees."

Understanding lit her features; while he peeled off his clothes, she rolled over and got to all fours, her sweet little ass facing him, thighs trembling as she waited. Dante slowly stroked his cock as he admired the view.

More than the blatant sexuality of the pose was the vulnerability, the trust, inherent in it. She was placing herself utterly in his hands, under his control. The knot in his belly loosened, then began to unravel entirely.

"Dante?" She glanced over her shoulder, her voice nervous.

"I'm here, *cara mia*, just looking at you. I like looking at you, Cassie. I told you that once already, tonight. You shouldn't make me repeat myself."

He climbed on the bed behind her and ran his fingers over her wet folds, spreading them apart, slipping a teasing fingertip over her clit, hard again, jutting out, searching for him.

"Do you like that?" he asked but all she did was moan in response, because he followed the question with two fingers pushed roughly inside her. "Answer me, Cassie."

But again she just moaned, a desperate edge to it, and rocked her hips back to enclose his fingers once more.

He covered her body with his, draping himself over her, their bodies in contact from chest to knees. He dropped a kiss on her scarred shoulder as he slid his fingers free of her grasping cunt, then smacked her ass, the sound as loud and sudden as the crack of a gunshot in the dim silence of the room. She groaned and shifted on her knees.

"Cassie, when I tell you to do something, you do it," he growled in her ear. "When I ask you something, you answer me. Do you understand?"

Frantically, she nodded, her satiny curls bobbing and brushing his cheek with the motion.

"I can't hear you, baby." He rubbed his hand over the warm, pinkened handprint he'd left on her ass cheek– to sooth it, and in warning.

"I understand, Dante," she said at last, her words more gasp than anything else.

"Good." He lined up his cock with her pussy and with no warning, no preamble, thrust inside her– hard.

"Fuck," he moaned; her interior muscles, wet and snug, spasmed around him as her body made him welcome.

That was the only pause he gave her; he withdrew, buried a hand in her hair, and slammed forward, pounding into her. Cassie punctuated each thrust with little whimpering pleas, begging him not to stop, to never stop, to make her come and come and come. He used his grip on her hair to pull her head back, making her back arch, and wondered what it would take to make her use the safe word.

No objection to the hair pulling, just more enthusiastic moaning, so he tugged harder, snapping his hips into her almost viciously. Instead of the safe word, that time, her cunt clamped around him like a vice.

"Fuck, you were made me for me," he groaned. "Made for my cock."

"Yes, Dante, god, yes." she agreed, breathless, almost babbling.

He pushed her back down into the bed, her head in the pillows, and continued to pound into her. The delicious give of her ass against his belly with each thrust, the damp heat of her skin against his, added to the sensory overload he was fast approaching.

He leaned back over her and pressed his cheek against hers, using her hair to steer her head so he could snatch away another hot, wet kiss. Her face was slack with passion, eyes shut tight, harsh breath drawn in past parted lips.

"Look at me, Cassie," he growled, and her eyes fluttered open. She waited for him, expectant, patient, wanting his instructions for what to do next. Oh, she was a good girl. She deserved a reward.

"Come." No sooner is the command spoken than she was climaxing, her body writhing as best it could under the heavy press of him over her, hoarse cries breaking from her. Inside, she was burning-hot, strangling-tight, and a fresh burst of wetness from her flowed down over his tight, aching balls.

His own orgasm was building, with the telltale tightening in the small of his back, and with his free hand he smacked her ass again. His other hand moved from her head to her throat, wrapping around it lightly, and then not-so-lightly, not gripping, not hurting– never hurting– but enough to make sure she knew who had her, was fucking her, *owned* her.

"That was good, Cassie," he purred, "but I think you can do it again." And he slapped her ass a third time, harder than the previous two.

She *howled*, obediently coming again, lurching so hard that he had to wrap an arm around her waist to keep her from thrashing away from him. Restraining her so tightly to himself dissolved the last cords of control he'd scraped together; his own climax hit him like a truck, fireworks bursting behind his eyes, his hips flying against hers in a blur.

He kept thrusting for a long time after they were done coming, unable to resist coaxing the last few drops of ecstasy from each of them, until her whimpers turned uncomfortable instead of passionate. He slid free of the slick grasp of her body and sank to the side, the bed's blissful comfort receiving him when his pleasure-flooded muscles finally gave out.

Cassie collapsed on the other side, limp as an overcooked noodle. Sweat made her skin gleam, even in the low light, and the sight reminded him of the need to get up, get a cool damp cloth so she could clean up, but... it could wait a minute. He pulled her body against his, dropping a kiss on her shoulder.

"Thank you," he murmured, because she had so generously given him what he asked for.

"Not needed," she mumbled back, face smooshed in the pillow. "I told you I wanted it, wanted all of you."

He kissed her cheek, relishing the downy softness of it against his sensitive lips. "Yes, you did, *cara mia*. Now, sleep."

Her breath deepened, evened out, and her limbs went lax. Dante took inventory of his own body and found it devoid of any tension anywhere, utterly limp in satisfaction.

His world outside that room might not be exactly as he wanted it, and he had an enemy he couldn't name coming for his family, but here, now, it was good. He was pleased.

In the intervening weeks, nothing had improved with the supply chain of their drugs; in fact, things had gotten worse. Over the last six weeks, four of the seven shipments had either been seized by police or hijacked.

The hijackings were concerning, because now their superior product was on the street, but with dealers that weren't theirs. The family was hemorrhaging money, and they still didn't know who was making it happen. For right now, the clubs and their legitimate businesses were keeping them afloat, but it couldn't be sustained for much longer.

Dante sat back in his chair, elbow on its arm, cheek propped on his fist, and thought. He might not have a college and law school education like Elias, but he was just as smart, more intuitive in his way. There had to be a reason for what was happening, and there had to be an equal solution for it. He just had to find it.

A knock on his door pulled him from his ruminations. "Come in," he said absently, still contemplating how the hijackers were succeeding in spite of their heavily guarded shipments.

"Hey." Cassie's small smile was a welcome break from his relentless search for answers.

"Come here," he directed. She rounded the desk and he pulled her into his lap before dropping a kiss on her lips.

"I missed you," Cassie murmured against his neck.

"You're the one who said you had to go home and be with Lucy," he teased, and squeezed her around the waist. Her presence, her touch, was relaxing him with a swiftness, a thoroughness, no one else had ever been able to achieve, and he wasn't ready to examine how it was possible. Not yet.

"You want to eat together later?" she asked.

He shook his head. "No, I've got a meeting with the managers." He had not yet shared with her the truth of what was occurring with the shipments, and he wasn't sure why not. Maybe on some level, he thought that if he didn't tell her about the danger, it couldn't touch her. That, too, was something he was not prepared to examine.

"Okay," she said easily, and with a final smacking kiss, slid off his lap. "I need to get through last month's orders tonight. I'm hoping that will help me pinpoint where the discrepancy is."

Cassie had found a large gap between the amount of liquor they ordered versus the number of drinks they sold. Someone– or several someones– were robbing him blind. Cassie hadn't figured out who, yet, but he had no doubt she would.

"Come home with me tonight?" This meeting hadn't even started yet and he was already on edge. A night with Cassie would go far in alleviating that.

"Of course." She smiled on her way out of the office.

"So that's the lovely Cassie?" said a voice almost as familiar to him as his own. His father walked into the office without knocking. Anyone else would have been reminded of their place, but... Dante may be his father's boss, but he would always be Luciano's son.

"Hey, Papa." Dante stood and hugged his old man. It was starting to become a more literal description, 'old man,' since his age had begun to show in the form of lines around his eyes and mouth, and liberal amounts of gray streaking his once jet-black hair. "Aren't we supposed to meet in a half hour?"

Dante resumed his seat behind his ornate desk, and his father dropped into one of the chairs on the other side of it.

"Yes, but I was hoping for a moment alone with you, to talk about what's going on." Then his father grinned. "And maybe I wanted to catch a glimpse at the woman who seems to have caught your attention."

Luciano di Ruggiero was a murderer, a professional hit man, a mobster from birth, as dangerous as they came, and rightly feared by many. But to Dante, he was just his father. Was it strange, to other people, that such a man could at the same time be a fond, doting parent?

"Who says she's caught my attention?" he said, deciding to play it cool.

"You tryin' that with me? I recognize the look on your face." His father grinned wider. "I *gave* you the look on your face."

His father always loved to gross out his sons with references to their conceptions. It was just as funny now as it ever had been— as in, not funny at all. Dante just barely kept from rolling his eyes. "What look?" he asked instead.

"Stupid, like you've been hit with a brick," his father replied promptly. "I wore the same stupid look the entire time I was blessed with your mother's love, may God rest her soul."

Luciano di Ruggerio's love for his wife, Marissa, was legendary, like something out of a fairytale. He adored her to the point of obsession, an obsession that lingered even years after her murder.

"It's not the same," Dante argued. He didn't love Cassie, not like his father loved his mother. Probably no one loved anyone like that. No, Dante wanted Cassie. He liked her, desired her, enjoyed her, but those were the best he could do.

"If you say so, son," his father said with a laugh.

Before Dante could reply, the door to his office opened again, revealing his two youngest brothers.

"Matty, Marco." Dante stood to welcome them, gesturing for them all to move to the larger table to the side, around which were eight chairs. Four more men arrived after that, the lieutenants who helped run his organization, and they got down to business.

"I've called you all here tonight because our problems have gotten worse," he began, surveying his men.

Tony had been with them for years, since Dante's grandfather, and was as loyal as they came. The same could be said for David; he had run the clubs and the drug routes under *Nonno* for years. He doubted it was either of them. They'd been tested repeatedly and never failed to prove they were body-and-soul loyal to the family.

That left Juan, Mikey, and Gino. Dante had brought them up from lower levels in the organization, all three smart and hungry, and Dante wondered which one– or more than one– was betraying him.

"Another shipment was hijacked two days ago–" he started, but the door to his office burst open. His temper, already primed from his father's teasing, descended a notch, from 'mediocre' to 'poor'.

Cassie was there, her expression anxious. "Dante–"

He tamped ruthlessly on the anger that arose. What the fuck was she doing? She knew better than to interrupt, especially without knocking and waiting for permission to enter.

"Cassie, I'm in a meeting," he said through gritted teeth and turned back to his men, expecting her to leave, but instead she stepped deeper into the office. "I'll talk to you later. Leave."

"Dante, please, it's important," she begged, her hands grasping at his arm.

Disbelieving at her behavior, he shook himself free. "Cassandra, I told you to go. I'll call you later."

"No, Dante, please, I just need a moment–" she protested.

A few of the men snickered and fury built in him, warring with disappointment. He'd thought she understood how to behave, especially as his woman; that she comprehended her role, her need to be deferent, to respect his business, to not make him look bad. He could afford no weakness, no fragile opening through which an enemy could thrust the tip of a spear in hopes of taking him down. To be seen catering to a wild-eyed female could be deadly to his reputation. He took her arm in a bruising grip and pulled her out of his office.

"Dante, please, just listen," she said, but he was already hauling her down the stairs to where he knew Manny was eating dinner.

"Cassie, enough," he hissed.

Manny stood up as they approached his small table in the corner of the club.

"Manny, please take Cassie home." His voice was clipped and hard.

"Dante, it's important! Please!"

He ignored her. "Manny, take her home *now*, to my apartment." He turned back to Cassie. She stared back, imploring. "I will see you later."

Her tragic expression melted into stubbornness, and an anger that might match his own.

"Ms. Cassie?" Manny asked, and Cassie shot Dante one last withering look before she stomped out of the club.

Dante took a steadying breath before returning to his office. He needed to be his most observant and Cassie barging in, demanding his attention in the middle of a meeting, undermined not only how his men saw him, but tanked his concentration.

"Energetic girl," Papa commented from the hallway in front of Dante's office as he approached.

"Not usually, she's not," Dante muttered. Her outburst had been very out-of-character for Cassie.

Dante's father's look turned thoughtful. "Well, what did she need?"

"I don't know. I sent her home."

Luciano laughed and shook his head and squeezed his son's shoulder. "Oh, *figlio mio*, you have a lot to learn."

Dante scowled, not in the mood for more teasing or any enigmatic words of wisdom. "What do you mean?"

"Just that if she's not usually like that, maybe you should've listened to her, is all." Luciano shrugged, clapping his eldest son on the shoulder, and disappeared into Dante's office, leaving Dante questioning his actions with Cassie.

He rubbed the back of his neck, trying to lessen the tension solidifying the muscles there into iron knots. One of the reasons he'd delayed finding a woman was because he only had so many mental resources, and most of them were occupied in running a multi-million-dollar operation spanning two countries, two families, and hundreds of employees, while navigating the tricky matter of most of it being extremely illegal. He didn't have the energy or patience for the drama that women brought into a man's life. They had never seemed worth the bother.

Cassie is worth the bother, mocked a tiny voice in the deepest recesses of his brain.

Maybe she was. But he didn't have the time to spare in figuring it out, not at the moment. All his faculties had to be directed toward solving the question of who was trying to bring down the di Ruggieros. Nothing else could matter to him, not now.

If Cassie were the right woman for him, she'd understand that. If she couldn't... well, maybe that was fate trying to tell him something.

CHAPTER

NINETEEN

CASSIE

Manny pulled up to Dante's building, and Cassie had no way to get inside. Things just were not going her way, that night.

"I don't have a key for the elevator," she told the driver with a sigh.

"Oh, that's okay, Ms. Cassie. Mr. Dante keeps a spare in the car." He reached into the glove compartment and pulled out an electronic key.

"Thank you, Manny." She reached for her purse and she realized that it, and her phone, were still in her office at the club. It only stoked her anger and irritation.

"Manny, can you do me a favor?" she asked, surprised at how normal her voice sounded. She felt on the verge of furious tears, her throat tightening almost painfully.

"Of course I can!" Manny said cheerfully. He was a good guy, Manny, like most of the people she had met who worked for Dante.

"I left my purse in my office at the club. When you bring Dante home, will you grab it for me?"

"Yes, of course," he replied, nodding.

She forced a weak smile at Manny and exited the car, making her way to the elevator without seeing much of her surroundings. Why had Dante wanted her to go to his place? He was obviously angry with her, and she was just as angry with him. She'd have thought he would send her to her own apartment, not wanting to even look at her any time too soon. She knew she wasn't too eager to see his face for a while, herself. But Dante's mind worked in mysterious ways, she'd learned. It was pointless to try to understand his motives about anything.

She opened his apartment door and stood for a moment in the foyer. It was odd, being there without him. It spoke of Dante, of his power, his wealth, his influence, but also his personality: everything was of the finest caliber but understated, no loud colors or funky pieces that drew attention. It was all quiet, solid, and very, very dark. Just like him.

Cassie didn't bother to turn on the lights as she made her way to the large window that dominated the space. Ambient light from the surrounding city illuminated the space well enough for her to navigate around the furniture without bumping into anything. She sat in one of the two large, ornate chairs that centered his living room. Dante had told her about them, when she'd inquired. They had belonged to Dante's grandparents, upholstered in peach velvet, with gilded arms and legs, and were the only things that didn't suit Dante's typical sleek aesthetic.

It was silly, but sitting in the chair made her feel closer, not just to Dante, but to being a part of his world, his family. She didn't know if she'd ever be that, in truth, and after their altercation earlier, it seemed less likely than ever.

As she sat there, her anger slowly melted into a sort of sad frustration at how things had occurred earlier. She could recognize her part in it, her mistake, to interrupt the meeting and make Dante look amusing to men who needed to respect and fear him. But she was hurt at how easily he'd dismissed her, that he didn't think enough of her to know she wouldn't have done it without a damned good reason, that he wouldn't even give her a moment to explain.

Did he truly think she was so stupid or irresponsible that she'd interrupt his meeting for no reason? He himself had impressed upon her the importance of learning the identity of the traitor within their midst... and she had. She had, and she'd gone right to Dante so he could have his meeting with the knowledge he needed. And instead of trusting her to have a valid reason to interrupt him, he'd dismissed her like an unruly child, sending her off to stew in the corner until he felt she'd done sufficient penance.

Well, she was stewing, alright. She stewed and stared blindly out the window, wondering if she'd done much harm to his image with her barging in, but also if his saving face in front of the men was worth not having the information she'd wanted to give him. Now, an hour after it had happened, she could see past the faded red haze of her anger to how risky a life he led, and how essential it was to appear completely and totally in control of everything at all times. If anyone got the slightest inkling that Dante might have a weakness, it could topple the entire precariously-perched empire his family had built over the course of generations.

And it would have been her fault.

A thrill of fear jittered up her spine, and her hand twitched toward the phone she only belatedly realized was not there. A need to know what had happened after her hasty departure grew until she couldn't contain it sitting down any longer, jumping from the chair to pace around.

After a while of that, she settled down and sat in the chair again. It really was comfortable, for all that it was 50 years out of style. She stroked the soft, aged velvet, and thought about the discovery she'd made.

The mole was Juan, the bartender, and it solved the mystery of why he'd been apprehensive to meet her, back when she'd taken over the club's books. It hadn't been her imagination, he really had been uneasy with her, and it was because he'd suspected she'd learn what he'd been doing.

She didn't know if he were the mole informing Dante's competitors, but he was certainly the one fudging the numbers and stealing both alcohol and money from the club. He would be in the meeting, at best a thief and at worst an active risk to the organization, and Dante was presumably divulging more sensitive information to him because she hadn't been able to reveal Juan's true motives.

A last feeble flash of annoyance went through her before winking out, as she sat there in his dark apartment, staring at the city lights of Dallas below. There was no point in anger; Dante was who he was, and his world was what it was. Justified or not, her interruption had made him look bad. The people he dealt with would not care about that justification.

She wasn't sure how long she sat there, mulling over what she'd learned, what she didn't know, and what could have gone wrong because Dante wouldn't let her speak. The traffic far below had slowed to a trickle, and the lights in many of the buildings had winked out, when finally she heard the door open, twisting in the chair to look back at who it was... though she already knew.

"Cassie?" Dante called out. Standing in the pool of light thrown by the chandelier over the door, he was limned in gold, looking ironically angelic.

"Here," she answered, twisting back around to face the windows once more.

It didn't take him long to find her.

"Why are you sitting in the dark?" He switched on a light, its sudden brightness making her flinch a little. He turned the switch again and it dimmed considerably, imparting only a faint glow to the room, and she lowered the hand she'd raised to protect her eyes from the glare.

Dante set her little black purse on the table at her elbow. "Thanks," she murmured. He nodded in return. "I was just thinking," she began. Might as well get it over with. Important things first.

He squatted down in front of her, his hands warm on her thighs. His face being on a level with hers, as she sat, gave her a perfect view of his elegant bone structure, the harmonious way all the angles fit together to create such a handsome man. Even when she was upset with him, he still stirred her as no other had... or probably ever could.

"About tonight," she began.

"Look, Cassie–" Dante interjected, but she touched her fingertips to his lips, silencing him.

"I'm sorry, Dante. I shouldn't have burst into your meeting, I know that. But I figured out who was skimming, and wanted to let you know right away."

His eyes widened and she could see the emotions flickering in them as he processed both of her revelations: the reason she'd interrupted the meeting, and that the mystery of who had been stealing from him was solved.

"Who?"

"Juan."

"Fuck." Dante stood with a curse and dug out his phone, stepping towards the window. She could see tension grow in his body, much like it had at the club when he hauled her out of his office, but this time it wasn't directed at her, and perversely she felt all the tension *she* had been carrying drain away.

"Marco?" Dante said, his voice cold and hard. "I need you to bring me Juan."

This was a Dante she hadn't seen yet, the mafia *don*. Gone was the Dante who had her drink juice to hydrate after an intense lovemaking session; nowhere to be seen was the Dante who worried about the lack of security at her building. In their place was a killer, pure and simple. He might not pull the trigger himself– though he was by no means incapable of it– but he was the one who commanded the deed be done.

"No, not at the club," Dante replied into the phone. He glanced at her over his shoulder for a moment and then turned back to gaze out the window. "We'll need more privacy."

Cassie wondered how much would be talk and how much would

be interrogation. She expected to feel sympathy for what awaited Juan, an understanding of how a person could make foolish choices when they were in need of money, but she felt none. He had betrayed Dante, who had treated him far better than any other club owner in Dallas would have, and whatever punishment he received for that betrayal, Juan deserved it.

"Call me when you've found him and I'll join you." Dante disconnected the call and turned to her. "I owe you an apology," Dante started and she waited, because he did. "I'm sorry, Cassie, I should've–"

"It's okay," she interrupted, standing and going to him, taking his hands in hers. "I should've found a better way to tell you. I was just so worried that you would give him information that could hurt you, but I should've found a differemmmmf."

He stopped her rambling with a kiss, his arms pulling her against his body.

"No, Cassie." He cupped her face in his hands. "I should've listened to you, should've trusted that you had something important to say. That what you were saying, how you were acting, was because you needed me to listen to you. Because you have my best interests at heart." He kissed her again, deep and tender, breaking free something inside that had been trying to get out for weeks.

"I love you," she whispered against his lips. He needed to know.

She didn't know what she thought he'd do in reaction. Probably not a similarly impassioned declaration, but certainly not physical withdrawal: he retracted his arms from around her and stepped back, out of the circle of light thrown by the lamp, into the shadows.

"Cassie," he said, then stopped. His voice was odd; gone was the warmth and desire she'd come to expect when he spoke to her. In its place was a detached, neutral, almost clinical tone, like he directed at the employees of the club. The *other* employees, rather. She was one of them, herself.

So, she had misread his actions, his words, the way he touched her, the way they made lo– had sex. The relationship between them had been built up in her mind to be something it wasn't.

He kept talking, each word a blow on her heart.

"It's not you," he was saying. "I can't love you, not in the way you want, not the kind of love my mother and father shared, or how my brother Elias loves his wife. I'm not capable of it."

His eyes searched hers, almost pleading for her to understand, and it felt weirdly like he was sharing more of himself with her in that moment than he ever had when they were in bed. He was baring himself, his soul, to her, begging her not to reject it.

"I can't promise you love, but I can promise you fidelity." He stepped back into the light. There was an earnestness on his face she'd never seen before, and it took her breath away. "I will be as loyal to you as you have proven you are to me. I will take care of you. Anything you want or need– that's within my power to give– will be yours."

She couldn't have stopped the smile that spread across her face, even if she tried. "But, Dante, isn't that love?" she asked, very gently, because that was what it sounded like to her. What else was love, but loyalty and care and sharing? That was what her experience of it had been to that point. What else could there be?

"I don't think so," he replied, sounding confused. "That's not what has been demanded of me before."

She leaned up and pressed a kiss to his lips. "Dante, will you continue to treat me as well as you always have? *Not* including earlier tonight, that is?"

"Of course," he replied automatically.

"You won't lie? You won't make promises you can't or won't keep?" She'd had empty words from her mother and even from Amber most of her life. What Dante gave her fulfilled her more than anyone's empty words ever could.

He frowned, looking insulted she'd even ask, and opened his mouth to reply, but his phone rang instead. He snatched it up and accepted the call.

"Marco." His eyes widened at what he heard. "What do you mean *gone*? Fuck! No, put ears to the ground. He probably knew when Cassie came into the office like that." He looked at her and the corners of his mouth twitched up just a little. "I should have listened to her. Not a mistake I will repeat." With a few quick words more to his brother, he was off the phone.

"What's wrong?" she asked, though she had an idea.

"Juan is missing," he growled. "He probably hit the road right after the meeting ended."

"I'm sorry, Dante." She should have been more persistent, even when he was adamant about refusing to hear her out.

"It's my fault, not yours," he told her with a sigh, reeling her back into his arms. "We'll find him, I promise you that. No one steals from me." He moved to kiss her, but she put her hand on his chest in a feeble attempt to stop him.

"Dante, I need to go home," she said, moaning when his persistent lips found a particularly sensitive spot on her neck.

"You know, if you moved in here, you wouldn't have to go home all the time," he mumbled against her skin.

"What— ahhh, what about Lucy?" She leaned her head to the side, granting his wicked lips more access to her neck, letting herself get lost in the feelings he stirred in her body, her mind, her heart.

"I assumed you two were a package deal," he teased. "I'll talk with the building concierge about their dog services. They're state-of-the-art, I've heard. Lucy will be treated like a princess."

He kissed his way up neck and used his teeth to tug on her earlobe.

"Well?" he probed when she didn't answer.

"You didn't actually ask me anything," Cassie replied pertly. She was capable of teasing him, too.

He heaved a put-upon sigh. "Cassie, will you and Lucy please move in with me?"

"Of course," she told him, sliding her arms around his neck and going up on tiptoe as his hands found her waist. "You only had to ask."

That must've been the right answer, because the kiss that followed made her toes curl. For the next few hours, nothing else existed, not Juan, not Amber, nothing. All that mattered was them: Cassie and Dante. Together.

CHAPTER

TWENTY

Three days later, Juan was still in the wind, nowhere to be found.

"You're telling me he has just disappeared without a trace." Dante paced his office. Marco, Matty and Tony sat around the table and watched his movement: past his desk, around the table, past his desk, along the bank of windows, past his desk...

"So it would seem," Marco said with a grin.

"Dammit, Marco, it's not funny." Dante whirled around on his brother who threw up his hands in mock surrender, but his eyes were still gleaming with mirth.

"Well, if you had just listened to Cassie..." Matty trailed off.

Dante sat back down in his chair. "I know. Trust me, I know." He pinched the bridge of his nose and sighed.

"We'll keep looking, boss," Tony injected between the brothers, as the phone began to ring.

Dante nodded grimly and took the call.

"Dante! How are you, *mi'jito?* How are your brothers?" Dante was surprised to hear his grandfather's voice; they had a scheduled call the next day, about a shipment due in, and his grandfather rarely deviated from the schedule.

"I'm doing good, as is everyone else, *welo*. How are things on the ranch?"

"Aye, you know it is. The rats are horrible this time of year." Dante sat up and put the phone on speaker.

"*Welo*, I'm in my office with Marco, Matty and Tony. I know they want to hear about your rat problem. We had a rat here in the club, but it got away."

"That's a shame, *mi'jito*. You've got to nip the problem in the bud before they breed and spread disease."

Dante made eye contact with Marco, knowing what that meant. "Were you able to get your rats under control?"

"Of course. This is nothing new. It happens. Unfortunately, I'm afraid they got into some boxes I was going to send you. Just make sure that when you get them, nothing is lurking about." Dante let the coded words seep in: their shipment in two days was compromised.

"Do you think it will be stopped at the post office?" Dante wanted to know if the shipment was going to be seized or hijacked.

"Oh, I don't think it's anything like that, but I'm afraid some rat droppings might be on the gifts."

Marco mouthed the word 'hijack' and Dante nodded in agreement.

"Well, I'm sure it will still be wonderful, whatever it is," he said.

"Of course, *mi'jito*. You know I'd never send you anything but the best," their grandfather said with a chuckle. "Call me when you get my package and tell me if you like it. If you don't, I can send you something else, this time safe from *las ratas*. Your package will arrive on Thursday, so be sure to check the mail." Without farewell, he hung up.

"So, hijacking?" Marco asked.

Dante nodded. "Sounds like it. *Welo* wouldn't give us bad information. The truck will be hijacked on Thursday, probably just like the others, when the trucks stop to refuel after crossing the border,"

"Where is the next truck supposed to enter from?" Tony asked.

"Reynosa, so the driver won't stop until he's passed the Falfurrias checkpoint... that would be where? A truck-stop in Alice?" Dante asked Matty, who shook his head.

"No, our guys don't stop in Alice. Too busy, too much oilfield traffic. They go to a truck stop in Premont. Smaller. No police presence."

Dante leaned back in his chair, thinking. They needed to catch who was doing the hijacking on this side of the border, find out what they knew. Who they were working for.

"What're we gonna do?" asked Matty.

"We are going to lay a trap, baby brother; bait the rats with some cheese, and get rid of this infestation once and for all."

Dante smiled and tapped his fingers on the leather arm of his chair. For the first time in months he felt like he wasn't shooting at noises in the dark, but like he might actually get a leg up on their foe.

Dante spent the entire night before they headed south with Cassie. He took her to dinner and then home, to his bed. Losing himself in her, in her skin, her hair, her scent and feel and taste, it was the only true respite he had from all the pressure, and she never denied his needs.

Oh, there had been a few things she hadn't liked. The first time he tied her to the bed, blindfolded, she had used her safe word and told him that she couldn't have two senses restricted, and he understood. He enjoyed looking in her eyes when they fucked, anyway. But in all the ways that mattered, she was exactly what he needed, and what was more, he was what she needed as well. They fit.

"Penny for your thoughts." His father's voice interrupted Dante's thoughts as they traversed the countryside in the SUV, Luciano at the wheel.

"I'm not sure they're worth that much," Dante answered, gaze upon the sprawling ranches and farmland that made up most of Texas between its cities and towns as they drove south.

"Oh, I have no doubt they're worth at least a penny, son."

Dante rolled his head on the headrest and looked at his father. "When did you know you were going to marry Mama?" That was the primary issue on his mind. He even had a ring burning a hole in his pocket– well, in his safe at the club– but something was holding him back.

"The first night I met her," his father answered promptly, without a hint of humor or exaggeration.

"Bullshit," Dante said with a laugh. Dante knew his mother had been engaged to another man when they first met. There was no way Luciano di Ruggiero had decided an unattainable woman would be his wife.

"No bullshit, Dante. I saw her across a smoke-filled wedding reception in Nuevo Laredo. She was laughing at something her sister had said. She tossed back her head and laughed, and I just stared. She was the most beautiful thing I had ever seen. Her long hair was pinned in a sleek updo and she had on this god-awful puffy pink bridesmaid dress that only the '80s could vomit up. I took one look and knew she would be the mother of my children.

"Then later, her father– the man I was supposed to be impressing, by killing his rival that weekend– introduced us. When I kissed the back of her hand, it was like a lightning strike. Something electric and profound. And she felt it, too."

Luciano took his eyes off the road for a moment and grinned at Dante in a way he hadn't seen since his mother had been murdered.

"And I *really* knew it later that night, when she let me fuck her in a janitor's closet."

Dante choked on the water he had just swallowed. "What! Mama always said it was a kiss, that she kissed you at the wedding,"

"Yeah, well, you boys got the sanitized version growing up. It was way more than a kiss." Luciano had the audacity to wink at him and Dante only just stopped himself from rolling his eyes. He wasn't fourteen anymore, though it was easy to feel that way in the presence of his father.

"A week later, her engagement was called off. A week and many phone calls after that, we were engaged, and married a month later. No huge wedding, like the one where I met her, but still in a church. And then, in the eyes of God and man, she was mine..."

His father trailed off, his voice growing wistful, a shattered grief vibrating along the words. Then Luciano cleared his throat, as though to swallow away unwanted emotions.

"Why all these questions, son?" His father glanced at him yet again, and Dante sighed.

"I want to propose to Cassie, but I'm concerned," Dante admitted. "Concerned about keeping her safe, about her knowing all my secrets."

Because as much as he had shared with Cassie, there were still things he was holding back. The longer he did so, the more he felt like he was lying to her, and he didn't want that. He didn't want them to start their life together on dishonesty and betrayal.

"Dante, no one in the world is ever truly safe. Our life is more dangerous than if you were a high school football coach, sure, but this life also allows you to protect her better and provide her with more."

"It didn't protect Mama," he said, and was shocked when his father laughed. That was *not* the reaction he had expected.

"Because your mother was who she was. I begged her to take security, but she refused. The café was her time, and I didn't argue. Your mother wasn't a stupid woman, and she was neck deep in our business. She knew the risks, grew up with them. Cassie may not be exactly like your mother, but I can see the same strength in her, the same fire and devotion."

His father reached over and squeezed his forearm.

"Don't be afraid to trust her. Your greatest strength in this life is a good, strong woman. A woman who can help you become and stay the powerful man I know you will be. Don't let fear keep you from happiness, because we all die, Dante. It's how we choose to live that makes this shit-show bearable."

Dante absorbed his words in silence. It was true that Cassie didn't just please him and make him happy; she gave him the peace and acceptance that he craved. He needed her, it was just that simple, and he was selfish enough to keep her.

"Besides, I want grandkids, and Elias and Sam don't seem to be in any hurry," his father added, laughing, and Dante grinned. It always boiled down to legacy with his family, but he needed that, too. And there wasn't anyone he could imagine as his wife but Cassie. Anyone he wanted as the mother of his children but Cassie.

"You know, Papa, for once you might be right," Dante teased.

"Son, I'm always right," his father bantered right back, with the rakish grin that had won his wife's heart all those years earlier.

The plan they developed was for Marco to switch places with the truck driver right past the checkpoint. That Marco knew how to operate a big rig was news to Dante, but Marco just shrugged.

"I wanted to learn. I've been kinda obsessed with them since I was a kid. *Nonno* had one of the men teach me, and I got my license. Given what we do, it didn't seem like a bad skill to have."

Now that he mentioned it, Dante recalled their childhood, and how thrilled Marco had always been to get trucks of any sort for his birthday and Christmas. Perhaps in another life, where Marco could have chosen his profession instead of having one decided for him by the family, he could have indulged his fascination and become a long-haul driver.

But that was not the life they lived. In this life, Marco was nothing but a killer, like their father but even colder, somehow. Dante was glad, in a way, to see that his little brother still had that interest, had interest in anything at all, because sometimes he seemed almost robotic in how remote and expressionless he appeared.

"Well, lucky for us you did." Dante slapped him on the back.

So there they were, Dante with Tony in one car, Matty and his father in another, waiting and watching. It had just gone full dark for the night, only marginally cooler than the oppressive, sticky heat of the day.

Tony shifted in his seat for what had to have been the tenth time in almost as many minutes.

"You okay over there, Tony?" Dante asked, not taking his eyes off the truck.

"Yeah, boss, sorry. Just antsy." Tony settled down and Dante opened up his mouth to say something when a woman got out of a nearby beat-up pickup truck.

Not unusual in and of itself, but what was noteworthy was that she didn't go inside the store, instead making a beeline for the lot where the big rigs were parked. Dante picked up his binoculars and studied her. She was dressed in very brief, very tight shorts and an equally tiny top. She wasn't the first woman to walk her way over to the idling trucks to see if any of the men, cooped up in their cramped trucks for days or weeks on end, might be lonely, but there was something familiar about this woman.

"Oh, fuck!" Tony, who was also looking through his own set of binoculars, screeched next to him.

"What?" Dante didn't look away from the woman sauntering over to the rig Marco was in.

Before Tony could answer, Dante's phone rang. It was Marco's number. Dante answered and put his phone on mute. This was part of the plan: Marco would call him with the phone on speaker, and he and Tony would listen in for anything suspicious.

"Hey, honey, you looking for some company?" A female voice, sultry and flirtatious, issued from the speaker of Dante's phone.

"Sure. What's your name, beautiful?" Marco asked.

"I'm Amber," she cooed.

Dante looked at Tony, eyes widening. "That's Cassie's sister, right?" Tony nodded. "And her little boyfriend that 'lost' the $15,000 was part of Juan's crew, wasn't he?"

Tony simply nodded again. The extent of Juan's duplicity to the family was becoming clearer and clearer.

"Why don't we leave the lot? It's a little bright, don't you think? I know a back road that's a lot more private." Amber's voice was sweet and light, a perfect example of guileless temptation.

She was good, he had to give her that. A faint pang of dismay for Cassie went through him. She'd be sad to learn what her sister was up to. He made a mental note to try to keep the extent of it from her. No need to upset her needlessly.

In the big rig, Marco agreed to drive to that back road. Dante nodded to Tony, who sent a text to Luciano and Matty, telling them to be ready– this was it.

The semi they were following was bright yellow, garish but effective for keeping track of in the night. Marco steered it out of the truck stop and turned down the local road, away from the highway.

This part of south Texas was desolate, surrounded by hundreds of thousands of acres of ranch land with only cows and wild animals for company. Dante waited a few beats so it wasn't obvious he was following them, then pulled out of the truck stop, pursuing the truck from a reasonable distance away.

Besides being an eye-searing yellow color, the rig itself had a GPS tracker, which had been disabled after the hijacking occurred. They'd turned it back on for this covert mission, however. Sure enough, the GPS showed the truck turning off of the main road, down a smaller ranch road, and then stopped.

"Isn't this better?" Amber's voice could be heard once again. The air brakes released, a telltale noise signaling the truck would be stopped for a while. "Now, what do you like, handsome?"

"I don't know. What do you like to do?" Marco asked and was answered with Amber's throaty laughter.

"With a man as hot as you, I like it aaaall," she drawled.

There was some rustling and shifting, the creaking of plastic upholstery and the whisper of fabric.

"It's a shame I can't actually do anything fun with you, handsome." When she spoke again, her voice was different, colder and lacking the coquettishness of earlier.

"Do you want my wallet? It doesn't have much cash, but you don't have to put a knife to my throat to get my money, beautiful." Marco was stalling, waiting for them to arrive.

Dante killed the lights of his SUV as he turned down the ranch road, the GPS tracker telling him the truck was only half a mile away.

"Oh, I don't want your cash, handsome." One of the rig's doors opened. "I want your truck."

"More importantly, we want the load you're carrying," said a male voice, one Dante recognized. That voice... it was Juan.

Then a gun cocked.

Dante pulled the car up to the rig, slamming it into park before jumping out, Tony on his heels. He was on Juan, his arm around his neck in a bruising chokehold, before the man even got a good-enough look at Marco to recognize him. The idiot dropped his gun and Tony quickly scooped it up. Juan gave up right away, his body falling limp in Dante's grip.

"Aww, Juan, I was hoping you would put up more of a fight than this," Dante seethed as his father and Matty, just arrived, strolled up to the scene.

Amber leaped from the truck and tried to run away but Matty went after her and was much faster, hauling her back none-too-gently by one skinny arm, unconcerned with how she struggled and dug her nails into his hand to make him release her.

"It's just the two of them," Dante's father said as he pulled some plastic zip ties from his back pocket. With the negligent ease of someone who has done it a hundred times, he secured Juan, then peeled Amber's claws from Matty and cuffed her as well.

"Let's get these two back to Dallas." Dante shoved Juan at Tony, who caught him roughly by the elbow and jerked him to a stop. "And this shipment to where it needs to go."

They got their captives into the SUVs, one in each so there was a man free to watch them while the other drove. Amber, in with Dante and Tony, wasn't putting up a fight. All the energy seemed to have gone out of her, and she sat limply against the seat, staring blindly out the window at the night, beautiful face expressionless.

They drove to a small private airfield. From there, Dante, Tony, and Luciano would fly with Amber and Juan to Dallas. They would deal with the would-be thieves while Matty and Marco got the truck where it needed to be.

"What are you going to do about the girl?" his father asked once they settled in the back of the plane with their two 'guests' blindfolded, gagged, and handcuffed to their seats a few rows in front of them.

"I have to tell Cassie what she did," Dante replied. "And what I'm going to do to her. I can't have a threat like her interfering with my family, but... how do I kill the sister of the woman I'm planning to marry? And how do I explain that to Cassie?" It seemed like an unsolvable dilemma.

"You protect the family the best you can," his father answered with a cryptic non-answer, typical for him. "And Cassie is family, Dante, or as good as. Remember that, no matter what you decide."

"How much do you think she knows?"

Luciano shrugged. "I don't know. I know she wasn't the mastermind behind this– she was Juan's pawn, just as Juan is someone else's pawn... but he's our captive, now." His grin was terrifying.

This was the part of the life his father enjoyed. Wet work, they called it. Dante tolerated it, knowing it was needed, and he didn't cry when a problem was eliminated, but he didn't enjoy it, either, not like his father or Marco, who seemed to thrive as the family's next generation of hit man.

Dante leaned his head back, closing his eyes. For the first time in his life, he was worried that something he considered his... wouldn't stay his.

CHAPTER

TWENTY- ONE

CASSIE

Cassie had been a total mess the two-and-a-half days Dante had been gone. He had shown up at her work, much to the delight of Tiffany and her coworkers, with an offer to take her to lunch. Cassie knew by the look in his eye and the tightness in his smile, however, that he wasn't just popping in to see her.

"What's wrong?" she asked the second they were alone in the car.

"We have a lead on Juan. I need to go out of town for a few days."

A cold dread fell over Cassie. Her first inclination was to beg him to stay behind and let the others handle it, to be safe at home with her, but she knew he wouldn't. He wasn't the type of man who let his employees venture into danger while he stayed home, comfortable and out of harm's way. It was one of the things she loved about him, in fact.

"Okay," she whispered, staring at her hands folded tightly in her lap, trying to keep her fear and worry at bay. They hadn't even left the parking lot yet.

"Cassie?" His hand cupped her cheek and coaxed her to meet his eyes.

"Yes?"

His eyes were a warm, molten bronze where the sunlight glanced off them. "I need your help while I'm out of town."

"Anything," she breathed, eager to prove her worth, to ease his burden... and if it happened to keep her busy so she didn't spend the whole time worrying about him, all the better.

"I need you and Miranda to manage things at the club. I'm taking Tony with me, and Juan would be the next person in charge. You don't have to do much, just make sure the place doesn't burn down while I'm gone."

He smiled at his little joke. She tried to smile back but it didn't work, her face wouldn't do what she told it. He sighed, leaning across the console and kissed her, his lips sweet and soft, and some of her anxiety melted away with that reassurance.

"Don't worry so much, *cara mia*. I'll be back before you know it," he murmured against her lips. "And I'm not going alone, Matty and Marco and our father will be there, too. I know what I'm doing. We all do."

She nodded. He was the farthest thing from reckless, and she'd never seen anything like the loyalty the di Ruggieros had for each other. With two of his brothers and their father along, there was little they couldn't withstand. This time, when she smiled, it was genuine.

She was entering purchase orders from a delivery two days later when Miranda knocked on her office door.

"Knock knock, boss." Miranda pushed open the door and entered the office, sitting in the lone chair next to Cassie's desk. "Working hard?"

Cassie nodded, attention remaining on the ledgers, engrossed in what she was doing.

"Cassie?"

"Hmmm?" Cassie acknowledged her friend without looking up.

"I just came up to tell you the main stage is on fire."

Cassie paused while that information filtered through her work-centered focus. Then, "What?"

"Finally," Miranda said, laughing as Cassie rubbed her eyes. "I came up here to see if you wanted some dinner. I know you've been here since six, and it's nearly midnight. I know you haven't eaten."

"I'm not hungry," she mumbled. It was true; the longer Dante was gone, the less inclination she had to eat.

"I don't care if you're not hungry," Miranda retorted. "Dante told me to keep an eye on you, and if you die from malnutrition, it will piss him off." She paused for effect, leaning in for some close eye contact. "And, Cassie, like all smart people in this city, I wake up every day with the main goal of *not* pissing off Dante di Ruggiero."

There was a knock at the door; Miranda stood and pushed Cassie's laptop closed.

"Hey!" Cassie protested weakly.

"Nope. Thirty-minute lunch break, mandatory." She opened the door to reveal two of the club's waitresses carrying trays laden with food.

"Thank you," Miranda said as the meals, chicken caesar salad and cold bottles of water, were placed on Cassie's desk. The sight of it roused Cassie's appetite and with surprising gusto, she dug in.

"So, how are you doing?" Miranda asked after a few minutes of silent eating.

"The club is doing well, now that we know what was wrong and eliminated it," Cassie said, dabbing her lips with a napkin. "I'm almost done implementing the new bookkeeping system."

"I didn't ask about the club, Cassie," Miranda said gently. "I asked how *you* were doing."

Cassie took a drink of her water and leaned back into her chair. "I'm okay," she said eventually. "I'm worried and I miss him, but I'm okay."

Miranda nodded, sympathetic, and rubbed her arm. "If you need me, just tell me."

"How's the crowd?" Cassie asked, changing the subject.

"Meh, it's okay. I've only made $900."

Cassie choked on her salad and looked at her watch. It was only ten minutes after midnight.

"You've only been on the floor three hours," Cassie exclaimed, still amazed at the money that the dancers made some nights.

"I had a regular come in who had been promising me a 'great night'," she used her well-manicured fingers for air quotes. "I even let him pick my outfit for the night. He comes in, I take him to the VIP room... and he only tips $30 above the minimum. I was annoyed."

"Well, the night is young, and it's not the weekend yet," Cassie said comfortingly, though internally she was still marveling over how blasé the other woman was about what Cassie considered huge sums of money.

Miranda smiled. "I like your optimism, my dear."

"I do, too," a deep voice said from the door.

"Dante!" Cassie shot up from her chair and launched herself into his arms.

"Hey, *cara mia*," he murmured into her hair, then kissed her temple. "Miranda," he said as he loosened his hold on Cassie. Her hungry gaze moved over him, taking a visual inventory.

There were no visible injuries, he wasn't holding himself or standing as if he were in pain... the tight band that had seemed to clench around her chest the last few days released with the proof that he was hale and whole and back with her again.

"Nice to have you back, boss." Miranda stood, taking her half-eaten meal and leaving the office.

As soon as the door closed, Dante was kissing her, his hands roaming her body, squeezing and grasping as if he would die if he couldn't touch her.

"I missed you," she whispered against his mouth.

"Mmmm, I missed you, too," he replied, but straightened and pulled away from her a little. "I need to talk to you." He sat down in her chair and pulled her into his lap.

"Did you find Juan?" she asked, concerned.

"Oh. Yes," he said, almost dismissively. That had her sense of foreboding spring to life. What else could have happened, if catching their thief merited such a bored response?

"What else, then?"

Dante chewed one corner of his mouth, clearly searching for the best words to describe what had occurred. Finally, he settled on, "Juan wasn't working alone."

"Someone else at the club?" she asked, paging through a mental list of any of the club's employees who Juan had treated preferentially.

"No, *cara mia*," he said softly, then pressed another kiss to her temple. He sighed. "He was working with Amber."

His words were a bucket of cold water tossed over her, shocking and unwelcome, making her suck in a breath as she struggled to absorb the news. She tried to stand, her first inclination to rescue her baby sister from danger yet again, but his arms were a band of steel holding her to his chest.

Cassie closed her eyes and made herself relax into him again, willing her rational mind to overcome her base instinct to protect Amber.

"Is she hurt?" she whispered, face pressed to his neck.

"She's jonesing for a hit of H, but she's okay," he answered, his words blunt but his tone soft. There was a tension in him that said the discussion wasn't yet over. What more could there be to say– oh.

Cassie wasn't stupid. Amber had helped Juan damage the organization. She knew the repercussions of such an act against a family like Dante's. Death was waiting for Juan, and now, the same fate was probably waiting for her sister. Amber had been stupid to play such a dangerous game with the di Ruggieros, not once but twice. Her sister had finally gone too far, getting herself neck-deep in a mess that Cassie could not extract her from.

If Cassie begged, Dante might spare Amber, maybe, but she would lose Dante if she made that request. There was no way he could run *la famiglia* and be merciful to those who acted against it. And he knew she knew it, how it worked, what the expectations were for him, how needful it was to maintain his fearsome image in order to command absolute respect and obedience.

This was her fork in the road. She knew it in her bones. She could once again try to save her sister, who would probably not change, and who would never go to the same lengths, make the same sacrifices, for Cassie the way Cassie had always done for her.

Or she could pick Dante, the flawed, dangerous man who would always be loyal to her if she was loyal to him, if she accepted him as he was, without trying to change him. The man she could build a life with... a life in a dark underworld empire, but a life. It was more than she'd ever had before. How could she give up her only opportunity for this kind of happiness? She knew it would never come again, that another man would not come again. Not like this, not like Dante.

She had given Amber chance after chances, and Amber had squandered them all. Cassie had lamented her sister's foolishness, her wasteful nonchalance at wasting the bounty the universe had granted her: beauty, charm, a sister who loved her. She could have gone so far, been so successful. Instead, she was an addict on the verge of execution for her crimes against the mafia.

Cassie now had a chance at happiness, and she wasn't going to repeat her sister's mistakes. She was not going to squander the bounty the universe had granted her: love– even if Dante insisted it wasn't– security, safety, family. A future. Contentment, at last, after being so long denied it.

To put it in terms her mathematical, business-oriented mind could best comprehend: Amber was a poor return-on-investment, but with Dante, she stood to gain a fortune.

Cassie swallowed against the lump in her throat as she processed her options, the repercussions of them, and made her decision.

She would choose Dante over Amber.

But she needed to say goodbye first. "Can I see her?" She opened her eyes and searched his. "Before you– before?"

"Of course, Cassie." He tucked a loose strand of hair behind her ear. " I'll take you to her now, if you'd like."

She nodded. "Yes, please."

One silent car ride later, Dante pulled up to a plain, nondescript house almost an hour outside of the city.

"Is Juan here, too?" she asked.

He shook his head. "No, *cara mia*, he's at another location with my father and Marco. In fact–" he paused, glancing at the dashboard for the time "–I need to leave you here and see what they've learned from him, but I thought you would want to see Amber."

She nodded gratefully and opened the car door, but Dante's hand on her arm stopped her from climbing out.

"Come here," he murmured and pulled her close, kissing her deeply, his lips caressing hers and his tongue stealing into her mouth. "I'll see you later."

" I've missed sleeping next to you, these last few days," she admitted.

"I've missed sleeping," he said with a laugh, then gave her a nudge toward the car door. "Tony and Matty are inside. Matty will take you home when you're done."

She walked to the boring little house in the middle of a boring little suburb. The grass was cut and there were even summer roses blooming along the porch. Who lived there? Or was it a place that the family kept for events like this? She rang the doorbell, and Matty opened it with his wide smile.

"Cassie! You're a sight for sore eyes." He stepped aside so she could enter, and gave her a big bear hug.

"Hi, Matty," she said, subdued, and patted his back till he released her.

"Did Dante fill you in?" he asked, his usually happy blue eyes dimmed.

"He just said that my sister was helping Juan, but no details."

He nodded and led her deeper into the house. As they passed the living room, Tony waved to her from the couch where he was watching TV, the telecaster describing how the Rangers had lost to the Astros that day.

"Rangers still sucking bathwater?" she asked, eager to postpone the conversation she was about to have with Amber, and Tony nodded.

"Yup, I'm gonna move to Houston and become an Astros fan," he grumbled. "At least they win."

She grinned. "That's blasphemy, Tony," she teased.

"True enough," he agreed. "I hate Houston. Smells funny."

They exchanged smiles and it occurred to her what a sea change had overcome them in the time since she had begun working at the club. She had hated Tony that first day, but she had grown to respect and even like the older man. He was good at his job and loyal to Dante, and that was most important to her.

But the task before her could not be delayed indefinitely. She took a deep breath and squared her shoulders. "Where is she?" she asked Matty.

His expression, usually so lively, was somber. He understood the gravity of what was about to happen between the sisters.

"Third door on the right," he replied quietly. "She's jonesing but not dope sick, yet."

Cassie made her way down the hallway and opened the door without knocking, unsurprised to find a disheveled and distraught Amber pacing the room.

"Cassie!" Amber ran to her, wrapping her in a frantic embrace, and Cassie did her best to memorize how it felt to be in her sister's arms. Amber's skin was clammy, her clothing damp with sweat even in the air-conditioned house, a symptom of her drug withdrawal.

Cassie had the bleak realization that since Amber's adolescence and throughout her adult life, Cassie really had only known addict Amber. She had never once been clean long enough since their foster parents died to just be an Amber unencumbered by addiction. The tragedy of it weighed heavily on Cassie's heart.

"Matty said you would come soon, he's much nicer than his thug brother– Marco– but not as hot. Still, the hotness doesn't make up for his attitude. Did you know that Marco sat with me for hours and never said a word? Not a single word. So frustrating." Her sister was rambling, from fear or withdrawal, Cassie didn't know. She just smiled and nodded and led her sister to sit on the rumpled bed that dominated the small bedroom.

Amber seemed to realize something had happened, with the lack of response on Cassie's part. She quieted for a moment, looking like she was processing facts. "Are you here to take me home?"

Cassie cupped her cheek in a trembling hand. "No, Amber, I'm not," she answered bluntly

Her sister shot up and began pacing again. "What do you mean, *no*? Cassie, I know Dante is fucking you, Juan told me." She paused in her pacing to run a disdainful glance over Cassie, then added, "Even though it's hard to see why."

"Hard to see?" Cassie tilted her head and watched her hollow-eyed, jittery, hostile sister, her only flesh and blood left in this world.

"Well, I mean... Cass, you know I love you, but... you're..."

"Yes, Amber? I'm what?" Cassie prodded, wanting to know what her sister really thought of her.

"Well, like– and don't take this the wrong way, but– you don't really do much with yourself, you know? And you're kind of, well, you don't party. You're... you're boring."

Amber must've seen something in Cassie's face, because she tried belatedly to cover her hurtful words with a smile. It was the same smile she always gave her sister, but Cassie saw the insincerity of it for the first time. How long had she been deluding herself about Amber, believing that there was a mutual love and respect between them?

"You're reliable and that's wonderful, but that's not what a man like Dante needs. Not really," Amber finished, a look of satisfaction on her face to have expressed herself well.

"How would you know what Dante needs? You know him that well?" Cassie asked, her voice light despite how, inside, she was fuming. She made pointed eye contact with her sister. "That's surprising to hear, because the only time he's mentioned you, it was to talk about the mess– messes– you've gotten yourself into."

Amber blinked, surprised dawning over her wan, but still lovely, features. "Oh... well, no, I don't know him at all, really," she stammered at first, but soon rallied, her self-confidence as resilient as ever. "But I know his kind, and they need someone a bit more confident. You know, sexy."

Two months ago, before Dante had proven that Cassie's appeal was plentiful if one cared to look for it, the cruelty edging Amber's smile would have made Cassie's stomach twist. Where was that resentment coming from? Had Cassie done something to make Amber feel this sort of antagonism towards her?

"Well, he doesn't seem to be complaining," Cassie replied dryly.

Amber studied her, her gaze cold and clear of the haze of withdrawal for a moment, seeming to be measuring which next move would be most beneficial to her. Like donning a new outfit, her stance and expression shifted, from haughty and contemptuous to warm enthusiasm. She flew back to the bed, sitting close to Cassie and grabbed her hands.

"That's great, Cass!" she burbled, face alight with hope. "That's so great! I mean, if he cares for you like you say, he's got to listen to you, right?"

She'd decided that browbeating Cassie into compliance was a no-go, so she was back to pleading and bargaining. Her mood swings– no, not mood swings, because they weren't shifts in genuine moods; they were only acts Amber was putting on, trying everything she could think of in desperation– were giving Cassie whiplash.

"I know he'll listen to what I have to say, because that's how good relationships work. They're a two-way street," Cassie said pointedly, but judging by her sister's manic smile, the undercurrent of the comment had missed its mark. Once again, Amber only saw what she wanted, and not the reality of the situation. Cassie would save her again, wouldn't she, because hadn't she always?

Cassie squeezed her sister's hands, then pulled away. She had done this so many times in their lives, had held Amber, had promised her everything would work out, that Cassie would fix the problem, she would make it better... and oh, how she had tried. She had done everything she could to save Amber from everyone who would hurt her, but the one person she couldn't save Amber from was herself.

"I love you, Amber," she said and stood.

"I love you too, Cassie!" Amber replied excitedly. "So you'll talk to Dante? Tell him I'll go back to that rehab." She dogged Cassie's steps to the door. "Or maybe a different one, they were really too much at that place." She laughed, high-pitched and a little crazed.

Goosebumps raced up Cassie's arms at the sound. She put her hand on the doorknob and closed her eyes to keep the tears from falling. It would be so easy to pick Amber, to fall back into comfortable old habits and the long-held identity of big-sister-riding-to-the-rescue. To ask Dante to betray what he stood for, betray his family to save hers, but she couldn't. She wouldn't.

For a moment she was back in that barren field, kneeling in the rock-strewn dirt, leaning into a burning car to save someone she couldn't save. Carol's words came to her again: "It's okay to let go, baby. I love you, and I know you love me. Save yourself. Move away, Cassie."

It was time for Cassie to move away from Amber, to keep from sacrificing her love, her future, for a sister who couldn't or wouldn't do the same for her.

"No, Amber," she said to the door, shoulders tense. "I won't."

"What? Cassie!" Amber screeched. "What do you mean?"

"I will tell him no such thing." Cassie turned and faced her sister for the last time. "I will not beg him to save you. I will not sacrifice anything for you anymore."

Amber's green eyes hardened, and then the person looking back wasn't her sister, at least not the sister Cassie had grown up with, the sister Cassie loved. No, this Amber was someone else entirely. Someone Cassie didn't know, someone who would steal drugs from a mafia drug cartel and somehow expect to survive anyway.

"Do you know who he is, Cassie? Do you know what he will do to me?" Amber demanded.

Cassie nodded. "I do know, yes."

"Cassie! I'm your sister! Your family! Please, *please* tell him." Amber threw her arms around Cassie's shoulders and squeezed tight. "Cassie, he will *kill* me," Amber whispered.

Cassie wondered if the shaking in her sister's body was withdrawal or fear. Did it matter? Either way, it was a symptom of Amber's foolishness and hubris. "I know," she replied.

Amber stilled in her arms and pulled away. "Then how can you–?"

"You betrayed the family, Amber, and you had to know the consequences of that," Cassie interrupted, a feeling of calm settling over her. She felt lighter than she had in years. Dumping the responsibility for saving her sister firmly on Amber's own shoulders, no longer bearing that burden for her, was like a mountain lifted from her.

"He's not *your* family, Cassandra," Amber growled. "I am."

Cassie shook her head. "He's done more for me, been better to me, in two months than you have in two decades. He's been a better family to me than you ever have." Amber jerked back as if she had slapped her, but Cassie forged on. "I'm choosing him. I will always choose him, because I know he would do the same for me. Just like I know you wouldn't."

The words fell between them like a portcullis slamming down, heavy, impassible. Cassie turned away, opened the door, paused. "Goodbye, Amber."

And just like that, it was over.

The walk back to the living room felt like she was leaving prison after a long sentence, finally served in full. Matty was at the end of the hallway, but she had no doubt he had heard at least some of it.

"You okay?" he asked, his words as soft and kind as the look on his face. She nodded quickly but couldn't get any words out. If she spoke, she risked falling apart entirely.

Matty pulled her into a quick but strong hug and then kept his arm slung over her shoulders as he walked her out of the house.

"Lock her in the room, Tony. I'm going to drive Cassie home, then I'll be back."

"Sure thing, Matty. Bye, Cassie."

She smiled fleetingly at Tony and let Matty lead her out to a car. Somehow, she held herself together until she got home to Dante's penthouse and the only soul to see her tears was Lucy.

CHAPTER

TWENTY- TWO

DANTE

Dante pulled up to the abandoned warehouse outside of the city where his father and Marco were holding Juan. A few of his most trusted men stood guard by the entrance. Dante nodded to the three that were on the door and went inside. The place was a dump, but that was irrelevant; he needed somewhere no one could hear Juan's screams as they interrogated him, not a showplace.

"Has he told you anything?" Dante asked as he approached Luciano, who was cleaning various tools laid out on a workbench. There were pliers and a couple of heavy wrenches, and his father was wiping down a small knife.

"Oh, he was very forthcoming when I started in on his fingers, but we only got to the good parts when Marco showed him a live feed of his three-year-old and his baby mama," Luciano answered, his tone matter-of-fact, like he was ticking off items on a to-do list.

"Did it have to go that far?" Dante didn't relish the idea of hurting a child; it was distasteful and the cruelty of it never garnered the kind of fear you really wanted to instill. But while it was a last resort, it was one that always had to be on the table, and if pushed, you sometimes had to follow through on threats.

"It did not. Juan is, thankfully, not that stupid... but he was also not very helpful." His father lit a cigarette and drew a long inhalation.

"What do you mean, not helpful?" Dante asked, eyeing the object of their conversation.

Juan was hanging in the middle of the shop from a steel beam, his head lolling to the side, barely conscious, struggling for each breath.

"He didn't know who hired him or who paid him," Luciano finally said. "It all came from an anonymous email. Marco got one of your tech guys on it, but they said something about the IPs being untraceable."

Dante swore under his breath. "How was he being paid?"

"Well, the first initial payments came from a wire transfer."

That was something. Wire transfers were traceable.

"Where?"

"A closed account in the Caymans, another dead end," his father lamented.

"Did you get anything? Anything at all?" Dante rubbed his forehead against the headache burgeoning there.

"Just a name: *La Viuda Negra.*"

"The Black Widow?" Dante's face screwed up in confusion. He had never heard of anyone being referred to or calling themselves that.

"Yeah, it was a new one for me too," Luciano quipped. He began to roll tools into individual cloths and drop them into a small duffle bag.

Marco strolled in and dropped onto a stool. "How's the girl?"

"Jonesing," Dante answered, his voice flat.

"What do you want to do with her?" his father asked, and Dante sighed.

"I don't know. I know we shouldn't leave any loose ends, but she's Cassie's sister."

Luciano nodded but said nothing, accepting Dante's statement without question. He wasn't the *capo*. It wasn't his place to make those kinds of decisions, just to enact them.

"There's a really stellar rehab in Italy," Marco said. "It's far enough away that she should break ties with every destructive influence, and if she runs... well, she's on another continent. She'd only be screwing herself."

"Who would take her? I'm not having Cassie do it again," Dante told his brother flatly. No, Cassie had done enough, given enough of herself, for Amber. Cassie was his now, his to protect, and that included protection from her soul-sucking sister.

"I'll do it," his brother replied. "I could use a couple of weeks away. I know it's an inopportune time, given all that's going on, but I'm feeling restless."

It was true that Marco was more of a caged animal than the rest of them, his violence barely contained on a good day. When his monsters started getting a little too close to the surface, Marco disappeared for a while, and then only Dante could always reach him, and only in a dire emergency. But Dante understood. He had his own demons. They all dealt with them in their own ways.

"Do it," Dante told him. "If anything happens, I'll be in contact. But finish this first." He gestured to Juan, who for the moment was still breathing.

"We're good at taking out the trash, son." His father's smile would give a lesser man chills, but Dante had grown up around his father's bloodlust. He merely nodded and headed back out into the night. It was a long drive home, and he needed the quiet to think.

Dante entered the apartment and was surprised Lucy wasn't there to greet him. In the last few weeks, Cassie wasn't the only one to make herself at home in his apartment. Lucy had, as well, with the addition of expensive new dog beds in the living room, his office, and their bedroom, where he had put his foot down about her sleeping on the bed.

It was a new experience for him, owning a pet. His mother had let her sons have fish, mainly because Elias had cried, and they each had horses on their *welo*'s farm, but dogs or cats in the house? Absolutely not, not in Marissa di Ruggerio's home.

So sharing his bed with Lucy was a hard *no* for him, and Cassie understood. Most nights, Lucy would sleep in the library while Dante debauched Cassie in almost every way known to man, but before they would fall into an exhausted sleep, Cassie would let the shaggy dog of dubious breeding into the room.

Lucy, true to her training, would lick Cassie's hands and face while Cassie told her goodnight and then fall asleep in her bed on the floor. And yet, somehow, every morning Dante would wake with the dog curled at the foot of the bed, her head on Cassie's feet or legs... and for some reason, he always let the dog stay.

Maybe it was Cassie's good-morning kisses while he sipped his coffee, or the look of pure happiness on her face as she took Lucy for a walk in the green space his building provided. He couldn't deny Cassie something that brought her so much joy, and Lucy obviously did.

So while he had expected to have to learn to tolerate Lucy, he'd also come to enjoy the dog's affection and companionship. Lucy, like him, enjoyed running, and Cassie did not. She had explained to him that was why they went to the dog park so much, she could throw a ball and Lucy would run and run and Cassie didn't have to. Dante began to forgo his treadmill in favor of a jog to the park three blocks away and Lucy, he found, was excellent company. Even though she was an older dog, she still had a lot of pep and she never asked him any questions, just trusted he knew how to get home. He enjoyed that.

So when Lucy didn't run to the door to greet him, he knew something was wrong. At first he was concerned that Cassie hadn't come home, or that she had gone somewhere, but he knew that wasn't the case. Matty had texted when he'd dropped her off forty-five minutes earlier, and her car had been in its spot beside Dante's own in the parking garage.

He checked the living room, thinking of that fitful night not even a week before, when she had waited for him in the dark, but she wasn't there.

"Cassie?" he called as he headed up the stairs two at a time. It was illogical to think something had happened to her while in the apartment; the building had the best security in Dallas. And a person needed a key to access the elevator leading to the penthouse.

But none of those facts stopped his heart from pounding. He still didn't know who was after the family, and until he did, until they were rotting in a hole somewhere, the danger was still present.

"Cassie?" He opened his office door, but it was dark and quiet. That left the bedroom. Maybe she was sleeping. He hoped she was. He would even let Lucy stay, if they were both curled on the bed.

He pushed open the door and was greeted by Lucy's head popping up from where it lay on Cassie's stomach as she idly stroked her fur. She wasn't sleeping and the only light in the room was provided by the moon and the city around them.

"Is it done?" she asked, her voice hollow.

"Is what done, *cara mia?*" he asked softly as relief washed over him. *Safe, she's safe.* He toed off his shoes and joined her on the bed, curling his body around hers.

"Amber?" She turned her face to his, and he was surprised to find it dry. He had expected tears, perhaps even pleading and bargaining for her sister, anything but this calm, resigned acceptance.

"Cassie, I don't–"

"Dante, just tell me. Is she dead?" she interrupted, and he just stared at her for a moment, shocked by not only her words but her calmness.

"Cassie, did you think I would kill your sister?"

"Of course," she replied, her tone matter-of-fact. "She hurt you, your business... Isn't that what's going to happen to Juan?" She looked at him as if he were stupid, like she couldn't imagine any other way to handle her sister and her actions.

"Well, yes, but Juan's betrayal was different. Deeper. He was my employee, and he turned on me. Amber is different."

She sat up, her face no longer calm but angry. It was the anger he had expected, but it seemed to be for a completely different reason.

"How is she different, Dante? How? She's volatile and stupid, and now that she knows she can hurt us, she will continue to do so." Cassie levered herself from the bed and paced in front of the window. "She won't be happy that I'm yours. You don't understand her, not really. Hell, I don't even think I do. The drugs, her addiction... she's a liability to us. I can't trust her, haven't been able to in a long time, Dante."

She stopped pacing and faced him. "I can't have her destroy this, us–" And this time, she did burst into tears.

Dante shot off the bed and took her in his arms. "Shhh, Cassie," he crooned into her ear, swaying with her until she quieted. "Cassie, baby, I'm not going to kill your sister."

She opened her mouth to argue, but he put a finger over her lips to silence her. "No, Cassie. I'm sending her to a rehab in Europe. My brother Marco is going to take her there, himself. It will be okay, baby. She won't be able to hurt anyone."

He kissed her lips softly. "I would never make you choose between your sister and me, Cassie."

She cupped his face in her hands and pulled far enough away to look him in the eye. "Dante, there is no choice. If it's between you and her, it's going to be you. It will always be you. That's what *my* love is, Dante." Her voice was soft but firm, and it both humbled and frightened him... and fear was not an emotion Dante often felt.

"I will always choose you, Dante," she continued, her eyes searching his. "Your world is my world, now. I don't need you to love me, I just need you to always choose me, too. To always promise me your honesty."

Something inside him was screaming, *tell her everything now*. He knew deep in his bones that Cassie would never betray him. He had known it before that night, but her words proved it. Still, though he couldn't bring himself to tell her. Maybe a not-so-small part of him thought that if she knew it all, knew every dark nook and cranny of what passed for his soul, she would leave. And he couldn't have that. If locking those dark parts away was what it took to keep her with him, so be it.

"I will always pick you, too, Cassie," he therefore said. It wasn't everything, but it was all he was willing to say. It would be enough. "Always."

CHAPTER

TWENTY- THREE

CASSIE

I t was almost six weeks since Cassie had discovered Juan's theft at the club, and not long after that situation had been dealt with, Dante came to her with the idea of her handling the finances of all the clubs.

"I don't think I can, Dante," she told him honestly.

She was working about seventy hours a week: forty at her regular job with Tiffany's firm, and twenty-five to thirty at Aphrodite's Palace, though that would decrease with the implementation of the new accounting and bookkeeping software she was having installed. Revamping the entire club– including training the bartenders, waitresses and kitchen staff on the new computer system– would go a long way to prevent the type of theft Juan had gotten away with for almost a year. But it was also what was taking most of her time, and she didn't think she could keep running on so little sleep for much longer.

"What do you mean, you can't?" He popped one of her fries in his mouth.

They were sharing their usual dinner in his office at the club, and she swore he ate his meal quickly so he could steal half of hers. A part of her didn't mind; she loved the small intimacies she got to share with him daily. The other part of her, the part that had just smacked the hand of one of the scariest men in Texas, didn't like to share her food.

"If you're still hungry, call down and order more," she told him. He pouted and shook his hand, as if her slap to his fingers had really hurt. "Dante, I'm exhausted. I can't keep working my day job and add more to what I'm doing here."

"So quit your day job," he said, shrugging, and then grinned as he snatched another fry when she took a sip of her water.

"What? Yours taste better." He blinked innocently at her.

She rolled her eyes. There wasn't an innocent bone in his body. "Dante, I can't just quit my job!"

"Why not?" he asked seriously, stealing a third fry.

She sighed and gave up, pushing her plate closer to him on the bistro table where they shared most dinners. She had told the kitchen weeks ago to always give her extra fries because she was in love with a fry thief.

"Dante, I still have bills. I have student loans and..." She floundered there, because since moving in with Dante, she really didn't have any bills. He had promised to take care of her, and he had fulfilled that promise, and then some. She didn't have a car payment or rent, or even a cell phone payment anymore.

Hell, he had even given her a credit card with permission to buy anything she wanted. When she had seen a first edition copy of his favorite poet at a used bookstore, she had called the credit card company to check her limit, and the woman had informed her that the black AmEx card had no limit. Cassie had almost fainted.

"How much are your loans, *cara mia*?" he asked, and she frowned, thinking.

"Um, a little under ten thousand." She had worked very hard not to accumulate a lot, but some semesters, the scholarships just didn't cover everything.

"Pff, that's nothing, Cassie. I'll pay them off tomorrow, if they worry you." He waved his hand as if she had just asked him to borrow twenty bucks.

She felt like she should argue with him about how it was wrong for him to pay off her student loans in addition to everything else he was footing the bill for, but she already knew how it would go: she'd protest, he'd insist, she'd protest again, he'd get all bossy-smoldery-sexy, they'd have sex, and the afterglow would make her agree to practically anything he said. She sighed in acceptance of losing that battle before it was fought, but forged on, wanting to make at least one valid point.

"Well, what about health insurance?" she challenged, feeling almost compelled to justify her need for paid employment. "I still have some expensive therapies for my scars." It was *kind* of true– she used a prescribed cream for her scars, but all the surgeries and therapies were behind her.

"You know I offer health insurance to my employees, right? Very good health insurance, at that." He grinned smugly, knowing he had her there– the insurance he offered those who worked for him was top-shelf and she knew it first-hand, having negotiated the rates with the insurance agents for the upcoming fiscal year herself.

"Cassie, look," Dante said, taking her hand. "I'm not sure what you're worried about. I want to hire you, baby." He pulled her into his lap and she ran her fingers through his hair, the thick, soft strands tickling her fingers.

"Why?"

"Because you're fucking brilliant." He kissed her mouth softly. "Juan ripped me off for how much?"

"Just over eighty-five thousand," she answered right away.

"And we had only just begun to notice when you walked in my door. What if that's happening at my other clubs? The laundromats or the restaurants?"

Her mind spun. She hadn't known he owned anything other than the clubs. But two more service industries were two more opportunities for theft and treachery.

"Look." He pulled her even closer, and she tightened her arms around his shoulders. "I try to only hire the best. The best dancers in

Dallas are downstairs entertaining oil barons and lawyers and musicians. I poached a chef from a two-star Michelin restaurant to run the kitchen here because I enjoyed his lobster bisque that much. And you... not only are you brilliant with numbers, in a way I will never understand, but I trust you."

Cassie didn't think she'd ever get used to– or tired of– the lavish compliments Dante heaped upon her. They filled the cracks in her parched soul, from all the times she'd craved acceptance, approval, affection... yet another thing Dante had given her without her needing to ask. She kissed him warmly in thanks.

He drew back after a moment to continue. "Keeping my legitimate businesses in good working order helps my not-so-legitimate businesses, too. I mean, look at Capone." He looked at her, expecting her to get the reference, but her confused expression had him adding, "They didn't get him for murder or bootleg liquor or anything like that. They got him for tax evasion."

"Oh!" she said, his motives clicking in her head. He needed her not just to ensure no one was stealing from him, but even more importantly, to keep *la famigilia*'s nose clean and not give the authorities any valid reasons to come sniffing around. With that essential a job to be done, no wonder he wanted the only person he could really trust to accomplish it.

"So say you'll be my numbers person, and if you need more help, you'll hire them, because I trust you and your judgement."

"Alright," she agreed. She'd miss Tiffany, but Danted needed her, so that was that. "But I've got to give Tiffany notice. I'm still in the middle of a big case. I can't leave until that's wrapped up."

He kissed her again, but before he could deepen it, she stood. Dante opened his mouth to argue, wanting his way, as always.

But Cassie had work to do, and she couldn't be distracted by his lips or wandering hands. She grabbed the last fry off her plate and shoved it in his mouth with a laugh as she spun away and left.

"I can't believe this is your last day." Tiffany's voice interrupted Cassie as she was cleaning out her cubicle. "I'll miss you, but I'm happy for you."

Tiffany knew she was leaving to handle the accounting for the *Palace*... and that Dante was the man Cassie was dating. She hadn't even tried to talk Cassie into staying; it was obvious to her where Cassie's interests and loyalties now lay.

"Thank you," Cassie said, smiling. "I'll miss you, too."

"But we'll keep in touch!" Tiffany insisted. "Don't forget dinner and drinks, tonight at Cliff's." She shot Cassie a sly, teasing glance. "Bring that sexy man of yours, too."

Cassie nodded with a laugh. "I'll try, but no promises." She knew better than to commit Dante to anything. No telling what appointments or meetings he might have set up for that evening.

After Tiffany had left the cubicle in a whirl of her gardenia perfume and silk jersey dress, Cassie resumed her task. There was only one thing left to put in the box: a framed photo of Amber and herself, from before things had gotten so bad. They were smiling, arms around each other, heads tilted together, the sun shining down on them. Cassie took a deep breath and wedged it carefully between the other things, to ensure the glass wouldn't crack.

She hadn't heard from Amber, but Marco had returned from Europe a couple of weeks earlier and assured Cassie that she was doing well. The complete change of scenery had been good, he said, and maybe it would be enough of a wake-up call to really sink in, this time.

But Cassie refused to hope. Hope had only ever broken her heart. This time, she was just going to wait and see. Amber was an adult, and she needed to forge her own way without Cassie.

Finally done, Cassie left. She opened the door, about to get in, but paused and looked back at the nondescript office building that had been her workplace for years. It had been a good job, and Tiffany had been excellent to her as both boss and friend. Cassie had needed that stability and safety as she established herself, but it was time to move on.

She drove straight to the club; it was only three in the afternoon, and a Thursday, but the late lunch crowd was in full swing and the parking lot was over half full. The club would be packed to the gills before the night was over. Cassie grabbed her box of belongings and closed the car door with a jaunty bump of the hip, her mood elevated from the wistfulness of her departure from Tiffany's to excitement at turning a new page in her life.

"Cassie." Chris, one of the newer bouncers, acknowledged her with a smile and held the door open.

"Hey, Chris," she replied, smiling back. Anticipation and eagerness filled her as she traversed the club to her office, her box balanced on her hip. She opened her office door, prepared to drop the box on the battered old desk she'd been using, and almost dropped it on the floor.

For the last few months she had shared the office with stacked boxes, extra chairs, and filing cabinets filled with years of paperwork from the club. But it had all been removed, and in its place... she wandered, wide-eyed and breathless, into the room, trying to take it all in.

The ancient, yellowing paint job had given way to wallpaper in ivory and gold. The chipped linoleum was still present, but had been covered in a seagrass rug that hid most of it from sight. The serviceable but old plastic blinds had been replaced with long, full curtains made from a creamy, translucent linen. Two tall gold étagère-style bookcases flanked the window, just waiting for her to style them to her heart's content. That battered old desk was gone, and in its place was a beautiful replacement with a glass top and gold legs, and an office chair of teal-blue velvet. Two guest chairs, in the same velvet, perched facing the desk. Elegant floor lamps stood in each corner, illuminating it– she flicked on the switch– with cheerful light making the entire place feel warm and comfortable There were even some beautiful plants stationed around the room, giving it some life and greenery.

Best of all, the crappy old laptop she'd been slogging away at for so long had been replaced with a sleek new all-in-one computer with a huge monitor. No more hunching forward and squinting, no more scrolling endlessly to the right to see all of her spreadsheets' columns.

"Do you like it?" Dante's deep voice asked behind her.

Cassie dropped the box on her new desk and spun around, launching herself into his arms, wrapping around him as tight as she could. He easily lifted her a few inches up so her feet dangled off the ground.

"I'll take that as a yes," he said, laughing.

She pulled her head back to look at him and nodded, her body thrumming with excitement and happiness. This man, this dark and complicated man who didn't think he was capable of love, had yet again showed her the depth of his caring for her.

"Yes, I like it." She smiled and gave him a pecking kiss.

"Good, cause some of the guys were a little pissed when I sprung it on them this morning that there were going to be a few changes in here."

Her eyes popped open wide. "You did this all in just today?"

Dante shrugged. "You throw enough money at a problem, you can get almost anything done in a day."

He set her down. With a final squeeze, she released him and went to sit behind her new desk, in her new chair that was like sitting on a cloud, the velvet as soft as kitten fur. Dante sat in one of the guest chairs facing her.

"So who do I need to thank for all of this?" she asked, smirking.

"Me, of course," Dante scoffed, and she rolled her eyes.

"No, silly, who picked out everything? The wallpaper, curtains, furniture? And who did the manual labor?" She had to thank everyone who had contributed.

"Miranda picked everything out. Matty, Tony, a couple of the bouncers were the ones who dragged out all the old stuff and dragged in the new stuff in after the wallpaper guys left." He leaned forward, eyes wide in a pretense at earnestness. "But, Cassie, *I* approved it all. Most importantly, I paid for it."

Cassie made a mental note to find out from Tony which, specifically, of the bouncers had helped, and to thank them all in addition to bringing in some pastries from Dante's favorite bakery. If there were one thing she'd learned about this *famiglia*, it was that they couldn't get their hands on enough *sfogliatelle*.

"Well, thank you, Dante. I love it." She couldn't stop smiling.

Dante looked entirely too pleased with himself. "If I'm going to have an on-site accountant, I might as well provide her with a decent office."

"If only you had thought of that when I started," she quipped, running her hands over the smooth glass of the new desk.

"Nah, I had to be sure you were gonna stay, first." He stood and circled the desk, leaning in for a kiss, but she pushed him away.

"No more kissing. I've got payroll today."

Dante heaved a theatrical sigh as he straightened. Just before he walked out the door, she remembered.

"Oh, Dante, Tiffany and some of my co-workers–" she caught herself and smiled a little, "–well, *former* coworkers, are having a goodbye dinner and drinks for me tonight at this little bar we go to. Would you... maybe... go with me?"

Even after several months together, she was still shy asking him to go places with her, though he seldom refused.

"What time, *cara mia?*" he asked, his tall, muscular frame leaning against the door jamb of her office. It drew attention to his wide shoulders and lean hips, and Cassie couldn't help but lick her lips at the delectable sight.

No, she scolded herself. *Payroll.*

"Oh, um, eight tonight."

"I have a meeting with Tony and Matty at seven. We may not be done in time."

She plastered a smile on her face to hide her disappointment. "That's okay, I understand."

In three quick strides, he was back in front of her, big hands tilting up her face, and his mouth was on hers. The kiss was deep and probing, sending her pulse racing. When he pulled away, she was breathing harder and her skin was flushed, as if she had just run a mile.

"I didn't say no," he told her with a hint of reproval. "I'll just be late and have to meet you there... unless you want to wait and go when I'm done?"

Dante looked at her, hopeful she'd agree to waiting. She knew he hated when she went places without him, somehow convinced that every man in the place was panting and desperate to make love to her. No matter how many times she'd told him, laughing and laughing, that that was *not* the case, he would not believe her.

She supposed that level of possessiveness would bother most women– hell, it should bother *her*– but it didn't. No, she relished it, because it meant she was so desirable to him that he couldn't believe he was the only one who wanted her to such a powerful, all-encompassing extent.

"No, I don't want everyone to have to wait for me," she told him. "It'll be fine, I'll just miss you until you get there."

"I'll meet you there by nine, then."

"Yes, please."

His eyes darkened; he liked when she said *please* to him. He looked at her lips, clearly wanting to take them again with his own, but he seemed to decide against another kiss and straightened.

"You'll be saying more of that tonight," he told her– warned her– and before she could respond, he was gone.

Cassandra spent the rest of the afternoon happily working away. Around seven, she decided to stop for the day and texted Tony that she was about to go. She wanted to freshen up before leaving, but before she could, Miranda popped her head in the door. Cassie was surprised to see her dressed in street clothes and not her normal floor attire.

"Hey, you busy?" she asked.

Cassie stood and went to her, wrapping her in a tight hug. "Thank you so much for helping with all of this." She waved a hand to encompass the huge change in her office. "I appreciate it so much. Your taste, as always, is exquisite."

Miranda gave her a squeeze in return. "You're welcome. It was my pleasure, and no more than you deserve."

"So what's up?" Cassie asked her, returning to her chair. "I thought you were working tonight?"

Miranda sat opposite her, in the seat Dante had vacated earlier, and nodded.

"I am, but I have to pick up my daughter. She needs a ride home from her friend's house, and no one else can do it." The corners of Miranda's pretty mouth took an uncharacteristic downturn. "And my stupid car won't start. It's my fault the battery has been acting up, but I thought it would last until tomorrow. Tony said you were leaving soon, and I thought you might give me a ride?"

"Girl, I'll do you one better," Cassie said. "Take my car." She rummaged in her purse for the keys and placed them on the desk before Miranda. "I was going to take a ride share to the bar, anyway, because I know I'm going to have a few drinks. And Dante is going to meet me there later, so I'll ride home with him."

Miranda opened her mouth to argue but Cassie stopped her with a wave of her hand.

"Take it, pick up your daughter. In the morning, I'll come here with Dante. You and I will jump-start your car, and you can get it to the repair shop."

The tension visibly left Miranda's shoulders. "Are you sure?" she hedged, even as she stood and closed her fist around the keys.

"Yes, Miranda, I'm sure. Go." Cassie made a shooing motion with her hands, laughing. Miranda laughed back and departed.

Cassie pulled up the ride-share app and ordered a car, then went to the restroom to freshen up. She had just returned to her office to grab her purse before leaving when a loud *boom* shook the building from somewhere nearby. She put her hand to the desk to steady herself as multiple car alarms began to sing the song of their people.

At first, she wasn't sure what had happened. They occasionally– very rarely– had earthquakes in Dallas, but it hadn't felt like an earthquake. Could it have been a freak lightning strike? She went to the window, expecting to see a charred mark on the pavement where a bolt might have touched down, but instead... her purse fell from slack fingers as the blood seemed to leave her body.

Unable to move or even breathe, frozen, Cassie stared in horror at the wreckage of the parking lot: her car was on fire.

No, the vehicles that had been parked around it were on fire. *Her* car was gone, completely gone. It had been an explosion, not lightning.

And it had been her car that had done the exploding.

CHAPTER

TWENTY- FOUR

DANTE

Dante was having a very good day.

Matty barged into his office, his white T-shirt sweat stained and streaked with dust. "Please explain to me why you aren't helping us move 30 years of crap out of Cassie's office?" he demanded.

"Because being the boss has its perks, little brother. Perks like not doing manual labor." Dante grinned as Matty guzzled a bottle of water.

"I can't believe she's been working there for all these months in that filthy cave of a room. You should be ashamed of yourself."

Dante shrugged. "I didn't expect her to stay."

"But she *is* staying?" Matty sat down, swiping a grimy forearm over his damp forehead.

Dante opened his desk drawer and pulled out the little black box that held the ring he'd commissioned a few weeks earlier. "I'm hoping forever, but I haven't asked yet."

Matty let out a low whistle at the two-carat princess-cut diamond solitaire set in a platinum band. It was elegant in its simplicity, much like the woman Dante bought it for.

"Not Mama's?" Matty asked, putting the ring back on the desk.

Dante shook his head as he replaced the box in the drawer. "No, I want Cassie to have something that's only hers. She hasn't gotten a lot of that, in the past."

"I get that," Matty said seriously, but then an impish grin spread across his face. "Look at my big brother, being sappy."

Dante leveled a look on him that would make a lot of men wet themselves, but Matty just smiled wider. "Don't you have more furniture to move?"

Matty rolled his eyes but stood. "I do, but it's because I like Cassie, not because I do what you say."

"Keep telling yourself that, little brother. One day I might believe it," Dante said sardonically and went back to work.

For the most part, things had returned to normal since the situation with Juan had been handled, but something in Dante's gut was eating at him, telling him not to let his guard down. He had been trying to fit together the puzzle pieces, the things that had been happening to his family starting with his mother's murder. So far, he had a lot of pieces but no picture was forming from them.

He had gone so far as to call Eli with his worries, even though he had promised to leave his brother out of it. And while Eli hadn't been pleased to hear from him, he had listened. They had come up with no new conclusions, but Eli told him to trust his gut.

"The big things– enemies, sickness, war– they don't just go away on their own. You've probably wounded whoever this 'black widow' is, but a wounded animal is twice as deadly, Dante," Eli said. "Look, Sam and I have some vacation coming up. We could come to Dallas–"

"No, Elias, don't do that. I promised you a clean break. I shouldn't have even called you, I just needed an outside perspective from someone I trusted."

"You still trust me?" Eli asked, sounding surprised.

"Let's just say, I'm learning what real betrayal is, even from a sibling, and what you did was more self-preservation than betrayal. I still think you're a weak little shit who's too cerebral for his own good, but you're also my brother and if the shit truly hit the fan, I know you would be here to do your part," Dante told his brother.

Knowing Cassie had opened up his mind in many ways. He understood, now, what Eli had felt when Dante had kidnapped his wife Samantha, to ensure Eli's obedience. He'd have been out of his mind if that had happened to Cassie.

"I forgive you, too, Dante," Eli replied after a moment.

That was enough brotherly bonding for Dante; he hung up the phone without a farewell and returned to pondering the issue with the black widow. He had nothing new on them so he would maintain a defensive stance and wait for them to strike. What else could he do?

He was telling Matty and Tony as much later that evening, when they went over the new shipment routes. He didn't want to rush the meeting, but he wanted to get to the bar and celebrate with Cassie, rejoice in her coming to work for him. He pulled open the drawer, once again, to stare at the little velvet box.

A plan had formed in his head after she'd told him about the get-together at the bar: him, proposing to her that very night, with all of her friends in attendance. Her world would narrow, as his wife– a trade-off he hoped she was ready for, and would feel was worth what she lost– but that night, she could have a normal thing like that.

Dante checked his watch. Matty and Tony had agreed to move up the meeting and they'd begun early, but they still had so much to discuss. It was a few minutes after seven. He hoped it wouldn't take much longer. He didn't want to disappoint Cassie.

"So the trucks coming in from Nuevo Lar—," Tony's words were cut off by a thundering *boom*, so loud that it rattled the thick bullet-proof windows in their casings.

"What the fuck?" Tony exclaimed. All three men were out of their seats in the next second.

Dante rushed to the window. Reason told him it was some kind of accident on the freeway, but the sinking feeling in his gut told him it wasn't. He knew that sound; he'd heard it once before, in Mexico as a child, when his *welo* took him to watch as they killed a government official who was trying to shut down the cartel.

He fought to control his breath as the realization of it settled into his bones: it was a—

"Was that a fucking *bomb?*" Matty demanded.

Dante's window did not provide a view of the parking lot, but a trail of smoke drifted into their line of sight on the wind, and an orange glow began illuminating the outer reaches of the parking lot.

Cassie's office did look directly down, however. Dante strode to it, flinging open the door, but the room was empty. If Cassie weren't there—

Heart in his throat, he rushed to the restroom, forcing the door open, hoping she'd be there. A moment of embarrassment was worth calming his sudden, relentless fear. He could make it up to her with a bracelet to match the ring—

She wasn't there. The restroom was empty. *Where is she where is she **where is she**—*

He bolted down the stairs, ignoring Matty's shout of "Dante!" He pushed his way through the club patrons pressing toward the exit, wanting to sate their curiosity about what had occurred. Prying himself free of the throng, he popped free of it like a champagne cork into a hellish scene of noise and heat, the crackling of flames and a hissing, as of air or gas escaping. In the air was a peculiar sweet stink, like pork burning.

It was all centered on a cluster of cars surrounding a particular spot, the spot where Cassie liked to park her car, the spot she said was far enough away to stretch her legs but not get too hot getting from place A to B—

His mind drew a conclusion. Everything went away, all of his senses except for sight, which narrowed in focus to the twisted, burning remains of Cassie's car, and then he was screaming her name.

He began to run to the car, only to be contained by two sets of powerful arms. He struggled and thrashed, trying to pull free, but it was like being held back by bands of steel. Why wouldn't they let him go to her? He couldn't let her stay there, had to get her out, get her to safety, to the hospital, he'd have the best doctors in the world there by morning, he'd–

"Boss! Calm down!" a voice shouted into his ear. It broke through the panicked haze in his head and he stopped fighting whoever was holding him back. Sound and sensation rushed back from the foggy void he'd been in; sirens were blaring in the distance, coming closer, and the heat from the flames bolstered that of the early evening temperature, making him sweat in his expensive suit. His shirt clung damply to his back and chest under the jacket. His tie was strangling him, he couldn't swallow, couldn't breathe–

He tore at it blindly, fumbling until hands slapped his aside and untangled it for him. He blinked, numbness cutting through his terror, making his brain work again. Matty was there, his face set into hard lines, undoing the tie with brisk motions, yanking it off and tossing it aside.

"Better?" Matty asked tightly. "Can they let you go now?"

"Yeah," Dante rasped. The steel-cable arms released him and he stepped back. Flanking him were two of the bouncers, one a newbie who Cassie had just hired.

Cassie. The anguish punched him in the stomach, made him stumble back into the bouncers. their rough hands were the only thing keeping him from falling to the ground.

"NO!" a female voice screamed and Dante turned toward it– it sounded like her, was it possible, could it be–

She flung herself at him, into his arms, driving the breath from his lungs but he didn't care, she hadn't been in the car, she was alive and with him, safe, she was safe, she was *safe*–

Dante closed his eyes and thanked a god he wasn't sure he believed in, then opened them again. Cassie's face was white, her eyes wide and horrified, but she was alive.

"Miranda!" she cried, tears spilling down her cheeks. "It's Miranda! We have to get her out!" She was trembling so hard he feared she would shake apart, and then he remembered: her foster parents. She had told him of the smell of burning rubber and charred flesh– suddenly, the burned pork stench made sense. Dante swallowed against the gorge rising in his throat.

"Dante, let me go!" She scratched and fought him, but he only pulled her closer. "She was in my car!"

Her struggling was fierce, and he almost lost his grip on her once, but the bouncers closed ranks around them. If she got away from him, they'd catch her. The fire department had arrived, by then, and more hissing rose in the cacophony, this the sound of water dousing the flames.

As the fire went out, so did the fury of Cassie's fighting. Eventually, she collapsed against him and he just held her as she sobbed. When she was able to walk again, he guided her back inside and up to his office, where he collapsed onto the sofa and pulled her to sit on his lap. She needed the comfort, but so did he; the rush of endorphins and the fade of adrenaline when he had realized she was alive had his head somehow both fuzzy and clear.

"Someone needs to call her mother," she whispered eventually, almost silent against his throat. "Let her know that someone else needs to pick up Nina."

"What happened?" he asked, passing his hand over her hair, down her back, in a repetitive motion that soothed both of them.

"Her car wouldn't start, so I lent her mine." She looked up at him, her dry and red-rimmed. "It was meant for me. It should have been me."

"No!" he growled, pulling her even more tightly against him. "No, Cassie. I'm sorry it was Miranda, but it shouldn't have been you. *Or* her."

Eventually the police showed up, one a detective who was friendly to the family, and after an hour of questioning, Dante finally got to take Cassie home.

"I want to make sure Miranda's daughter is cared for, Dante," she told him in the dark of his car. "I don't care how we do it, but we do it." She stared at him, her eyes full of a fire that hadn't been there in hours, and he nodded.

"Of course, *cara mia.*" He brought her hand to his lips and kissed the back of it. "We'll do whatever you think should be done, for Nina, for Miranda's mother, all of them."

She dropped her head to his shoulder, shuddering with after-shocks of grief and horror, and Dante knew he had to work harder than ever to figure out what the hell was happening, before someone else got hurt.

Before Cassie got hurt.

Cassie had just gotten in the shower, and Dante was contemplating what to do about the ring and his proposal– it was definitely the wrong night, now, to do it– when his phone buzzed. It was a text from a number he didn't recognize.

No hay furia infernal como una mujer despreciada– La Viuda Negra

'Hell hath no fury like a woman scorned,' the text read in Spanish. Dante stared at it. Who had he scorned? He couldn't think of a woman he'd hurt in the past who would be so angry, and powerful enough to hurt him.

Dante tossed his phone as if it had burned him and set the ring box next to it. Cassie had been the target. This was personal. He just didn't know why.

What he did know was that it had been done to punish him, to get to him. It was clear that being his girlfriend, eventually his wife, was a dangerous proposition. And all of Dante's money and influence, all the fear he instilled, were still not enough to keep her safe. He had deluded himself, had forgotten the significance of his mother's death, how it meant no one was safe, not even the daughter and wife of two of the most powerful criminals in the country.

He didn't want to be without her, but it wasn't fair to have her in this life. Not while this person was actively hunting them, hunting *her*. He leaned his head back in the chair and closed his eyes, the heightened emotions of the day taking their toll.

The water shut off in the bathroom. Soon, Cassie exited the bathroom, her bare feet padding softly on the carpet as she approached. He opened his eyes and took her in.

Her wet hair was dripping onto a ragged old robe that looked as if it had once been pink, but had since faded to a murky gray. She was pale, drawn, her eyes still red. To Dante she was the most beautiful thing he had ever seen. And she was alive. He meant to keep her that way.

"Come 'ere," he said, smiling a little when she curled her slight body into his lap.

"I love you," she whispered and placed a gentle kiss on his lips, then resting her head on his shoulder. She didn't wait for him to say it back because she knew he couldn't— but didn't he? Wasn't that what the panic of earlier had been, when he had thought she'd been the one in the car? Wasn't that what the knee-weakening relief had been, to know she was safe? Wasn't that what the delighted anticipation had been, when he'd contemplated how to propose to her?

He really wished he knew. But the poetry books had yet to reveal the truth of it to him with their verses. It was all still a baffling puzzle to him. All he knew was that he was too weak to break up with Cassie, to ensure her safety by forcing her to leave him, but that he needed to tell her the truth. She deserved to make her own choices, and to have all the information to make smart ones.

"I need to tell you something," he told her, voice muffled against her damp, clean-smelling hair.

She lifted her head from his shoulder to look him in the face. "Okay," she whispered, her eyes tender and soft.

"I know you know some of my business. I know you know about the drugs, but... you don't know it all," he admitted softly.

"Dante." Cassie put one hand on his cheek and smiled. "I know. I know it all. I know about your family, and how powerful you are.

Shanna mentioned it at the fight, and then... well, the internet is my friend. And I don't care. We could lose all this–" she gestured around his bedroom, "–and I wouldn't care, as long as I had you."

"But what if you lose me?" he asked. Her brow furrowed at his words. He traced her lips with the pad of his thumb. "What if I'm arrested or killed? Can you survive that?"

"Dante, I can't predict the future. I've experienced unexpected loss, like you have. They were different kinds of loss, my foster parents in an accident and your mother to a bullet, but equally devastating in their ways. And while I will pray every day for a long, long life with you," she smiled again and ran her fingers through his hair, soothing him. "I would prefer spending even a short time with you, than living forever apart."

Dante's throat tightened. When had anyone ever declared their loyalty to him like that? He'd had employees declare their loyalty, but that was more due to greed for what he paid them or fear of what he could do to them. His family was rock-solid in terms of fidelity, but the affection shown was an obligation, given and shown because it was expected, because they shared blood. Cassie was the first person who cared for him without hopes of compensation, without worry of reprisals, without having to because they were related.

He pulled her to him and kissed her again, swallowing the happy little hum she made. When it ended, she leaned back, then patted his chest, right over where the ring box had been stashed in his breast pocket.

"So... is that for me?" she asked.

How had she– Dante shook his head. He had to stop underestimating her. She was probably smarter than all four di Ruggiero brothers put together.

"It is, but I'm not sure you're going to want it," he admitted.

"Of course I want it, Dante!" she told him incredulously. "Just ask me."

"You said you researched my family. And that you know about

my mother, and how my father went to prison for killing the man that killed her."

"Yes, but Dante–"

He pressed his thumb against her mouth, stopping her words. "My father didn't kill him. I did," he told her, his eyes never leaving hers, and for a moment neither of them breathed. Dante was sure this would be one step too far. This lovely, kind, generous woman would judge him rightly–

"Good," she said at last.

Dante stared at her in shock. "*Good?*" he croaked, bewildered.

"Yes, Dante, *good*. I'm not stupid or idealistic. The man killed a woman in broad daylight. I understand that justice in your world is different, and," she lifted one shoulder in an almost nonchalant way, "he can't hurt us now, can he?"

Something swelled within him, some indefinable sensation of wanting-needing-admiring, of relief-desire-safety, and then suddenly all the poems made sense. No wonder he hadn't comprehended love: he'd thought it was a single emotion, not an overwhelming tangle of all of them at the same time. It didn't seem possible to contain them all. And yet he did.

I could keep even the stars within me, Rilke had written, *so immense my heart seems to me.*

He understood it, now.

"I love you," he told her, softly, softly, and pulled the box from his pocket, plucked the ring from its velvet bed. She sucked in a breath, eyes wide and shocked, unresisting as he slid the ring on her third finger.

Dante was flawed. Some would say that he was the perfect product of his environment and who raised him, but as a human being, he was far from normal. That had always suited Dante just fine, because his life had a purpose that lifted him far above normal. He had just thought he'd be living it alone, because it didn't seem possible there was a woman out there who could not only accept his flaws, but love him in spite of them... or because of them.

He hadn't counted on Cassie.

He pulled the robe from her shoulders and worshipped her body, that night, imbuing all he felt into his touches and caresses. He knew she felt it, that she believed it. When she held onto the headboard, grasping it as she came, first on his tongue and then around his cock, the ring caught the soft light of the moon. The intensity, the bond, between them flowed back and forth, a completed feedback loop, as they made love.

And in the early hours, as the sun broke through the night and she sat astride him and took him deep inside her body once more, he knew it might not be a typical love, but it was his, the love he was made to give and receive, and that he would sacrifice anything for it.

EPILOGUE

Three months later

It was the first time Cassie had ever been to Italy, and she was lamenting she was making the trip without Dante, but Marco wasn't a terrible escort. Besides, it wasn't for a vacation; it was Amber's first family therapy session, and Amber herself had called Cassie to ask her to attend.

"I'm not sure if you can, or even if you'd want to." Amber's voice was clearer than it had been in years, and it was all Cassie could do not to cry. "But I would like it if you came. I owe you a few–" Amber's voice broke off in a fit of nervous laughter but she regained her composure quickly. "–a lot of apologies, and I don't want to say them over the phone. Plus, I think maybe you could use an unbiased ear, too? My therapists and counselors here are really good."

"Just tell me when," Cassie had said, tears running silently down her face.

Now, three weeks later, she was the passenger in a slinky little car navigating the rolling hills of the Italian countryside.

"I know it's a long drive, but the rehab is located in an old tuber-culosis clinic, so it's kind of out of the way." Marco was relaxed, one arm on the open window, the other casually gripping the steering wheel. He drove effortlessly, as if he were part of the vehicle. His aviator sunglasses and dark hair and classic Italian features made him look like a local.

"I don't mind," replied Cassie. "It gives me time to get my thoughts together."

The last she'd seen Amber, it had been with the assumption that Dante would execute her for her actions against his family. Cassie had made her peace with it, because after a lifetime of trying and trying, of making excuses and giving second and third and tenth and twentieth chances, she was done– Amber, finally, had to bear the consequences of her choices and actions.

Fortunately– for Amber, if not for Cassie– Marco and Dante had taken it upon themselves to help Amber save herself. The authority they had established over her– *go to rehab or we'll kill you*– had gone far in gaining her compliance, in a way Cassie had not been able to accomplish. A year earlier, she'd have been horrified at how everything had gone, and the steps taken to get them where they were on that day, but now? Now, she agreed with every bit of it.

At last Marco turned down a long driveway with a venerable stone fence and a tall gate of curlicued wrought iron. After speaking to a guard in Italian, Marco drove them up a long paved drive to a massive historic building, its walls of creamy-gold stone looking like they'd been there since the beginning of time. It was exactly what an American would think of when they thought of old Italian villas.

Several other cars were parked in a small lot off to the side of the building in a jarring juxtaposition of history and modernity.

"It was built in the sixteenth century," Marco told her as he parked the car and they got out. "Then in the late 1800s until the 1920s, it was a respite home for people with TB and other lung conditions."

The gravel crunched under their feet as they approached a serviceable side door that seemed to be the main entrance, instead of the grand and elaborate portico and double doors at the front of the building.

"How do you know so much about it?" she asked after Marco spoke to a woman sitting at the front desk and signed them in.

"I own the building," he said with a shrug once they had been pointed in the right direction.

Cassie's mouth dropped open as they began walking. "You *what?*"

"I own the building," he repeated easily, as if he had just admitted to buying a pair of shoes. She still wasn't used to the wealth Dante and his brothers came from and earned, and doubted she ever would be. "Bought it straight out of college. It was supposed to be just an investment, at first, but then a good friend of mine from school died of a drug overdose."

He pushed open another door. Where what once had probably been a grand entryway now looked more like a dorm rec room. There were a few bookcases, several sofas, a few TVs, and lots of people milling around, hugging and crying, some talking somberly, some excitedly. It was a scene Cassie had witnessed many times, under different circumstances in her life, thanks to Amber. Only the setting was different. They found a vacant bench and sank onto it.

"So your friend died of an overdose and you were like, 'let me open a rehab'?" she asked, astonished and confused. His family sold drugs, profited from the very people in this room, from their weakness and reliance on mood-altering substances.

"It wasn't exactly like that. The friend died from drugs we supplied, and I felt some guilt for that. Guilt I had trouble reconciling because–" He grinned and his eyes crinkled in the same way Dante's did, but his were a lighter brown, almost golden in color. "Well, you know why."

Cassie nodded, hoping Marco would continue but not pressuring him.

"Well, I spoke to my mother about it. She was a little like you, you know." Cassie gave him a quizzical look and he chuckled a little. "More than a little, really," he said affectionately. "She told me if I had guilt about my friend and our way of life, to do something good.

'Life is about balance' she always said, and this," he gestured around them, "is my way of offering balance."

Cassie thought that a more efficient way of offering balance might be to not deal the drugs in the first place, but that topic was a losing battle. Instead, she gave Marco a kiss on the cheek and smiled. "Thank you."

"For what?" he asked, amused.

"This balancing act of yours might save my sister, when I had given up." Her eyes burned with unshed tears, and Marco gave her a warm brotherly hug.

"No thanks needed. You're family, now." It was just that simple for him, for all the di Ruggieros. Once you were family, that was it.

"Cassie!"

Cassie turned and saw her sister, healthier and happier than she had seen in years. She stood and hurried to her, wrapping her in an encompassing hug.

"Amber," she whispered, crying into her hair.

"Gosh, don't cry, not yet. We haven't even started therapy!" Amber teased, only making Cassie cry harder. She hadn't wanted to lose her sister that horrible day months ago, but she didn't regret choosing herself over Amber, either. In truth, she hadn't been helping her sister, hadn't for a long time. She had enabled Amber, and it was time for Cassie to own her part in her sister's addiction as well.

She pulled back and held Amber's face in her hands. Her eyes were clear of the shadows that had consumed them for the better part of a decade, and Cassie had the overwhelming sense that, even with the work ahead of them, it would all somehow end up okay. She had Dante, and now she had her sister back, and everything else were just details to get hammered out.

Dante

Dante blinked as he walked into a dusty barn, eyes acclimating from the sudden shift from bright midday sun to the darker interior. It was more of a shack, really; it hadn't held a horse or anything along those lines in years, and the air was hot and dusty in a way only Chihuahua ever was.

In the middle of the dilapidated structure, a man sat tied to a chair, a bloodstained flour bag over his head. He was shirtless, his hands tied behind his back, and his chest was cut and mottled with bruises. Observing him with flat black eyes was one of *Welo*'s most trusted men.

"Has he given you anything?" Dante addressed Benifacio in Spanish.

The man stubbed his cigarette out under his boot. "Nah, he said he would only speak to you. *El jefe* told us to wait, so we waited."

Just like Dante was the *don* of his family, *el jefe* was what his grandfather's men called his *abuelo*. 'The boss'... some things were universal after all.

Dante nodded and approached the prisoner. As he got closer, he could see the word *rata* carved into the man's chest. His *welo*'s men were brutal, that was sure. Dante pulled the sack from the man's head and studied his battered face, hoping to recognize him beneath all the contusions and lacerations, but he was a stranger. In truth, he was just another low-level flunky who had been offered money from the Black Widow to give her information. Dante understood it. The man would still die, but he understood it.

"What did you need to tell me?" Dante asked him.

The man smiled, his teeth jagged and broken, mouth full of blood from his beating.

"The Widow wants you to know that she doesn't just want your trade routes and your drugs, she wants revenge. You and your family, you wronged her. She's coming for you all, and she won't stop until you're dead."

The man laughed, spraying bloody saliva. Dante barely kept from rolling his eyes; if he had a dollar for every time some so-called tough guy tried to intimidate him, he'd be twice as wealthy as he already was. Turning on his heel, he walked away.

"Take out the trash," Dante told Benifacio. "Put it out as a warning for any other rats, that they don't want to come at us."

Benifacio nodded in response and Dante was almost to his truck when he heard the shot.

This new war was far from over; no, it had only just begun. But that was fine, because the di Ruggieros were the spear in the darkness, and they didn't lose.

THE END

ABOUT THE AUTHOR

While Laura Sutton may be new to writing romance she is not new to the romance world. She has been reading romances since her pre-teen years when her mother would leave her to her own devices at their local used bookstores.

Today you will find her in her home state of Texas living by the beach with her dogs and a book still in her hand. Though now her days are also full of putting the stories that once only existed in her head down on the page.

Connect with Laura Sutton:
Website: https://laurasuttonauthor.com/
E-newsletter: shorturl.at/iyJMQ
Facebook Group: shorturl.at/dqAN2

facebook.com/LauraSuttonAuthor

twitter.com/suttonauthor

instagram.com/laurasuttonauthor

bookbub.com/authors/laura-sutton

amazon.com/author/Laura-Sutton

ALSO BY

THE DIRUGGIERO MAFIA FAMILY SAGA

La Famiglia: Elias

La Famiglia: Dante

La Famiglia: Matteo (Coming July 10th, 2021!)

TEXAS THREE-STEP SERIES

To Love her Cowboys

The Power of Love

Love on the Coast

www.ingramcontent.com/pod-product-compliance
Lightning Source LLC
Chambersburg PA
CBHW061242120726
48001CB00001B/94